The Averoigne Chronicles

THE
AVEROIGNE
CHRONICLES

THE COMPLETE AVEROIGNE STORIES OF
Clark Ashton Smith

EDITED BY
Ronald S. Hilger

HIPPOCAMPUS PRESS
NEW YORK

Published by Hippocampus Press
P.O. Box 641, New York, NY 10156.
www.hippocampuspress.com

Cover art and title page spread, "The Enchantress of Sylaire," © by
David Ho, used by gracious permission of the artist.
Cover design by Daniel V. Sauer, dansauerdesign.com
Hippocampus Press logo designed by Anastasia Damianakos.

First Paperback Edition
1 3 5 7 9 8 6 4 2

ISBN 978-1-61498-320-0

To Lin Carter
(1930–1988)
and Gahan Wilson
(1930–2019)
in memoriam.

CONTENTS

Introduction, *by Gahan Wilson*...9

A Note on the Text, *by Ron Hilger*..13

Averoigne 23

A Night In Malnéant..25

The Nevermore-to-be...32

The Maker of Gargoyles..33

The Broken Lute 49

The Holiness of Azédarac...50

In Cocaigne 73

The Colossus of Ylourgne 74

Necromancy 115

The Enchantress of Sylaire 116

Amithaine 133

The Beast of Averoigne..135

Song of the Necromancer...151

Mother of Toads...153

The Witch with Eyes of Amber 162

A Rendezvous in Averoigne 163

The Dark Château..180

The Mandrakes 182

Canticle 190

The Satyr..191

Cambion 198

The Disinterment of Venus...199

"O Golden-Tongued Romance" 210

The End of the Story...212

To Klarkash-Ton, Lord of Averoigne, *by H. P. Lovecraft*..............232

Averoigne: An Afterword, *by Donald Sidney-Fryer* 233

Acknowledgments...251

INTRODUCTION

Of all Smith's worlds of fantasy—those specific, defined worlds such as "Xiccarph" and "Zothique"—the one closest to this world of flesh and blood was that which he named "Averoigne."

Part of this is doubtless because the stories and poems with which he celebrated it take place in a world something like a world which actually did exist, or at least did seem to exist in the minds of its participants, in real history and in a real place. There was a Dark Ages, there was a French version of it, and some of the last did occur in a geographical area recognizably like the one depicted as Averoigne, namely the Auvergne, which is also rich in poetic folk, and old, strange beliefs.

But I think it would be a very great mistake to imply that these stories are really about a particular region. They are not, in that sense, like the stories of Smith's good friend Howard Phillips Lovecraft. Lovecraft was a regionalist and he very carefully and lovingly crafted a kind of dark analogue of his cherished New England in order to make a stage for the horrendously doleful events he did so like to write about.

A very reasonable version of Lovecraft's Arkham, for instance, may be walked through by any tourist to Salem who is careful in choosing his routes, but tramp through France how you may, you will find no Ximes, you will come across no Ylourgne.

Do not despair. Visit a little country restaurant near Périgon some sunny afternoon and share a demie or two with an elderly local. Sit on the terrace looking out over the valley at the ancient stone village beyond as you listen to the growly French words and smell the harsh French tobacco, and you are very likely to hear a little more of the doings of Azédarac or Mère Antoinette.

9

And there are many physical traces, many leavings behind, of Averoigne, even though it did not and does not exist. The careful seeker will come across numerous treasures which obviously come from that special region and none other, even though their geographic origins may be quite diverse. Those tapestries of gorgeously-costumed nobles hunting unicorns and boars were clearly woven there, and the masons who carved the gargoyles on Notre Dame in Paris were Averoignese to a man, I have no doubt; particularly, I suspect, that one who chopped out the sidewise gazing monster with the bone in its mouth which is called "The Gnawer," and of course, so were those ancient dreamers who wrote that wistful music with the lutes, and the strummings in minor keys, and the slow, sad lyrics in old French which wail over the lover who will not be persuaded.

The people in Smith's other worlds are often distant, though for very good reasons. The citizens of Zothique, for example, are always fascinating; but they are as cold as their dying world and something in their race has expired beyond their wisest necromancer's arts of resurrection. In Smith's interstellar adventures his astronauts' encounters with the diversely grotesque denizens and environments of other planets are absorbing, and the explorers' courage and fortitude always admirable and convincing, but they have been, as they very likely will turn out to be in real life, when that sort of thing moves along from fantasy to fact, by and large dehumanized by their technology.

The humanity of the people in Smith's Averoigne, on the other hand, is in full flower. They sweat and smell of garlic and wine; they have orgasms and rumbling stomachs; they fumble at important moments; their faith fails them exactly when they need it most, and they boast and brag just when they should have kept their mouths shut.

It is very easy to empathize with these olden men and women and even with the supernatural entities which move darkly and malignantly among them, and that's fortunate for us because Smith lures us close enough to them to feel their body warmth—or lack of it!—and he does it with that impartial, but remarkably kindly and forgiving, detachment that was always so typical of him and which continues to get him into trouble with the general public, who persist in grossly misreading him as a cynic.

You sigh for the poor young man ensnared by the witch, but at the same time you also sigh for the witch, weird and horrible and singularly repulsive though she may be. You blush for the innocent priest who is being made a fool of by the sophisticated and sinister plottings of his religious superior, but that does not stop you from understanding only too well the weight of those irretraceable steps which led his deceiver into his present hopeless villainy.

Of course, above everything else, Averoigne is beautiful and magical. Clark Ashton Smith was a poet of vast talent and his powers seem particularly evident when he sets them to evoking this strange, medieval land and its wonders. All of his stories resonate and haunt—you are far from finished with them when you've read them and put them down— but the spells woven by these tales seem to have a particular persistence.

All the legends make it quite clear that anyone rash enough to visit a real fairyland will never quite manage to leave it again entirely, and, in that fairy sense, Averoigne is real. Once you've read this book you'll find you've been authentically enchanted by a master sorcerer and for the rest of your life you must expect to be periodically wafted willy-nilly far away from ordinary things. One moment you'll be on a crowded bus, and the next you'll be wandering down a flowery pathway by the River Isoile; another time when you've almost gotten yourself to sleep in some lonely hotel room, you'll suddenly be lost amid tall, grey trees perilously close to the tomb of Malinbois; and staring fixedly into space with your mind on nothing in particular, will almost certainly cause you to revisit that interesting Inn near Sylaire.

But do not worry—as a traveler of some experience in those regions, I assure you, you'll enjoy every minute of it. Clark Ashton Smith is remarkably kindly to dreamers.

—GAHAN WILSON

A Note on the Text

Of the many imaginary realms created by the California poet and author Clark Ashton Smith, perhaps the most enchanting and romantic of all may be found within his chronicles of Averoigne. Smith's delightful yet horrific conception of medieval France was apparently derived from the historical province of Auvergne, located in the Massif Central of south-central France which rises abruptly just west of the Rhône-Saône valley, and inclining north to the Paris basin and west to the basin of Aquitaine. This sparsely populated region is indeed semi-mountainous, well forested, and the source of many French rivers as the poet-author describes it, but here the correlation ends and Smith's fertile imagination takes over. Aside from acknowledging certain powerful influences such as the Druids and Paganism, the Romans and the Holy Roman Church, Averoigne owes little or nothing to actual French history—yet retains the full flavor of medieval France.

Ashton Smith conceived the idea of collecting his tales of Averoigne together in book form around 1933, as indicated by this excerpt from a letter to August Derleth in the summer of that year. ". . . I will have a series totaling 60,000 words, all dealing with the future continent of Zothique. These could be collected with a brief note as to supposed geography and chronology. My Averoigne series also lacks about two more tales to bring it to book-size." About this same time, Smith also created a list of twelve titles in his literary notebook under the heading "Averoigne Chronicles." Unfortunately, he would never complete the last three titles, "The Sorceress of Averoigne," "The Oracle of Sadoqua," and "The Doom of Azédarac," although "The Sorceress of Averoigne" was apparently reworked into "The Enchantress of Sylaire" around 1940. The interested reader should refer to *The Black Book of Clark Ashton Smith* (Arkham House, 1979) items 48, 49, and 60, and also *Strange Shadows* (Greenwood Press, 1989) for the plot-sketch of "The Sorceress of Averoigne," as well as many other synopses relating to the Averoigne cycle.

It is lamentable that this concept of collecting Smith's tales together according to their settings (i.e. Zothique, Averoigne, Hyperborea, etc.) was never fully realized during his lifetime, thus giving him the incentive to complete more tales in these excellent fantastic realms, and also, perhaps, to create a greater cohesion within each story-cycle. But this did not occur, and it was not until 1970, nine years after the author's death, that Lin Carter edited a collection of sixteen tales comprising the Zothique cycle for inclusion in the celebrated "Adult Fantasy" series published by Ballantine books. This marked the very first paperback edition of tales by CAS, and was soon followed by three more titles: *Hyperborea*, *Xiccarph*, and *Poseidonis*. A future volume to be entitled *Averoigne* was planned by Carter, but once again the *Averoigne* book failed to materialize. Ballantine books published the last volume of its "Adult Fantasy" series in 1974, and the Averoigne collection lapsed again into oblivion.

In collecting the materials for this volume, I have included all the completed tales of Averoigne, interspersed with selections from Smith's finely crafted lyric poetry, carefully chosen for its medieval setting and thematic compatibility. Although not generally considered one of the Averoigne cycle, "A Night in Malnéant" introduces the series because of its closely related setting and super-romantic theme. This short, poignant story is steeped in a melancholy atmosphere that Edgar Allan Poe could easily have penned; in fact, Smith regarded this tale so highly that he included it as one of only six stories in his first collection of tales *The Double Shadow and Other Fantasies*, self-published in 1933. This first appearance stands free of the subsequent editing that marks the later version which appeared in both *Weird Tales* and Smith's first Arkham

House collection *Out of Space and Time*, and appears here in its original form for the first time since the publication of that scarce pamphlet.

The text for "Mother of Toads" has also been restored to its original version. After repeated rejections, Smith had been forced to excise some of the more erotic passages in order to ensure acceptance by *Weird Tales* editor Farnsworth Wright. This restored version results in a much more readable and enjoyable tale, as originally conceived by the author.

Farnsworth Wright also initially rejected "The Beast of Averoigne," prompting these comments by Smith in a letter to August Derleth on July 10, 1932. "Personally, I don't quite see why it was rejected, unless the documentary mode of presentation may have led me into more archaism than was palatable to Wright. The abbot's letter to Thérèse might be cut out, thus deepening the mystery; but I can't quite make up my mind on this." Smith would indeed cut out the abbot's letter, removing some 1,400 words from the tale. He also added "a new twist to the climax," which by all accounts is an improvement over the original, but which also presents a more complicated dilemma than merely restoring the original text would resolve. In the hope of following the author's wishes regarding this tale, the original text stands here restored, but also incorporates the new improved ending, resulting in a text that contains the best of both versions.

The texts used here in *The Averoigne Chronicles* come from the corrected texts used in the "Collected Fantasies of Clark Ashton Smith" edited by Scott Connors and myself. These texts are now recognized as the most definitive available, having been compared to the original manuscripts, various drafts and first appearances, also checking Smith's existing letters in order follow as closely as possible the author's wishes in this regard. Many thanks to Mr Rah Hoffman of Los Angeles for his kind assistance in providing photocopies of the texts in their original magazine appearances as well as from Smith's first three Arkham House collections—complete with corrections and annotations by Rah as well as by Klarkash-Ton himself!

Any collection such as *The Averoigne Chronicles* that presents itself as a history of a certain region would do well to include a few words explaining its chronology. In arranging the sequence of tales I am indebted to Mr T. G. L. Cockcroft of New Zealand, whose research has revealed that six of the tales contain specific dates, while two others contain approximate dating clues. "The Mandrakes" takes place during the Fifteenth Century and "The Satyr" introduces Olivier du Montoir as a possible rival of Ronsard, the leader of the group of poets known as the "Pléiade." Pierre de Ronsard lived 1524–1585, placing "The Satyr" around the middle of the Sixteenth Century.

The remaining tales contain no dating clues, specific or approximate, and therefore make their appearance inconspicuously near the middle of the sequence. "A Night in Malnéant" is placed first as a sort of prologue to the series proper, as it contains no specific link to the other tales.

The map of Averoigne has been drawn by taking the basic boundaries and general geologic features of historic Auvergne, and filling them with the towns, monasteries, forests, and rivers described within the tales of Averoigne. When comparing this map to one of modern France, the reader may notice that the Allier River corresponds somewhat to the Isoile, and Clermont-Ferrand to Vyônes. Another similarity: the names "Vyônes" and "Ximes" seem to echo "Lyon" and "Nimes," two towns near the Auvergne region. However, I have not attempted to associate any towns in Averoigne with corresponding cities in modern France (or historic Auvergne) because it is unlikely that Smith intended such parallels to be drawn, other than in the broadest of terms.

Instead, the towns, rivers, etc, have been located according to the information given within the Averoigne cycle. For example, in "The Holiness of Azédarac" when Brother Ambrose must travel from Ximes through the Averoigne Forest to Vyônes, the trip is expected to take a day and a half. Consequently, Vyônes appears at a considerable distance from Ximes, with the forest in between; the Inn of Bonne Jouissance lies somewhat more than halfway along his route. Another example: "The Colossus of Ylourgne" indicates that the ruinous castle of Ylourgne lies eastward of Vyônes, reportedly some forty miles distant, with much of the journey passing through the forest and along the River Isoile toward its fountainhead in the rocky valley below Ylourgne. Therefore, Ylourgne is situated well to the east of Vyônes, "beyond the werewolf-haunted forest, in the outlying, semi-mountainous hills of Averoigne." The River Isoile springs from the valley below the ruinous castle, and the Cistercian Monastery lies on the opposite side of the valley from Ylourgne.

Another bit of information comes from "The Disinterment of Venus," where Smith describes Sainte Zénobie as a neighboring village of Périgon; also, both seem located near Vyônes, chief city of the province. Finally, in "The Mandrakes" we learn of the marshes in lower Averoigne, fed by the slackening waters of the Isoile. "Mother of Toads" is also set down in the marshes, not far from the village of Les Hiboux.

Obviously, it is impossible to create a real geography out of an imaginary setting. Indeed, a few discrepancies may seem to exist between this map and certain descriptive passages by Smith. This should not seem surprising when we consider that Smith never used, and probably did not anticipate the creation of, such a map. Instead, he simply placed the towns and various geologic features wherever required by plot or atmosphere, and thus nearly all the tales lie within the shadow of the Averoigne Forest or along the banks of the River Isoile.

The gorgeously detailed descriptions common to all Smith's best prose made this map relatively easy to complete; the geography seemed to suggest itself. A general map of France is also included, in order to show the size and location of Averoigne relative to the rest of the country.

Among Smith's story-cycles, the tales of Averoigne stand out as the closest to our own milieu, having both a real historical time and place, that of mediaeval France. Perhaps for this reason he felt obliged to more fully develop the humanity of these characters, describing in close detail their hopes and fears, their failings as well as their triumphs; the all-too-human emotions that we all possess. It is also known that Smith enjoyed associating his cabin in the woods on the outskirts of Auburn with the forest of Averoigne. He referred to the Catholic novitiate near his home as "The Nunnery of Averoigne" and fans and writers who visited him there also commented that Smith lived within this primeval forest. H.P. Lovecraft himself wrote a very moving poem entitled "To Klarkash-Ton, Lord of Averoigne" as a tribute to his friend and kindred spirit whom he never met in person, yet became one of his closest friends through correspondence alone. Is it not possible then (or even likely) that these tales of Averoigne have a more autobiographical nature than those stories set in Zothique, Hyperborea, or Poseidonis? After all, many of the protagonists in his Averoigne stories are either poets or hermits; this may be a coincidence, perhaps, but I prefer to think otherwise!

Clark Ashton Smith was an intensely private man, so we will leave any speculation regarding his love life alone. Still, it's easy for me to imagine a warm spring day some one hundred years ago, when a young bard of Auburn hurried through the woods on some prearranged ren-dezvous, with his mind full of verses and his heart full of anticipation. Or perhaps some sweltering summer evening as he headed down to the American river (which from his cabin was an easy walk away) to escape the heat and relax in the cooling waters, that he may have en-countered a beautiful enchantress bathing in his favorite swimming hole. . . . Who knows? But if we have learned anything from the Lord of Averoigne, it is that all things are possible within the endless realms of the imagination!

—RON HILGER

While researching and compiling *The Averoigne Chronicles* I consulted with Donald Sidney-Fryer (who holds a degree in French language and literature) regarding certain French words coined by Smith, resulting in the following pronunciation guide. The somewhat Anglicized pronunciations of "Averoigne" and "Ylourgne" follow those used by the author himself. Other pronunciations have also been slightly Anglicized in deference to Anglophones, particularly in reference to the "half N" ending such French words as "Périgon" and "Malnéant."

—R. H.

AVEROIGNE	av-er-RON
AZÉDARAC	a-zay-da-RAHK
FAUSSESFLAMMES	fohs-flahm
ISOILE	ee-ZWAHL
LA FRÊNAIE	la frer-NAY
LES HIBOUX	lay ee-BOO
MALINBOIS	mal-in-BWAH
MALNÉANT	mal-nay-AHN
MORIAMIS	mor-ee-a-MEES
PÉRIGON	pay-ree-GON
SAINTE ZÉNOBIE	SANT zay-no-BEE
SYLAIRE	see-LAIR
VYÔNES	vee-OHN
YLOURGNE	ee-LORN or ee-LOORN

France

Paris

Averoigne

Spain

Les H

Sainte Zénobie

To Paris

Cistercian Monastery

Ylourgne

usses
lammes

Vyônes

La Frênaie

Tomb of
Malinbois

Isoile River

Tower of
Morlamis

Inn of
Bonne
Jouissance

Sylaire

Château of Azédarac

Ximes

Les

Oracle of
Sadoqua

To Malnéant

ort

Les
Hiboux

Marshes

Averoigne

AVEROIGNE

In Averoigne the enchantress weaves
Weird spells that call a changeling sun,
Or hale the moon of Hecate
Down to the ivy-hooded towers.
At evening, from her nightshade bowers,
The bidden vipers creep, to be
The envoys of her malison;
And philtres drained from tomb-fat leaves
Drip through her silver sieves.

In Averoigne swart phantoms flown
From pestilent moat and stagnant lake
Glide through the garish festival
In torch-lit cities far from time.
Whether for death or birth, the chime
Of changeless bells equivocal
Clangs forth, while carven satyrs make
With mouths of sullen, sombre stone
Unending silent moan.

In Averoigne abides the mage.
So deep the silence of his cell,
He hears the termless monarchies
That walk with thunder-echoing shoon
In iron castles past the moon—
Fast-moated with eternities;
And hears the shrewish laughters swell
Of Norns that plot the impested age
And wars that suns shall wage.

In Averoigne the lamia sings
To lyres restored from tombs antique,
And lets her coiling tresses fall
Before a necromantic glass.
She sees her vein-drawn lovers pass,
Faintly they cry to her, and all
The bale they find, the bliss they seek,
Is echoed in the tarnished strings
That tell archaic things.

A Night In Malnéant

My brief sojourn in the city of Malnéant occurred during a period of my life that is dim and dubious even as that city itself and the misty regions lying thereabouts. I have no precise recollection of its locality, nor can I remember exactly when and how I came to visit it. But I had heard vaguely that such a place was situated along my route; and when I came to the fog-enfolded river that flows beside its walls, and heard beyond the river the mortuary tolling of many bells, I surmised that I was approaching Malnéant. On reaching the grey, colossal bridge that crosses the river at this point, I could have continued at will on other roads leading to remoter cities: but it seemed to me that I might as well enter Malnéant as any other place. And so it was that I set foot on the bridge of shadowy arches, under which the black waters flowed in stealthy division and were joined again in a silence as of Styx and Acheron.

That period of my life, I have said, was dim and dubious—mainly so, perhaps, on account of my need for forgetfulness, my persistent and at times partially rewarded search for oblivion. And that which I needed to forget above all was the death of the lady Mariel, and the fact that I myself had slain her as surely as if I had done the deed with my own hand. For she had loved me with an affection that was deeper and purer and more stable than mine; and my changeable temper, my fits of cruel indifference or ferocious irritability, had broken her gentle heart. So it was that she had sought the anodyne of a lethal poison; and after she was laid to rest in the somber marble vaults of her ancestors, I had become a wanderer, followed and forever tortured by a belated remorse. For months, or years, I am uncertain which, I roamed from place to place, from old-world city to city, heeding little where I went,

25

if only wine and the other agents of oblivion were available. . . . And thus it was that I came, somewhile in my indefinite journeying, to the dim environs of Malnéant.

The sun (if ever there was a sun above this region) had been lost for I knew not how long in a sky of leaden vapors; the day was drear and sullen at best. But now, by the thickening of the shadows and the mist, I felt that evening must be near; and the bells I had heard in Malnéant, however heavy and sepulchral their tolling, gave at least the assurance of prospective shelter for the night. So I crossed the long bridge, and entered the grimly yawning gate with a quickening of my footsteps even if with no alacrity of spirit.

The dusk had gathered behind the grey walls, but there were few lights in the city. Also, few people were abroad, and these went upon their way with a sort of solemn haste, as if on some funereal errand that would admit of no delay. The streets were narrow, the houses high, with overhanging balconies and heavily curtained or shuttered windows. All was very silent, except for the bells, which tolled recurrently, sometimes faint and far off, and sometimes with a loud and startling clangor that seemed to come almost from overhead.

As I plunged among the shadowy mansions, along the streets from which a visible twilight issued to envelop me, it seemed that I was going further and further away from my memories at every step. For this reason I did not immediately inquire my way to a tavern, but was content to lose myself more and more in the grey labyrinth of buildings, which grew vaguer and vaguer amid the ever-mounting darkness and fog, as if they were about to dissolve in oblivion.

I think my soul would have been almost at peace with itself during that first hour in Malnéant, if it had not been for the reiterant ringing of the bells, which were like all bells that toll for the repose of the dead, and therefore set me to remembering those that had rung for Mariel. But whenever they ceased, my thoughts would soon drift back with an indolent ease, a recovered security, to the all-surrounding vagueness, and I would walk the length of many dark alleys, past many of the shrouded and mysterious mansions, in whose interior I could somehow imagine nothing but cobwebs and silence and slumber, before the hateful pealing began once more. Also, I deemed that the sound of the bells receded and became fainter with each repetition; and I hoped that I would presently lose it altogether, along with my troublous memories.

I have no idea how far I had gone in Malnéant, nor how long I had roamed among those houses that hardly seemed as if they could be peopled by any but the sleeping or the dead. At last, however, I became aware that I was very tired, and bethought me of food and wine and a lodging for the night. But nowhere in my wanderings had I noticed the sign-board of an inn; so I resolved to ask the next passer-by for the desired direction.

As I have said before, there were few people abroad—how few, I had apparently not realized. For when I made up my mind to address one of them, it appeared that there was no one at all; and I walked onward through street after street in my futile search for a living face.

At length I met two women, clothed in grey that was cold and dim as the folds of the fog, and veiled withal, who were hurrying along the street with the same funereal intentness I had perceived in all other denizens of that city. I made bold to accost them, asking if they could direct me to an inn.

Scarcely pausing or even turning their heads, they answered: "We cannot tell you. We are shroud-weavers, and we have been busy making a shroud for the lady Mariel."

Now, at that name, which of all names in the world was the one I should least have expected or cared to hear, an unspeakable chill invaded my heart, and I felt a dreadful surprise, a dismay like the breath of the tomb. It was indeed strange that in this dim city, so far in time and space from all I had fled to escape, a woman should have recently died who was also named Mariel. The coincidence appeared so sinister, that an odd fear of the streets through which I wandered was born suddenly in my soul; for the name had evoked, with a more irrevocable fatality than the tolling of the bells, all that I wished to forget; and the dying coals of my remorse were fanned to a ravening flame.

As I went onward, with paces that had become more hurried, more feverish than those of the people of Malnéant, I met two men, who were likewise dressed from head to foot in grey, and I asked of them the same question I had asked of the shroud-weavers.

"We cannot tell you," they replied. "We are coffin-makers, and we have been busy making a coffin for the lady Mariel."

As they spoke, and hastened on, the bells rang out again, this time very near at hand, with a more leaden and sepulchral menace in their dismal tolling. And everything about me, the tall and misty houses, the rare and wraith-like figures, became as if part of the obscure confusion and fear and bafflement of a nightmare. Moment by moment, the co-incidence on which I had stumbled appeared all too bizarre for belief, and I was troubled now by the monstrous and absurd idea that the Mariel I knew had only just died, and this fantastic city was in some unsurmisable manner connected with her death. But this, of course, my reason rejected summarily, and I kept repeating to myself: "The Mariel of whom they speak is another Mariel." And it irritated me be-yond all measure that a doubt so enormous and ludicrous should re-turn when my logic had dismissed it.

I met no more people of whom to inquire my way. But at length, as I fought with my shadowy perplexity and my burning memories, I found that I had paused almost beneath the weather-beaten sign of an inn, on which the lettering had been half-effaced by time and the brown lichens. The building was obviously very old, like all the houses in Malnéant; its upper stories were lost in the swirling fog, except for a few furtive lights that glowed obscurely down; and a vague and musty odor of antiquity came forth to greet me as I mounted the steps and tried to open the ponderous door. But the door had been locked or bolted, so I began to pound upon it with my fists, to attract the attention of those within. After much delay, the door was opened slowly and grudgingly, and a cadaverous-looking individual peered forth, frowning with portentous gravity as he saw me.

"What do you desire?" he queried, in tones that were both brusk and solemn.

"A room for the night, and wine," I answered.

"We cannot accommodate you. All the rooms are now occupied by people who have come to attend the obsequies of the lady Mariel; and all the wine in the house has been requisitioned for their use. You will have to go elsewhere." He closed the door quickly, after the last words.

I turned to resume my wanderings, and all that had troubled me before was now intensified a hundredfold. The grey mists and the greyer houses were full of the menace of memory, they were like traitorous tombs from which the cadavers of dead hours poured forth to assail me with envenomed fangs and talons. I cursed the hour when I had entered Malnéant, for it seemed to me now that in so doing I had merely completed a funereal, sinister circle through time, and had returned to the day of Mariel's death. And certainly, all my recollections of Mariel, of her final agony and her entombment, had assumed the frightful vitality of present things. But my reason still maintained, of course, that the Mariel who lay dead somewhere in Malnéant, and for whom all these obsequial preparations were being made, was not the lady whom I had loved, but another.

After threading many streets that were still darker and narrower than those before traversed, I found a second inn, bearing a similar weather-worn sign, and in all other respects very much like the first. The door was also barred, and I knocked thereon in much trepidation, and was in no manner surprised when a second individual with a cadaverous face informed me in tones of mortuary solemnity:

"We cannot accommodate you. All the rooms have been taken by musicians and mourners who will serve at the obsequies of the lady Mariel; and all the wine has been reserved for their use."

Now I began to dread the city about me with a manifold fear: for apparently the whole business of the people of Malnéant consisted of preparations for the funeral of this lady Mariel, whether or not she was the same Mariel whom I had known. And it began to be obvious that I must walk the streets of the city all night because of these same preparations. All at once, an overwhelming weariness was mingled with my nightmare terror and perplexity.

I had not long continued my peregrinations, after leaving the second inn, when the bells were tolled once more. For the first time, I found it possible to identify their source: they were in the spires of a great cathedral which loomed immediately before me through the fog. Some people were entering the cathedral, and a curiosity, which I knew to be both morbid and perilous, prompted me to follow them. Here, I somehow felt, I should be able to learn more regarding the mystery that tormented me.

All was dim within, and the light of many tapers scarcely served to illuminate the vast nave and altar. Masses were being said by priests in black whose faces I could not see distinctly; and to me, their chanting was like words in a dream; and I could hear nothing, and nothing was plainly visible in all the place, except a bier of opulent fabrics, on which there lay a motionless form in white. Flowers of many hues had already been strewn upon the bier, and their fragrance filled the air with a drowsy languor, with an anodyne that seemed to drug my heart and brain. Such flowers had been cast on the bier of Mariel; and even thus, at her funeral, I had been overcome by a momentary dulling of the senses because of their perfume.

I became dimly aware that someone was at my elbow. With eyes still intent on the bier, I asked:

"Who is it that lies yonder, for whom these masses are being said, and these bells are rung?" And a slow, sepulchral voice replied:

"It is the lady Mariel, who died yesterday, and who will be interred tomorrow in the vaults of her ancestors. If you wish, you may go forward and gaze upon her."

So I went down the aisle of the cathedral, even to the side of the bier, whose opulent fabrics trailed on the cold flags. And the face of her who lay thereon, with a tranquil smile about the lips and tender shadows upon the shut eyelids, was the face of the Mariel I had loved, and of none other. The tides of time were frozen in their flowing; and all that was or had been or could be, all of the world that existed aside from her, became as fading shadows; and even as once before (was it aeons or instants ago?) my soul was locked in the marble hell of a hopeless grief and regret. I could not move. I could not cry out or even weep, for my very tears were turned to ice. And now I knew with a terrible certitude that this one event, the death of the lady Mariel, had drawn apart from all other happenings, had broken away from the sequence of time and had found for itself a setting of appropriate gloom and solemnity; or perhaps had even built around itself the whole enormous maze of that spectral city, in which to abide my destined return among the mists of a deceptive oblivion.

At length, with an awful effort of will, I turned my eyes away and leaving the cathedral with steps that were both hurried and leaden, I sought to find an egress from the dismal labyrinth of Malnéant to the gate by which I had entered. But this was by no means easy, and I must have roamed for hours in alleys blind and stifling as tombs, and along the tortuous, self-reverting thoroughfares, ere I came to a familiar street and was able henceforward to direct my paces with something of surety. And a dull and sunless daylight was dawning behind the mists when I crossed the bridge and came again to the road that would lead me away from that fatal city.

Since then, I have wandered long and in many places. But never again have I cared to revisit those old-world realms of fog and mist, for fear that I should come once more to Malnéant, and find that its people are still busied with their preparations for the obsequies of the lady Mariel.

THE NEVERMORE-TO-BE

Lady, be the châtelaine
Of my vagrant dreams and vain:
Knowing naught is true and fair
Save the love that is despair,
In thy heart's withholden visne
Share with me the might-have-been,
Weave with me the sorcery
Of the nevermore-to-be.

Lady, let us pluck delight
Only from a forfeit night,
From the bedded myrtles strewn
'Neath a never-risen moon.
From the coil of years made free
In the climes of reverie,
Flee we to the phantom Troy
Of a time-forbidden joy.

Lady, be the châtelaine
Of my vagrant dreams and vain:
Be thou true and be thou kind
To the love we shall not find—
Sweet as aught the sirens sang:
Time shall bring no dearer pang
Nor a mightier sorcery
Than the nevermore-to-be.

THE MAKER OF GARGOYLES

I

Among the many gargoyles that frowned or leered from the roof of the new-built cathedral of Vyônes, two were pre-eminent above the rest by virtue of their fine workmanship and their supreme grotesquery. These two had been wrought by the stone-carver Blaise Reynard, a native of Vyônes, who had lately returned from a long sojourn in the cities of Provence, and had secured employment on the cathedral when the three years' task of its construction and ornamentation was well-nigh completed. In view of the wonderful artistry shown by Reynard, it was regretted by Ambrosius, the archbishop, that it had not been possible to commit the execution of all the gargoyles to this delicate and accomplished workman; but other people, with less liberal tastes than Ambrosius, were heard to express a different opinion.

This opinion, perhaps, was tinged by the personal dislike that had been generally felt toward Reynard in Vyônes even from his boyhood; and which had been revived with some virulence on his return. Whether rightly or unjustly, his very physiognomy had always marked him out for public disfavor: he was inordinately dark, with hair and beard of a preternatural bluish-black, and slanting, ill-matched eyes that gave him a sinister and cunning air. His taciturn and saturnine ways were such as a superstitious people would identify with necromantic knowledge or complicity; and there were those who covertly accused him of being in league with Satan; though the accusations were little more than vague, anonymous rumors, even to the end, through lack of veritable evidence.

However, the people who suspected Reynard of diabolic affiliations were wont for awhile to instance the two gargoyles as sufficient proof. No man, they contended, who was not inspired by the Arch-Enemy, could have carven anything so sheerly evil and malignant, could have embodied so consummately in mere stone the living lineaments of the most demoniacal of all the deadly Sins.

The two gargoyles were perched on opposite corners of a high tower of the cathedral. One was a snarling, murderous, cat-headed monster, with retracted lips revealing formidable fangs, and eyes that glared intolerable hatred from beneath ferine brows. This creature had the claws and wings of a griffin, and seemed as if it were poised in readiness to swoop down on the city of Vyônes, like a harpy on its prey. Its companion was a horned satyr, with the vans of some great bat such as might roam the nether caverns, with sharp, clenching talons, and a look of Satanically brooding lust, as if it were gloating above the helpless object of its unclean desire. Both figures were complete, even to the hindquarters, and were not mere conventional adjuncts of the roof. One would have expected them to start at any moment from the stone in which they were mortised.

Ambrosius, a lover of art, had been openly delighted with these creations, because of their high technical merit and their verisimilitude as works of sculpture. But others, including many humbler dignitaries of the Church, were more or less scandalized, and said that the workman had informed these figures with the visible likeness of his own vices, to the glory of Belial rather than of God, and thus had perpetrated a sort of blasphemy. Of course, they admitted, a certain amount of grotesquery was requisite in gargoyles; but in this case the allowable bounds had been egregiously over-passed.

However, with the completion of the cathedral, and in spite of all this adverse criticism, the high-poised gargoyles of Blaise Reynard, like all other details of the building, were soon taken for granted through mere everyday familiarity; and eventually they were almost forgotten.

The scandal of opposition died down, and the stone-carver himself, though the town-folk continued to eye him askance, was able to secure other work through the favor of discriminating patrons. He remained in Vyônes; and paid his addresses, albeit without visible success, to a taverner's daughter, one Nicolette Villom, of whom, it was said, he had long been enamored in his own surly and reticent fashion.

But Reynard himself had not forgotten the gargoyles. Often, in passing the superb pile of the cathedral, he would gaze up at them with a secret satisfaction whose cause he could hardly have assigned or de-limited. They seemed to retain for him a rare and mystical meaning, to signalize an obscure but pleasurable triumph.

He would have said, if asked for the reason for his satisfaction, that he was proud of a skillful piece of handiwork. He would not have said, and perhaps would not even have known, that in one of the gar-goyles he had imprisoned all his festering rancor, all his answering spleen and hatred toward the people of Vyônes, who had always hated him; and had set the image of this rancor to peer venomously down for ever from a lofty place. And perhaps he would not even have dreamt that in the second gargoyle he had somehow expressed his own dour and satyrlike passion for the girl Nicolette—a passion that had brought him back to the detested city of his youth after years of wan-dering; a passion singularly tenacious of one object, and differing in this regard from the ordinary lusts of a nature so brutal as Reynard's.

Always to the stone-cutter, even more than to those who had criti-cized and abhorred his productions, the gargoyles were alive, they pos-sessed a vitality and a sentiency of their own. And most of all did they seem to live when the summer drew to an end and the autumn rains had gathered upon Vyônes. Then, when the full cathedral gutters poured above the streets, one might have thought that the actual spit-tle of a foul malevolence, the very slaver of an impure lust, had some-how been mingled with the water that ran in rills from the mouths of the gargoyles.

II

At that time, in the year of our Lord, 1138, Vyônes was the principal town of the province of Averoigne. On two sides the great, shadow-haunted forest, a place of equivocal legends, of *loups-garous* and phantoms, approached to the very walls and flung its umbrage upon them at early forenoon and evening. On the other sides there lay cultivated fields, and gentle streams that meandered among willows or poplars, and roads that ran through an open plain to the high châteaux of noble lords and to regions beyond Averoigne.

The town itself was prosperous, and had never shared in the ill-fame of the bordering forest. It had long been sanctified by the presence of two nunneries and a monastery; and now, with the completion of the long-planned cathedral, it was thought that Vyônes would have henceforward the additional protection of a more august holiness; that demon and *stryge* and incubus would keep their distance from its heaven-favored purlieus with a more meticulous caution than before.

Of course, as in all mediaeval towns, there had been occasional instances of alleged sorcery or demoniacal possession; and, once or twice, the perilous temptations of succubi had made their inroads on the pious virtue of Vyônes. But this was nothing more than might be expected, in a world where the Devil and his works were always more or less rampant. No one could possibly have anticipated the reign of infernal horrors that was to make hideous the latter months of autumn, following the cathedral's erection.

To make the matter even more inexplicable, and more blasphemously dreadful than it would otherwise have been, the first of these horrors occurred in the neighborhood of the cathedral itself and almost beneath its sheltering shadow.

Two men, a respectable clothier named Guillaume Maspier and an equally reputable cooper, one Gérôme Mazzal, were returning to their lodgings in the late hours of a November eve, after imbibing both the red and white wines of the countryside in more than one tavern. According to Maspier, who alone survived to tell the tale, they were passing along a street that skirted the cathedral square, and could see the bulk of the great building against the stars, when a flying monster, black as the soot of Abaddon, had descended upon them from the heavens and assailed Gérôme Mazzal, beating him down with its heavily flapping wings and seizing him with its inch-long teeth and talons.

Maspier was unable to describe the creature with minuteness, for he had seen it but dimly and partially in the unlit street; and moreover, the fate of his companion, who had fallen to the cobblestones with the black devil snarling and tearing at his throat, had not induced Maspier to linger in that vicinity. He had betaken himself from the scene with all the celerity of which he was capable, and had stopped only at the house of a priest, many streets away, where he had related his adventure between shudderings and hiccoughings.

Armed with holy water and aspergillums, and accompanied by many of the towns-people carrying torches and staves and halberds, the priest was led by Maspier to the place of the horror; and there they found the body of Mazzal, with fearfully mangled face, and throat and bosom lined with bloody lacerations. The demoniac assailant had flown, and it was not seen or encountered again that night; but those who had beheld its work returned aghast to their homes, feeling that a creature of nethermost hell had come to visit the city, and perchance to abide therein.

Consternation was rife on the morrow, when the story became generally known; and rites of exorcism against the invading demon were performed by the clergy in all public places and before thresholds. But the sprinkling of holy water and the mumbling of the stated forms were futile; for the evil spirit was still abroad, and its malignity was proved once more, on the night following the ghastly death of Gérôme Mazzal.

This time, it claimed two victims, burghers of high probity and some consequence, on whom it descended in a narrow alley, slaying one of them instantaneously, and dragging down the other from behind as he sought to flee. The shrill cries of the helpless men, and the guttural growling of the demon, were heard by people in the houses along the alley; and some, who were hardy enough to peer from their windows, had seen the departure of the infamous assailant, blotting out the autumn stars with the sable and misshapen foulness of its wings, and hovering in execrable menace above the house-tops.

After this, few people would venture abroad at night, unless in case of dire and exigent need; and those who did venture went in armed companies and were all furnished with flambeaux, thinking thus to frighten away the demon, which they adjudged a creature of darkness that would abhor the light and shrink therefrom, through the nature of its kind. But the boldness of this fiend was beyond measure; for it proceeded to attack more than one company of worthy citizens, disregarding the flaring torches that were thrust in its face, or putting them out with the stenchful wind of its wide vans.

Evidently it was a spirit of homicidal hate, for all the people on whom it seized were grievously mangled or torn to numberless shreds by its teeth and talons. Those who saw it, and survived, were wont to describe it variously and with much ambiguity; but all agreed in attributing to it the head of a ferocious animal and the wings of a monstrous bird. Some, the most learned in demonology, were fain to identify it with Modo, the spirit of murder; and others took it for one of the great lieutenants of Satan, perhaps Amaimon or Alastor, gone mad with exasperation at the impregnable supremacy of Christ in the holy city of Vyônes.

The terror that soon prevailed, beneath the widening scope of these Satanical incursions and depredations, was beyond all belief—a clotted, seething, devil-ridden gloom of superstitious obsession, not to be hinted at in modern language. Even by daylight, the Gothic wings of nightmare seemed to brood in undeparting oppression above the city; and fear was everywhere, like the foul contagion of some epidemic plague. The inhabitants went their way in prayer and trembling; and the Archbishop himself, as well as the subordinate clergy, confessed an inability to cope with the ever-growing horror. An emissary was sent to Rome, to procure water that had been specially sanctified by the Pope. This alone, it was thought, would be efficacious enough to drive away the dreadful visitant.

In the meanwhile, the horror waxed, and mounted to its culmination. One eve, toward the middle of November, the abbot of the local monastery of Cordeliers, who had gone forth to administer extreme unction to a dying friend, was seized by the black devil just as he approached the threshold of his destination, and was slain in the same atrocious manner as the other victims.

To this doubly infamous deed, a scarce-believable blasphemy was soon added. On the very next night, while the torn body of the abbot lay on a rich catafalque in the cathedral, and masses were being said and tapers burnt, the demon invaded the high nave through the open door, extinguished all the candles with one flap of its sooty wings, and dragged down no less than three of the officiating priests to an unholy death in the darkness.

Everyone now felt that a truly formidable assault was being made by the powers of Evil on the Christian probity of Vyônes. In the condition of abject terror, of extreme disorder and demoralization that followed upon this new atrocity, there was a deplorable outbreak of human crime, of murder and rapine and thievery, together with covert manifestations of Satanism, and celebrations of the Black Mass attended by many neophytes.

Then, in the midst of all this pandemoniacal fear and confusion, it was rumored that a second devil had been seen in Vyônes; that the murderous fiend was accompanied by a spirit of equal deformity and darkness, whose intentions were those of lechery, and which molested none but women. This creature had frightened several dames and demoiselles and maid-servants into a veritable hysteria by peering through their bedroom windows; and had sidled lasciviously, with uncouth mows and grimaces, and grotesque flappings of its bat-shaped wings, toward others who had occasion to fare from house to house across the nocturnal streets.

However, strange to say, there were no authentic instances in which the chastity of any woman had suffered actual harm from this noisome incubus. Many were approached by it, and were terrified immoderately by the hideousness and lustfulness of its demeanor; but no one was ever touched. Even in that time of horror, both spiritual and corporeal, there were those who made a ribald jest of this singular abstention on the part of the demon, and said it was seeking throughout Vyônes for someone whom it had not yet found.

III

The lodgings of Blaise Reynard were separated only by the length of a dark and crooked alley from the tavern kept by Jean Villom, the father of Nicolette. In this tavern, Reynard had been wont to spend his evenings; though his suit was frowned upon by Jean Villom, and had received but scant encouragement from the girl herself. However, because of his well-filled purse and his almost illimitable capacity for wine, Reynard was tolerated. He came early each night, with the falling of darkness, and would sit in silence hour after hour, staring with hot and sullen eyes at Nicolette, and gulping joylessly the potent vintages of Averoigne. Apart from their desire to retain his custom, the people of the tavern were a little afraid of him, on account of his dubious and semi-sorcerous reputation, and also because of his surly temper. They did not wish to antagonize him more than was necessary.

Like everyone else in Vyônes, Reynard had felt the suffocating burden of superstitious terror during those nights when the fiendish marauder was hovering above the town and might descend on the luckless wayfarer at any moment, in any locality. Nothing less urgent and imperative than the obsession of his half-bestial longing for Nicolette could have induced him to traverse after dark the length of the winding alley to the tavern door. The autumn nights had been moonless. Now, on the evening that followed the desecration of the cathedral itself by the murderous devil, a new-born crescent was lowering its fragile, sanguine-colored horn beyond the house-tops as Reynard went forth from his lodgings at the accustomed hour. He lost sight of its comforting beam in the high-walled and narrow alley, and shivered with dread as he hastened onward through shadows that were dissipated only by the rare and timid ray from some lofty window. It seemed to him, at each turn and angle, that the gloom was curded by the unclean umbrage of Satanic wings, and might reveal in another instant the gleaming of abhorrent eyes ignited by the everlasting coals of the Pit. When he came forth at the alley's end, he saw with a start of fresh panic that the crescent moon was blotted out by a cloud that had the semblance of uncouthly arched and pointed wings.

He reached the tavern with a sense of supreme relief, for he had begun to feel a distinct intuition that someone or something was following him, unheard and invisible—a presence that seemed to load the dusk with prodigious menace. He entered, and closed the door behind him very quickly, as if he were shutting it in the face of a dread pursuer.

There were few people in the tavern that evening. The girl Nicolette was serving wine to a mercer's assistant, one Raoul Coupain, a personable youth and a newcomer in the neighborhood, and she was laughing with what Reynard considered unseemly gayety at the broad jests and amorous sallies of this Raoul. Jean Villom was discussing in a low voice the latest enormities of the demons with two cronies at a table in the farthest corner, and was drinking fully as much liquor as his customers.

Glowering with jealousy at the presence of Raoul Coupain, whom he suspected of being a favored rival, Reynard seated himself in silence and stared malignly at the flirtatious couple. No one seemed to have noticed his entrance; for Villom went on talking to his cronies without pause or interruption, and Nicolette and her companion were equally oblivious. To his jealous rage, Reynard soon added the resentment of one who feels that he is being deliberately ignored. He began to pound on the table with his heavy fists, to attract attention.

Villom, who had been sitting all the while with his back turned, now called out to Nicolette without even troubling to face around on his stool, telling her to serve Reynard. Giving a backward smile at Coupain, she came slowly and with open reluctance to the stone-carver's table.

She was small and buxom, with reddish-gold hair that curled luxuriantly above the short, delicious oval of her face; and she was gowned in a tight-fitting dress of apple-green that revealed the firm, seductive outlines of her hips and bosom. Her air was disdainful and a little cold, for she did not like Reynard and had taken small pains at any time to conceal her aversion. But to Reynard she was lovelier and more desirable than ever, and he felt a savage impulse to seize her in his arms and carry her bodily away from the tavern before the eyes of Raoul Coupain and her father.

"Bring me a pitcher of La Frênaie," he ordered gruffly, in a voice that betrayed his mingled resentment and desire.

Tossing her head lightly and scornfully, with more glances at Coupain, the girl obeyed. She placed the fiery, blood-dark wine before Reynard without speaking, and then went back to resume her bantering with the mercer's assistant.

Reynard began to drink, and the potent vintage merely served to inflame his smouldering enmity and passion. His eyes became venomous, his curling lips malignant as those of the gargoyles he had carved on the new cathedral. A baleful, primordial anger, like the rage of some morose and thwarted faun, burned within him with its slow red fire; but he strove to repress it, and sat silent and motionless, except for the frequent filling and emptying of his wine-cup.

Raoul Coupain had also consumed a liberal quantity of wine. As a result, he soon became bolder in his love-making, and strove to kiss the hand of Nicolette, who had now seated herself on the bench beside him. The hand was playfully withheld; and then, after its owner had cuffed Raoul very lightly and briskly, was granted to the claimant in a fashion that struck Reynard as being no less than wanton.

Snarling inarticulately, with a mad impulse to rush forward and slay the successful rival with his bare hands, he started to his feet and stepped toward the playful pair. His movement was noted by one of the men in the far corner, who spoke warningly to Villom. The tavern-keeper arose, lurching a little from his potations, and came warily across the room with his eyes on Reynard, ready to interfere in case of violence.

Reynard paused with momentary irresolution, and then went on, half-insane with a mounting hatred for them all. He longed to kill Villom and Coupain, to kill the hateful cronies who sat staring from the corner, and then, above their throttled corpses, to ravage with fierce kisses and vehement caresses the shrinking lips and body of Nicolette.

Seeing the approach of the stone-carver, and knowing his evil temper and dark jealousy, Coupain also rose to his feet and plucked stealthily beneath his cloak at the hilt of a little dagger which he carried. In the meanwhile, Jean Villom had interposed his burly bulk between the rivals. For the sake of the tavern's good repute, he wished to prevent the possible brawl.

"Back to your table, stone-cutter," he roared belligerently at Reynard.

Being unarmed, and seeing himself outnumbered, Reynard paused again, though his anger still simmered within him like the contents of a sorcerer's cauldron. With ruddy points of murderous flame in his hollow, slitted eyes, he glared at the three people before him, and saw beyond them, with instinctive rather than conscious awareness, the leaded panes of the tavern window, in whose glass the room was dimly reflected with its glowing tapers, its glimmering table-ware, the heads of Coupain and Villom and the girl Nicolette, and his own shadowy face among them.

Strangely, and, it would seem, inconsequently, he remembered at that moment the dark, ambiguous cloud he had seen across the moon, and the insistent feeling of obscure pursuit while he had traversed the alley.

Then, as he gazed irresolutely at the group before him, and its vague reflection in the glass beyond, there came a thunderous crash, and the panes of the window with their pictured scene were shattered inward in a score of fragments. Ere the litter of falling glass had reached the tavern floor, a swart and monstrous form flew into the room, with a beating of heavy vans that caused the tapers to flare troublously, and the shadows to dance like a sabbat of misshapen devils. The thing hovered for a moment, and seemed to tower in a great darkness higher than the ceiling above the heads of Reynard and the others as they turned toward it. They saw the malignant burning of its eyes, like coals in the depth of Tartarean pits, and the curling of its hateful lips on the bared teeth that were longer and sharper than serpent-fangs.

Behind it now, another shadowy flying monster came in through the broken window with a loud flapping of its ribbed and pointed wings. There was something lascivious in the very motion of its flight, even as homicidal hatred and malignity were manifest in the flight of the other. Its satyr-like face was twisted in a horrible, never-changing leer, and its lustful eyes were fixed on Nicolette as it hung in air beside the first intruder.

Reynard, as well as the other men, was petrified by a feeling of astonishment and consternation so extreme as almost to preclude terror. Voiceless and motionless, they beheld the demoniac intrusion; and the consternation of Reynard, in particular, was mingled with an element of unspeakable surprise, together with a dreadful recognizance. But the girl Nicolette, with a mad scream of horror, turned and started to flee across the room.

As if her cry had been the one provocation needed, the two demons swooped upon their victims. One, with a ferocious slash of its outstretched claws, tore open the throat of Jean Villom, who fell with a gurgling, blood-choked groan; and then, in the same fashion, it assailed Raoul Coupain. The other, in the meanwhile, had pursued and overtaken the fleeing girl, and had seized her in its bestial forearms, with the ribbed wings enfolding her like a hellish drapery.

The room was filled by a moaning whirlwind, by a chaos of wild cries and tossing struggling shadows. Reynard heard the guttural snarling of the murderous monster, muffled by the body of Coupain, whom it was tearing with its teeth; and he heard the lubricious laughter of the incubus, above the shrieks of the hysterically frightened girl. Then the grotesquely flaring tapers went out in a gust of swirling air, and Reynard received a violent blow in the darkness—the blow of some rushing object, perhaps of a passing wing, that was hard and heavy as stone. He fell, and became insensible.

IV

Dully and confusedly, with much effort, Reynard struggled back to consciousness. For a brief interim, he could not remember where he was nor what had happened. He was troubled by the painful throbbing of his head, by the humming of agitated voices about him, by the glaring of many lights and the thronging of many faces when he opened his eyes; and, above all, by the sense of nameless but grievous calamity and uttermost horror that weighed him down from the first dawning of sentiency.

Memory returned to him, laggard and reluctant; and with it, a full awareness of his surroundings and situation. He was lying on the tavern floor, and his own warm, sticky blood was rilling across his face from the wound on his aching head. The long room was half-filled

with people of the neighborhood, bearing torches and knives and halberds, who had entered and were peering at the corpses of Villom and
Coupain, which lay amid pools of wine-diluted blood and the wreckage
of the shattered furniture and table-ware.

Nicolette, with her green gown in shreds, and her body crushed by
the embraces of the demon, was moaning feebly while women crowded about her with ineffectual cries and questions which she could not
even hear or understand. The two cronies of Villom, horribly clawed
and mangled, were dead beside their overturned table.

Stupefied with horror, and still dizzy from the blow that had laid
him unconscious, Reynard staggered to his feet, and found himself surrounded at once by inquiring faces and voices. Some of the people were
a little suspicious of him, since he was the sole survivor in the tavern,
and bore an ill repute; but his replies to their questions soon convinced
them that the new crime was wholly the work of the same demons that
had plagued Vyônes in so monstrous a fashion for weeks past.

Reynard, however, was unable to tell them all that he had seen, or
to confess the ultimate sources of his fear and stupefaction. The secret
of that which he knew was locked in the seething pit of his tortured
and devil-ridden soul.

Somehow, he left the ravaged inn, he pushed his way through the
gathering crowd with its terror-muted murmurs, and found himself
alone on the midnight streets. Heedless of his own possible peril, and
scarcely knowing where he went, he wandered through Vyônes for
many hours; and somewhile in his wanderings, he came to his own
workshop. With no assignable reason for the act, he entered, and re-
emerged with a heavy hammer, which he carried with him during his
subsequent peregrinations. Then, driven by his awful and unremissive
torture, he went on till the pale dawn had touched the spires and the
house-tops with a ghostly glimmering.

By a half-conscious compulsion, his steps had led him to the
square before the cathedral. Ignoring the amazed verger, who had just

opened the doors, he entered and sought a stairway that wound tortuously upward to the tower on which his own gargoyles were ensconced.

In the chill and livid light of sunless morning, he emerged on the
roof; and leaning perilously from the verge, he examined the carven
figures. He felt no surprise, only the hideous confirmation of a fear too
ghastly to be named, when he saw that the teeth and claws of the malign, cat-headed griffin were stained with darkening blood; and that
shreds of apple-green cloth were hanging from the talons of the lustful, bat-winged satyr.

It seemed to Reynard, in the dim ashen light, that a look of unspeakable triumph, of intolerable irony, was imprinted on the face of
this latter creature. He stared at it with fearful and agonizing fascination, while impotent rage, abhorrence, and repentance deeper than that
of the damned arose within him in a smothering flood. He was hardly
aware that he had raised the iron hammer and had struck wildly at the
satyr's horned profile, till he heard the sullen, angry clang of impact, and
found that he was tottering on the edge of the roof to retain his balance.

The furious blow had merely chipped the features of the gargoyle,
and had not wiped away the malignant lust and exultation. Again
Reynard raised the heavy hammer.

It fell on empty air; for, even as he struck, the stone-carver felt
himself lifted and drawn backward by something that sank into his
flesh like many separate knives. He staggered helplessly, his feet
slipped, and then he was lying on the granite verge, with his head and
shoulders over the dark, deserted street.

Half-swooning, and sick with pain, he saw above him the other
gargoyle, the claws of whose right foreleg were firmly embedded in his
shoulder. They tore deeper, as if with a dreadful clenching. The monster seemed to tower like some fabulous beast above its prey; and he
felt himself slipping dizzily across the cathedral gutter, with the gargoyle twisting and turning as if to resume its normal position over the

gulf. Its slow, inexorable movement seemed to be part of his vertigo. The very tower was tilting and revolving beneath him in some unnatural nightmare fashion.

Dimly, in a daze of fear and agony, Reynard saw the remorseless tiger-face bending toward him with its horrid teeth laid bare in an eternal rictus of diabolic hate. Somehow, he had retained the hammer. With an instinctive impulse to defend himself, he struck at the gargoyle, whose cruel features seemed to approach him like something seen in the ultimate madness and distortion of delirium.

Even as he struck, the vertiginous turning movement continued, and he felt the talons dragging him outward on empty air. In his cramped, recumbent position, the blow fell short of the hateful face and came down with a dull clangor on the foreleg whose curving talons were fixed in his shoulder like meat-hooks. The clangor ended in a sharp cracking sound; and the leaning gargoyle vanished from Reynard's vision as he fell. He saw nothing more, except the dark mass of the cathedral tower, that seemed to soar away from him and to rush upward unbelievably in the livid, starless heavens to which the belated sun had not yet risen.

It was the Archbishop Ambrosius, on his way to early Mass, who found the shattered body of Reynard lying face downward in the square. Ambrosius crossed himself in startled horror at the sight; and then, when he saw the object that was still clinging to Reynard's shoulder, he repeated the gesture with a more than pious promptness.

He bent down to examine the thing. With the infallible memory of a true art-lover, he recognized it at once. Then, through the same clearness of recollection, he saw that the stone foreleg, whose claws were so deeply buried in Reynard's flesh, had somehow undergone a most unnatural alteration. The paw, as he remembered it, should have been slightly bent and relaxed; but now it was stiffly outthrust and elongated, as if, like the paw of a living limb, it had reached for something, or had dragged a heavy burden with its ferine talons.

THE BROKEN LUTE

Because you are silent to my lyric prayers, deaf to the melodies I have made from the sighs and murmurs of a wounded love, I have broken my golden lute, and cast it away, tarnished and unstrung, among the red leaves and faded roses of the September garden. Silence, the silver dust of lilies, the mournful muted wind of autumn, and the fitfully drifting leaves, have claimed it for their own. Seeing it there, as you pass on your queenly way amid the crumbling roses, will you not echo in your heart one sigh of the many sighs, which, as a music for your pleasure, were breathed from its chords, during the summer's half-forgotten days?

The Holiness of Azédarac

I

"By the Ram with a Thousand Ewes! By the Tail of Dagon and the Horns of Derceto!" said Azédarac, as he fingered the tiny, pot-bellied vial of vermilion liquid on the table before him. "Something will have to be done with this pestilential Brother Ambrose. I have now learned that he was sent to Ximes by the Archbishop of Averoigne for no other purpose than to gather proof of my subterraneous connection with Azazel and the Old Ones. He has spied upon my evocations in the vaults, he has heard the hidden formulae, and beheld the veritable manifestation of Lilit, and even of Iog-Sotôt and Sodagui, those demons who are more ancient than the world; and this very morning, an hour agone, he has mounted his white ass for the return journey to Vyônes. There are two ways—or, in a sense, there is one way—in which I can avoid the pother and inconvenience of a trial for sorcery, the contents of this vial must be administered to Ambrose before he has reached his journey's end—or, failing this, I myself shall be compelled to make use of a similar medicament."

Jehan Mauvaissoir looked at the vial and then at Azédarac. He was not at all horrified, nor even surprised, by the nonepiscopal oaths and the somewhat uncanonical statements which he had just heard from the Bishop of Ximes. He had known the Bishop too long and too intimately, and had rendered him too many services of an unconventional nature, to be surprised at anything. In fact, he had known Azédarac long before the sorcerer had ever dreamt of becoming a prelate, in a phase of his existence that was wholly unsuspected by the people of

Ximes; and Azédarac had not troubled to keep many secrets from Jehan at any time.

"I understand," said Jehan. "You can depend upon it that the contents of the vial will be administered. Brother Ambrose will hardly travel post-haste on that ambling white ass; and he will not reach Vyônes before tomorrow noon. There is abundant time to overtake him. Of course, he knows me—at least, he knows Jehan Mauvaissoir . . . But that can easily be remedied."

Azédarac smiled confidently. "I leave the affair—and the vial—in your hands, Jehan. Of course, no matter what the eventuation, with all the Satanic and pre-Satanic facilities at my disposal, I should be in no great danger from these addlepated bigots. However, I am very comfortably situated here in Ximes; and the lot of a Christian Bishop who lives in the odor of incense and piety, and maintains in the meanwhile a private understanding with the Adversary, is certainly preferable to the mischancy life of a hedge-sorcerer. I do not care to be annoyed or disturbed, or ousted from my sinecure, if such can be avoided.

"May Moloch devour that sanctimonious little milksop of an Ambrose," he went on. "I must be growing old and dull, not to have suspected him before this. It was the horror-stricken and averted look he has been wearing lately that made me think he had peered through the keyhole on the subterranean rites. Then, when I heard he was leaving, I wisely thought to review my library; and I have found that the *Book of Eibon*, which contains the oldest incantations, and the secret, man-forgotten lore of Iog-Sotôt and Sodagui, is now missing. As you know, I had replaced the former binding of aboriginal, sub-human skin with the sheep-leather of a Christian missal, and had surrounded the volume with rows of legitimate prayer-books. Ambrose is carrying it away under his robe as proof conclusive that I am addicted to the Black Arts. No one in Averoigne will be able to read the immemorial Hyperborean script; but the dragons'-blood illuminations and drawings will be enough to damn me."

Master and servant regarded each other for an interval of signifi-
cant silence. Jehan eyed with profound respect the haughty stature, the
grimly lined lineaments, the grizzled tonsure, the odd, ruddy, crescent
scar on the pallid brow of Azédarac, and the sultry points of orange-
yellow fire that seemed to burn deep down in the chill and liquid ebon
of his eyes. Azédarac, in his turn, considered with confidence the vul-
pine features and discreet, inexpressive air of Jehan, who might have
been—and could be, if necessary—anything from a mercer to a cleric.

"It is regrettable," resumed Azédarac, "that any question of my holiness and devotional probity should have been raised among the clergy
of Averoigne. But I suppose it was inevitable sooner or later—even
though the chief difference between myself and many other ecclesias-
tics is, that I serve the Devil wittingly and of my own free will, while
they do the same in sanctimonious blindness. . . . However, we must
do what we can to delay the evil hour of public scandal, and eviction
from our neatly feathered nest. Ambrose alone could prove anything
to my detriment at present; and you, Jehan, will remove Ambrose to a
realm wherein his monkish tattlings will be of small consequence. After that, I shall be doubly vigilant. The next emissary from Vyônes, I
assure you, will find nothing to report but saintliness and bead-telling."

II

The thoughts of Brother Ambrose were sorely troubled, and at vari-
ance with the tranquil beauty of the sylvan scene, as he rode onward
through the forest of Averoigne between Ximes and Vyônes. Horror
was nesting in his heart like a knot of malignant vipers; and the evil
Book of Eibon, that primordial manual of sorcery, seemed to burn beneath his robe like a huge, hot, Satanic sigil pressed against his bosom.
Not for the first time, there occurred to him the wish that Clément,
the Archbishop, had delegated someone else to investigate the Ere-
bean turpitude of Azédarac. Sojourning for a month in the Bishop's

household, Ambrose had learned too much for the peace of mind of any pious cleric, and had seen things that were like a secret blot of shame and terror on the white page of his memory. To find that a Christian prelate could serve the powers of nethermost perdition, could entertain in privity the foulnesses that are older than Asmodai, was abysmally disturbing to his devout soul; and ever since then he had seemed to smell corruption everywhere, and had felt on every side the serpentine encroachment of the dark Adversary.

As he rode on among the somber pines and verdant beeches, he wished also that he were mounted on something swifter than the gentle, milk-white ass appointed for his use by the Archbishop. He was dogged by the shadowy intimation of leering gargoyle faces, of invisible cloven feet, that followed him behind the thronging trees and along the umbrageous meanderings of the road. In the oblique rays, the elongated webs of shadow wrought by the dying afternoon, the forest seemed to attend with bated breath the noisome and furtive passing of innominable things. Nevertheless, Ambrose had met no one for miles; and he had seen neither bird nor beast nor viper in the summer woods.

His thoughts returned with fearful insistence to Azédarac, who appeared to him as a tall, prodigious Antichrist, uprearing his sable vans and giant figure from out the flaming mire of Abaddon. Again he saw the vaults beneath the Bishop's mansion, wherein he had peered one night on a scene of infernal terror and loathliness, had beheld the Bishop swathed in the gorgeous, coiling fumes of unholy censers, that mingled in mid-air with the sulfurous and bituminous vapors of the Pit; and through the vapors had seen the lasciviously swaying limbs, the bellying and dissolving features of foul, enormous entities . . . Recalling them, again he trembled at the pre-Adamite lubriciousness of Lilit, again he shuddered at the trans-galactic horror of the demon Sodagui, and the ultra-dimensional hideousness of that being known as Iog-Sotôt to the sorcerers of Averoigne.

How balefully potent and subversive, he thought, were these immemorial devils, who had placed their servant Azédarac in the very bosom of the Church, in a position of high and holy trust. For nine years the evil prelate had held an unchallenged and unsuspected tenure, had befouled the bishopric of Ximes with infidelities that were worse than those of the Paynims. Then, somehow, through anonymous channels, a rumor had reached Clément—a warning whisper that not even the Archbishop had dared to voice aloud; and Ambrose, a young Benedictine monk, the nephew of Clément, had been dispatched to examine privily the festering foulness that threatened the integrity of the Church. Only at that time did anyone recall how little was actually known regarding the antecedents of Azédarac; how tenuous were his claims to ecclesiastical preferment, or even to mere priestship; how veiled and doubtful were the steps by which he had attained his office. It was then realized that a formidable wizardry had been at work.

Uneasily, Ambrose wondered if Azédarac had already discovered the removal of the *Book of Eibon* from among the missals contaminated by its blasphemous presence. Even more uneasily, he wondered what Azédarac would do in that event, and how long it would take him to connect the absence of the volume with his visitor's departure.

At this point, the meditations of Ambrose were interrupted by the hard clatter of galloping hoofs that approached from behind. The emergence of a centaur from the oldest wood of paganism could scarcely have startled him to a keener panic; and he peered apprehensively over his shoulder at the nearing horseman. This person, mounted on a fine black steed with opulent trappings, was a bushy-bearded man of obvious consequence; for his gay garments were those of a noble or a courtier. He overtook Ambrose and passed on with a polite nod, seeming to be wholly intent on his own affairs. The monk was immensely reassured, though vaguely troubled for some moments by a feeling that he had seen elsewhere, under circumstances which he was now unable to recall, the narrow eyes and sharp profile that contrasted so oddly with the bluff beard of the horseman. However, he was comfortably sure that he had never seen the man in Ximes.

The rider soon vanished beyond a leafy turn of the arboreal highway. Ambrose returned to the pious horror and apprehensiveness of his former soliloquy.

As he went on, it seemed to him that the sun had gone down with untimely and appalling swiftness. Though the heavens above were innocent of cloud, and the low-lying air was free from vapors, the woods were embrowned by an inexplicable gloom that gathered visibly on all sides. In this gloom, the trunks of the trees were strangely distorted, and the low masses of foliage assumed unnatural and disquieting forms. It appeared to Ambrose that the silence around him was a fragile film through which the raucous rumble and mutter of diabolic voices might break at any moment, even as the foul and sunken driftage that rises anon above the surface of a smoothly flowing river.

With much relief, he remembered that he was not far from a wayside tavern, known as the Inn of Bonne Jouissance. Here, since his journey to Vyônes was little more than half completed, he resolved to tarry for the night.

A minute more, and he saw the lights of the inn. Before their benign and golden radiance, the equivocal forest shadows that attended him seemed to halt and retire and he gained the haven of the tavern courtyard with the feeling of one who has barely escaped from an army of goblin perils.

Committing his mount to the care of a stable-servant, Ambrose entered the main room of the inn. Here he was greeted with the deference due to his cloth by the stout and unctuous taverner; and, being assured that the best accommodations of the place were at his disposal, he seated himself at one of several tables where other guests had already gathered to await the evening meal.

Among them, Ambrose recognized the bluff-bearded horseman who had overtaken him in the woods an hour agone. This person was sitting alone, and a little apart. The other guests, a couple of travelling mercers, a notary, and two soldiers, acknowledged the presence of the monk with all due civility; but the horseman arose from his table, and coming over to Ambrose, began immediately to make overtures that were more than those of common courtesy.

"Will you not dine with me, sir monk?" he invited, in a gruff but ingratiating voice that was perplexingly familiar to Ambrose, and yet, like the wolfish profile, was irrecognizable at the time.

"I am the Sieur des Émaux, from Touraine, at your service," the man went on. "It would seem that we are travelling the same road— possibly to the same destination. Mine is the cathedral city of Vyônes. And yours?"

Though he was vaguely perturbed, and even a little suspicious, Ambrose found himself unable to decline the invitation. In reply to the last question, he admitted that he also was on his way to Vyônes. He did not altogether like the Sieur des Émaux, whose slitted eyes gave back the candle-light of the inn with a covert glitter, and whose manner was somewhat effusive, not to say fulsome. But there seemed to be no ostensible reason for refusing a courtesy that was doubtless well-meant and genuine. He accompanied his host to their separate table.

"You belong to the Benedictine order, I observe," said the Sieur des Émaux, eyeing the monk with an odd smile that was tinged with furtive irony. "It is an order that I have always admired greatly—a most noble and worthy brotherhood. May I not inquire your name?"

Ambrose gave the requested information with a curious reluctance.

"Well, then, Brother Ambrose," said the Sieur des Émaux, "I suggest that we drink to your health and the prosperity of your order in the red wine of Averoigne while we are waiting for supper to be served. Wine is always welcome, following a long journey, and is no less beneficial before a good meal than after."

Ambrose mumbled an unwilling assent. He could not have told why, but the personality of the man was more and more distasteful to him. He seemed to detect a sinister undertone in the purring voice, to surprise an evil meaning in the low-lidded glance. And all the while his brain was tantalized by intimations of a forgotten memory. Had he seen his interlocutor in Ximes? Was the self-styled Sieur des Émaux a henchman of Azédarac in disguise?

Wine was now ordered by his host, who left the table to confer with the inn-keeper for this purpose, and even insisted on paying a visit to the cellar, that he might select a suitable vintage in person. Noting the obeisance paid to the man by the people of the tavern, who addressed him by name, Ambrose felt a certain measure of reassurance. When the taverner, followed by the Sieur des Émaux, returned with two earthen pitchers of wine, he had well-nigh succeeded in dismissing his vague doubts and vaguer fears.

Two large goblets were now placed on the table, and the Sieur des Émaux filled them immediately from one of the pitchers. It seemed to Ambrose that the first of the goblets already contained a small amount of some sanguine fluid, before the wine was poured into it; but he could not have sworn to this in the dim light, and thought that he must have been mistaken.

"Here are two matchless vintages," said the Sieur des Émaux, indicating the pitchers. "Both are so excellent that I was unable to choose between them; but you, Brother Ambrose, are perhaps capable of deciding their merits with a finer palate than mine."

He pushed one of the filled goblets toward Ambrose. "This is the wine of La Frênaie," he said. "Drink, it will verily transport you from the world by virtue of the mighty fire that slumbers in its heart."

Ambrose took the proffered goblet, and raised it to his lips. The Sieur des Émaux was bending forward above his own wine to inhale its bouquet; and something in his posture was terrifyingly familiar to Ambrose. In a chill flash of horror, his memory told him that the thin, pointed features behind the square beard were dubiously similar to those of Jehan Mauvaissoir, whom he had often seen in the household of Azédarac, and who, as he had reason to believe, was implicated in the Bishop's sorceries. He wondered why he had not placed the resemblance before, and what wizardry had drugged his powers of recollection. Even now he was not sure; but the mere suspicion terrified him as if some deadly serpent had reared its head across the table.

"Drink, Brother Ambrose," urged the Sieur des Émaux, draining his own goblet. "To your welfare and that of all good Benedictines."

Ambrose hesitated. The cold, hypnotic eyes of his interlocutor were upon him, and he was powerless to refuse, in spite of all his apprehensions. Shuddering slightly, with the sense of some irresistible compulsion, and feeling that he might drop dead from the virulent working of a sudden poison, he emptied his goblet.

An instant more, and he felt that his worst fears had been justified. The wine burned like the liquid flames of Phlegethon in his throat and on his lips, it seemed to fill his veins with a hot, infernal quicksilver. Then, all at once, an unbearable cold had inundated his being; an icy whirlwind wrapped him round with coils of roaring air, the chair melted beneath him, and he was falling through endless glacial gulfs. The walls of the inn had flown like receding vapors; the lights went out like stars in the black mist of a marish; and the face of the Sieur des Émaux faded with them on the swirling shadows, even as a bubble that breaks on the milling of midnight waters.

III

It was with some difficulty that Ambrose assured himself that he was not dead. He had seemed to fall eternally, through a grey night that was peopled with ever-changing forms, with blurred unstable masses that dissolved to other masses before they could assume definitude. For a moment, he thought there were walls about him once more, and then he was plunging from terrace to terrace of a world of phantom trees. At whiles, he thought also that there were human faces; but all was doubtful and evanescent, all was drifting smoke and surging shadow.

Abruptly, with no sense of transition or impact, he found that he was no longer falling. The vague phantasmagoria around him had returned to an actual scene—but a scene in which there was no trace of the Inn of Bonne Jouissance, or the Sieur des Émaux.

Ambrose peered about with incredulous eyes on a situation that was truly unbelievable. He was sitting in broad daylight on a large square block of roughly hewn granite. Around him, at a little distance, beyond the open space of a grassy glade, were the lofty pines and spreading beeches of an elder forest, whose boughs were already touched by the gold of the declining sun. Immediately before him, several men were standing.

These men appeared to regard Ambrose with a profound and almost religious amazement. They were bearded and savage of aspect, with white robes of a fashion he had never before seen. Their hair was long and matted, like tangles of black snakes; and their eyes burned with a frenetic fire. Each of them bore in his right hand a rude knife of sharply chiselled stone.

Ambrose wondered if he had died after all, and if these beings were the strange devils of some unlisted hell. In the face of what had happened, and the light of Ambrose's own beliefs, it was a far from unreasonable conjecture. He peered with fearful trepidation at the supposed demons, and began to mumble a prayer to the God who had abandoned him so inexplicably to his spiritual foes. Then he remembered the necromantic powers of Azédarac, and conceived another surmise—that he had been spirited bodily away from the Inn of Bonne Jouissance, and delivered into the hands of those pre-Satanic entities that served the sorcerous Bishop. Becoming convinced of his own physical solidity and integrity, and reflecting that such was scarcely the appropriate condition of a disincarnate soul, and also that the sylvan scene about him was hardly characteristic of the infernal regions, he accepted this as the true explanation. He was still alive, and still on earth, though the circumstances of his situation were more than mysterious, and were fraught with dire, unknowable danger.

The strange beings had maintained an utter silence, as if they were too dumfounded for speech. Hearing the prayerful murmurs of Ambrose, they seemed to recover from their surprise, and became not only articulate but vociferous. Ambrose could make nothing of their harsh vocables, in which sibilants and aspirates and gutterals were often combined in a manner difficult for the normal human tongue to imitate. However, he caught the word *taranit*, several times repeated, and wondered if it were the name of an especially malevolent demon.

The speech of the weird beings began to assume a sort of rude rhythm, like the intonations of some primordial chant. Two of them stepped forward and seized Ambrose, while the voices of their companions rose in a shrill, triumphant litany.

Scarcely knowing what had happened, and still less what was to follow, Ambrose was flung supine on the granite block, and was held down by one of his captors, while the other raised aloft the keen blade of chiselled flint which he carried. The blade was poised in air above Ambrose's heart, and the monk realized in sudden terror that it would fall with dire velocity and pierce him through before the lapse of another moment.

Then, above the demoniac chanting, which had risen to a mad, malignant frenzy, he heard the sweet and imperious cry of a woman's voice. In the wild confusion of his terror, the words were strange and meaningless to him; but plainly they were understood by his captors, and were taken as an undeniable command. The stone knife was lowered sullenly, and Ambrose was permitted to resume a sitting posture on the flat slab.

His rescuer was standing on the edge of the open glade, in the wide-flung umbrage of an ancient pine. She came forward now; and the white-garmented beings fell back with evident respect before her. She was very tall, with a fearless and regal demeanor, and was gowned in a dark, shimmering blue, like the star-laden blue of nocturnal summer skies. Her hair was knotted in a long golden-brown braid, heavy as the glistening coils of some eastern serpent. Her eyes were a strange amber, her lips a vermilion touched with the coolness of woodland shadow, and her skin was of alabastrine fairness. Ambrose saw that she was beautiful; but she inspired him with the same awe that he would have felt before a queen, together with something of the fear and consternation which a virtuous young monk would conceive in the perilous presence of an alluring succubus.

"Come with me," she said to Ambrose, in a tongue that his monastic studies enabled him to recognize as an obsolete variant of the French of Averoigne—a tongue that no man had supposedly spoken for many hundred years. Obediently and in great wonder, he arose and followed her, with no hindrance from his glowering and reluctant captors.

The woman led him to a narrow path that wound sinuously away through the deep forest. In a few moments, the glade, the granite block, and the cluster of white-robed men were lost to sight behind the heavy foliage.

"Who are you?" asked the lady, turning to Ambrose. "You look like one of those crazy missionaries who are beginning to enter Averoigne nowadays. I believe that people call them Christians. The Druids have sacrificed so many of them to Taranit, that I marvel at your temerity in coming here."

Ambrose found it difficult to comprehend the archaic phrasing; and the import of her words was so utterly strange and baffling that he felt sure he must have misunderstood her.

"I am Brother Ambrose," he replied, expressing himself slowly and awkwardly in the long-disused dialect. "Of course, I am a Christian; but I confess that I fail to understand you. I have heard of the pagan Druids; but surely they were all driven from Averoigne many centuries ago."

The woman stared at Ambrose, with open amazement and pity. Her brownish-yellow eyes were bright and clear as a mellowed wine.

"Poor little one," she said. "I fear your dreadful experiences have served to unsettle you. It was fortunate that I came along when I did, and decided to intervene. I seldom interfere with the Druids and their sacrifices; but I saw you sitting on their altar a little while agone, and was struck by your youth and comeliness."

Ambrose felt more and more that he had been made the victim of a most peculiar sorcery; but, even yet, he was far from suspecting the true magnitude of this sorcery. Amid his bemusement and consternation, however, he realized that he owed his life to the singular and lovely woman beside him, and began to stammer out his gratitude.

"You need not thank me," said the lady, with a dulcet smile. "I am Moriamis, the enchantress, and the Druids fear my magic, which is more sovereign and more excellent than theirs, though I use it only for the welfare of men and not for their bale or bane."

The monk was dismayed to learn that his fair rescuer was a sorceress, even though her powers were professedly benignant. The knowledge added to his alarm; but he felt that it would be politic to conceal his emotions in this regard.

"Indeed, I am grateful to you," he protested. "And now, if you can tell me the way to the Inn of Bonne Jouissance, which I left not long ago, I shall owe you a further debt."

Moriamis knitted her light brows. "I have never heard of the Inn of Bonne Jouissance. There is no such place in this region."

"But this is the forest of Averoigne, is it not?" inquired the puzzled Ambrose. "And surely we are not far from the road that runs between the town of Ximes and the city of Vyônes?"

"I have never heard of Ximes, or Vyônes, either," said Moriamis. "Truly, the land is known as Averoigne, and this forest is the great wood of Averoigne, which men have called by that name from primeval years. But there are no towns such as the ones whereof you speak, Brother Ambrose, I fear that you still wander a little in your mind."

Ambrose was aware of a maddening perplexity. "I have been most damnably beguiled," he said, half to himself. "It is all the doing of that abominable sorcerer, Azédarac, I am sure."

The woman started as if she had been stung by a wild bee. There was something both eager and severe in the searching gaze that she turned upon Ambrose.

"Azédarac?" she queried. "What do you know of Azédarac? I was once acquainted with someone by that name; and I wonder if it could be the same person. Is he tall and a little grey, with hot, dark eyes, and a proud, half-angry air, and a crescent scar on the brow?"

Greatly mystified, and more troubled than ever, Ambrose admitted the veracity of her description. Realizing that in some unknown way he had stumbled upon the hidden antecedents of the sorcerer, he confided the story of his adventures to Moriamis, hoping that she would reciprocate with further information concerning Azédarac.

The woman listened with the air of one who is much interested but not at all surprised.

"I understand now," she observed, when he had finished. "Anon I shall explain everything that mystifies and troubles you. I think I know this Jehan Mauvaissoir, also; he has long been the man-servant of Azédarac, though his name was Melchire in other days. These two have always been the underlings of evil, and have served the Old Ones in ways forgotten or never known by the Druids."

"Indeed, I hope you can explain what has happened," said Ambrose. "It is a fearsome and strange and ungodly thing, to drink a draft of wine in a tavern at eventide, and then find one's self in the heart of the forest by afternoon daylight, among demons such as those from whom you succored me."

"Yea," countered Moriamis, "it is even stranger than you dream. Tell me, Brother Ambrose, what was the year in which you entered the Inn of Bonne Jouissance?"

"Why, it is the year of our Lord, 1175, of course. What other year could it be?"

"The Druids use a different chronology," replied Moriamis, "and their notation would mean nothing to you. But, according to that which the Christian missionaries would now introduce in Averoigne, the present year is 475 A.D. You have been sent back no less than seven hundred years into what the people of your era would regard as the past. The Druid altar on which I found you lying is probably located on the future site of the Inn of Bonne Jouissance."

Ambrose was more than dumbfounded. His mind was unable to grasp the entire import of Moriamis' words.

"But how can such things be?" he cried. "How can a man go backward in time, among years and people that have long turned to dust?"

"That, mayhap, is a mystery for Azédarac to unriddle. However, the past and the future co-exist with what we call the present, and are merely the two segments of the circle of time. We see them and name them according to our own position in the circle."

Ambrose felt that he had fallen among necromancies of a most unhallowed and unexampled sort, and had been made the victim of diableries unknown to the Christian catalogues.

Tongue-tied by a consciousness that all comment, all protest or even prayer would prove inadequate to the situation, he saw that a stone tower with small lozenge-shaped windows was now visible above the turrets of pine along the path which he and Moriamis were following.

"This is my home," said Moriamis, as they came forth from beneath the thinning trees at the foot of a little knoll on which the tower was situated. "Brother Ambrose, you must be my guest."

Ambrose was unable to decline the proffered hospitality, in spite of his feeling that Moriamis was hardly the most suitable of châtelaines for a chaste and god-fearing monk. However, the pious misgivings with which she inspired him were not unmingled with fascination. Also, like a lost child, he clung to the only available protection in a land of fearful perils and astounding mysteries.

The interior of the tower was neat and clean and home-like, though with furniture of a ruder sort than that to which Ambrose was accustomed, and rich but roughly woven arrases. A serving-woman, tall as Moriamis herself, but darker, brought to him a huge bowl of milk and wheaten bread, and the monk was now able to assuage the hunger that had gone unsatisfied in the Inn of Bonne Jouissance.

As he seated himself before the simple fare, he realized that the *Book of Eibon* was still heavy in the bosom of his gown. He removed the volume, and gave it gingerly to Moriamis. Her eyes widened, but she made no comment until he had finished his meal. Then she said:

"This volume is indeed the property of Azédarac, who was formerly a neighbor of mine. I knew the scoundrel quite well—in fact, I knew him all too well." Her bosom heaved with an obscure emotion as she paused for a moment. "He was the wisest and the mightiest of sorcerers, and the most secret withal; for no one knew the time and the manner of his coming into Averoigne, or the fashion in which he had procured the immemorial *Book of Eibon*, whose runic writings were beyond the lore of all other wizards. He was a master of all enchantments and all demons, and likewise a compounder of mighty potions. Among these were certain philters, blended with potent spells and possessed of unique virtue, that would send the drinker backward or forward in time. One of them, I believe, was administered to you by Melchire, or Jehan Mauvaissoir; and Azédarac himself, together with this man-servant, made use of another—perhaps not for the first time—when they went onward from the present age of the Druids into that age of Christian authority to which you belong. There was a blood-crimson vial for the past, and a green for the future. Behold! I possess one of each—though Azédarac was unaware that I knew of their existence."

She opened a little cupboard, in which were the various charms and medicaments, the sun-dried herbs and moon-compounded essences that a sorceress would employ. From among them she brought out the two vials, one of which contained a sanguine-colored liquid, and the other a fluid of emerald brightness.

"I stole them one day, out of womanly curiosity, from his hidden store of philters and elixirs and magistrals," continued Moriamis. "I could have followed the rascal when he disappeared into the future, if I had chosen to do so. But I am well enough content with my own age; and moreover, I am not the sort of woman who pursues a wearied and reluctant lover. . . ."

"Then," said Ambrose, more bewildered than ever, but hopeful, "if I were to drink the contents of the green vial, I should return to my own epoch."

"Precisely. And I am sure, from what you have told me, that your return would be a source of much annoyance to Azédarac. It is like the fellow, to have established himself in a fat prelacy. He was ever the master of circumstance, with an eye to his own accommodation and comfort. It would hardly please him, I am sure, if you were to reach the Archbishop. . . . I am not revengeful by nature . . . but on the other hand . . ."

"It is hard to understand how anyone could have wearied of you," said Ambrose, gallantly, as he began to comprehend the situation.

Moriamis smiled. "That is prettily said. And you are really a charming youth, in spite of that dismal-looking robe. I am glad that I rescued you from the Druids, who would have torn your heart out and offered it to their demon, Taranit."

"And now you will send me back?"

Moriamis frowned a little, and then assumed her most seductive air.

"Are you in such a hurry to leave your hostess? Now that you are living in another century than your own, a day, a week, or a month will make no difference in the date of your return. I have also retained the formulas of Azédarac; and I know how to graduate the potion, if necessary. The usual period of transportation is exactly seven hundred years; but the philter can be strengthened or weakened a little."

The sun had fallen beyond the pines, and a soft twilight was beginning to invade the tower. The maidservant had left the room. Moriamis came over and seated herself beside Ambrose on the rough bench he was occupying. Still smiling, she fixed her amber eyes upon him, with a languid flame in their depths—a flame that seemed to brighten as the dusk grew stronger. Without speaking, she began slowly to unbraid her heavy hair, from which there emanated a perfume that was subtle and delicious as the perfume of grape-flowers.

Ambrose was embarrassed by this delightful proximity. "I am not sure that it would be right for me to remain, after all. What would the Archbishop think?"

"My dear child, the Archbishop will not even be born for at least six hundred and fifty years. And it will be still longer before you are born. And when you return, anything that you have done during your stay with me will have happened no less than seven centuries ago . . . which should be long enough to procure the remission of any sin, no matter how often repeated."

Like a man who has been taken in the toils of some fantastic dream, and finds that the dream is not altogether disagreeable, Ambrose yielded to this feminine and irrefutable reasoning. He hardly knew what was to happen; but, under the exceptional circumstances indicated by Moriamis, the rigors of monastic discipline might well be relaxed to almost any conceivable degree, without entailing spiritual perdition or even a serious breach of vows.

IV

A month later, Moriamis and Ambrose were standing beside the Druid altar. It was late in the evening; and a slightly gibbous moon had risen upon the deserted glade and was fringing the tree-tops with wefted silver. The warm breath of the summer night was gentle as the sighing of a woman in slumber.

"Must you go, after all?" said Moriamis, in a pleading and regretful voice.

"It is my duty. I must return to Clément with the *Book of Eibon* and the other evidence I have collected against Azédarac." The words sounded a little unreal to Ambrose as he uttered them; and he tried very hard, but vainly, to convince himself of the cogency and validity of his arguments. The idyl of his stay with Moriamis, to which he was oddly unable to attach any true conviction of sin, had given to all that had preceded it a certain dismal insubstantiality. Free from all responsibility or restraint, in the sheer obliviousness of dreams, he had lived like a happy pagan; and now he must go back to the drear existence of a medieval monk, beneath the prompting of an obscure sense of duty.

"I shall not try to hold you," Moriamis sighed. "But I shall miss you, and remember you as a worthy lover and a pleasant playmate. Here is the philter."

The green essence was cold and almost hueless in the moonlight, as Moriamis poured it into a little cup and gave it to Ambrose.

"Are you sure of its precise efficacy?" the monk inquired. "Are you sure that I shall return to the Inn of Bonne Jouissance, at a time not far subsequent to that of my departure therefrom?"

"Yea," said Moriamis, "for the potion is infallible. But stay, I have also brought along the other vial—the vial of the past. Take it with you—for who knows, you may sometime wish to return and visit me again."

Ambrose accepted the red vial and placed it in his robe beside the ancient manual of Hyperborean sorcery. Then, after an appropriate farewell to Moriamis, he drained with sudden resolution the contents of the cup.

The moonlit glade, the grey altar, and Moriamis, all vanished in a swirl of flame and shadow. It seemed to Ambrose that he was soaring endlessly through phantasmagoric gulfs, amid the ceaseless shifting and melting of unstable things, the transient forming and fading of irresoluble worlds.

At the end, he found himself sitting once more in the Inn of Bonne Jouissance, at what he assumed to be the very same table before which he had sat with the Sieur des Émaux. It was daylight, and the room was full of people, among whom he looked in vain for the rubicund face of the inn-keeper, or the servants and fellow-guests he had previously seen. All were unfamiliar to him; and the furniture was strangely worn, and was grimier than he remembered it.

Perceiving the presence of Ambrose, the people began to eye him with open curiosity and wonderment. A tall man with dolorous eyes and lantern jaws came hastily forward and bowed before him with an air that was half-servile but full of a prying impertinence.

"What do you wish?" he asked.

"Is this the Inn of Bonne Jouissance?"

The innkeeper stared at Ambrose. "Nay, it is the Inn of Haute Espérance, of which I have been the taverner these thirty years. Could you not read the sign? It was called the Inn of Bonne Jouissance in my father's time, but the name was changed after his death."

Ambrose was filled with consternation. "But the inn was differently named, and was kept by another man when I visited it not long ago," he cried in bewilderment. "The owner was a stout, jovial man, not in the least like you."

"That would answer the description of my father," said the taverner, eyeing Ambrose more dubiously than ever. "He has been dead for the full thirty years of which I speak; and surely you were not even born at the time of his decease."

Ambrose began to realize what had happened. The emerald potion, by some error or excess of potency, had taken him many years beyond his own time into the future!

"I must resume my journey to Vyônes," he said in a bewildered voice, without fully comprehending the implications of his situation. "I have a message for the Archbishop Clément—and must not delay longer in delivering it."

"But Clément has been dead even longer than my father," exclaimed the inn-keeper. "From whence do you come, that you are ignorant of this?" It was plain from his manner that he had begun to doubt the sanity of Ambrose. Others, overhearing the strange discussion, had begun to crowd about, and were plying the monk with jocular and sometimes ribald questions.

"And what of Azédarac, the Bishop of Ximes? Is he dead, too?" inquired Ambrose, desperately.

"You mean St. Azédarac, no doubt. He outlived Clément, but nevertheless he has been dead and duly canonized for thirty-two years. Some say that he did not die, but was transported to heaven alive, and that his body was never buried in the great mausoleum reared for him at Ximes. But that is probably a mere legend."

Ambrose was overwhelmed with unspeakable desolation and confusion. In the meanwhile, the crowd about him had increased, and in spite of his monkish robe, he was being made the subject of rude remarks and jeers.

"The good brother has lost his wits," cried some. "The wines of Averoigne are too strong for him," said others.

"What year is this?" demanded Ambrose, in his desperation.

"The year of our Lord, 1230," replied the taverner, breaking into a derisive laugh. "And what year did you think it was?"

"It was the year 1175 when I last visited the Inn of Bonne Jouissance," admitted Ambrose.

His declaration was greeted with fresh jeers and laughter. "Hola, young sir, you were not even conceived at that time," the taverner said. Then, seeming to remember something, he went on in a more thoughtful tone: "When I was a child, my father told me of a young monk, about your age, who came to the Inn of Bonne Jouissance one evening in the summer of 1175, and vanished inexplicably after drinking a draught of red wine. I believe his name was Ambrose. Perhaps you are Ambrose, and have only just returned from a visit to nowhere." He gave a derisory wink, and the new jest was taken up and bandied from mouth to mouth among the frequenters of the tavern.

Ambrose was trying to realize the full import of his predicament. His mission was now useless, through the death or disappearance of Azédarac; and no one would remain in all Averoigne to recognize him or believe his story. He felt the hopelessness of his alienation among unknown years and people.

Suddenly he remembered the red vial given him at parting by Moriamis. The potion, like the green philter, might prove uncertain in its effect; but he was seized by an all-consuming desire to escape from the weird embarrassment and wilderment of his present position. Also, he longed for Moriamis like a lost child for its mother; and the charm of his sojourn in the past was upon him with an irresistible spell. Ignoring the ribald faces and voices about him, he drew the vial from his bosom, uncorked it, and swallowed the contents. . . .

V

He was back in the forest glade, by the gigantic altar. Moriamis was beside him again, lovely and warm and breathing; and the moon was still rising above the pine-tops. It seemed that no more than a few moments could have elapsed since he had said farewell to the beloved enchantress. "I thought you might return," said Moriamis. "And I waited a little while."

Ambrose told her of the singular mishap that had attended his journey in time.

Moriamis nodded gravely. "The green philter was more potent than I had supposed," she remarked. "It is fortunate, though, that the red philter was equivalently strong, and could bring you back to me through all those added years. You will have to remain with me now, for I possessed only the two vials. I hope you are not sorry."

Ambrose proceeded to prove, in a somewhat unmonastic manner, that her hope was fully justified.

Neither then nor at any other time did Moriamis tell him that she herself had strengthened slightly and equally the two philters by means of the private formula which she had also stolen from Azédarac.

IN COCAIGNE

It was a windless afternoon of April, beneath skies that were tender as the smile of love, when we went forth, you and I, to seek the fabulous and fortunate realm of Cocaigne. Past leafing oaks with foliage of bronze and chrysolite, through zones of yellow and white and red and purple flowers, like a landscape seen through a prism, we fared with hopeful and tremulous hearts, forgetting all save the dream we had cherished. * * * At last we came to the lonely woods, the pines with their depth of balmy, cool, compassionate shadow, which are sacred to the genius of that land. There, for the first time I was bold to take your hand in mine, and led you to a slope where the woodland lilies, with petals of white and yellow ivory, gleamed among the fallen needles. As in a dream, I found that my arms were about you, as in a dream I kissed your yielding lips, and the ardent pallor of your cheeks and throat. Motionless, you clung to me, and a flush arose beneath my kisses like a delicate stain, and lingered softly. Your eyes deepened to my gaze like the brown pools of the forest at evening, and far within them, as in immensity itself, trembled and shone the steadfast stars of your love. As a ship that has wandered beneath stormy suns and disastrous moons, but comes at last to the arms of the shielding harbour, my head lay on the gentle heaving of your delicious breast, and I knew that we had found Cocaigne.

THE COLOSSUS OF YLOURGNE

THE FLIGHT OF THE NECROMANCER

The thrice-infamous Nathaire, alchemist, astrologer and necromancer, with his ten devil-given pupils, had departed very suddenly and under circumstances of strict secrecy from the town of Vyônes. It was widely thought, among the people of that vicinage, that his departure had been prompted by a salutary fear of ecclesiastical thumbscrews and fagots. Other wizards, less notorious than he, had already gone to the stake during a year of unusual inquisitory zeal; and it was well-known that Nathaire had incurred the reprobation of the Church. Few, therefore, considered the reason of his going a mystery; but the means of transit which he had employed, as well as the destination of the sorcerer and his pupils, were regarded as more than problematic.

A thousand dark and superstitious rumors were abroad; and passers made the sign of the Cross when they neared the tall, gloomy house which Nathaire had built in blasphemous proximity to the great cathedral and had filled with a furniture of Satanic luxury and strangeness. Two daring thieves, who had entered the mansion when the fact of its desertion became well established, reported that much of this furniture, as well as the books and other paraphernalia of Nathaire, had seemingly departed with its owner, doubtless to the same fiery bourn. This served to augment the unholy mystery: for it was patently impossible that Nathaire and his ten apprentices, with several cartloads of household belongings, could have passed the ever-guarded city gates in any legitimate manner without the knowledge of the custodians.

It was said by the more devout and religious moiety that the Arch-fiend, with a legion of bat-winged assistants, had borne them away bodily at moonless midnight. There were clerics, and also reputable burghers, who professed to have seen the flight of dark, man-like shapes upon the blotted stars together with others that were not men, and to have heard the wailing cries of the hell-bound crew as they passed in an evil cloud over the roofs and city walls.

Others believed that the sorcerers had transported themselves from Vyônes through their own diabolic arts, and had withdrawn to some unfrequented fastness where Nathaire, who had long been in feeble health, could hope to die in such peace and serenity as might be enjoyed by one who stood between the flames of the *auto-da-fé* and those of Abaddon. It was thought that he had lately cast his own horoscope, for the first time in his fifty-odd years, and had read therein an impending conjunction of disastrous planets, signifying early death.

Others still, among whom were certain rival astrologers and enchanters, said that Nathaire had retired from the public view merely that he might commune without interruption with various coadjutive demons; and thus might weave, unmolested, the black spells of a supreme and lycanthropic malice. These spells, they hinted, would in due time be visited upon Vyônes and perhaps upon the entire region of Averoigne; and would no doubt take the form of a fearsome pestilence or a wholesale invultuation or a realm-wide incursion of succubi and incubi.

Amid the seething of strange rumors, many half-forgotten tales were recalled, and new legends were created overnight. Much was made of the obscure nativity of Nathaire and his dubitable wanderings before he had settled, six years previous, in Vyônes. People said that he was fiend-begotten, like the fabled Merlin: his father being no less a personage than Alastor, demon of revenge; and his mother a deformed and dwarfish sorceress. From the former, he had taken his spitefulness and malignity; from the latter, his squat, puny physique.

He had travelled in Orient lands, and had learned from Egyptian or Saracenic masters the unhallowed art of necromancy, in whose practice he was unrivalled. There were black whispers anent the use he had made of long-dead bodies, of fleshless bones, and the service he had wrung from buried men that the angel of doom alone could lawfully raise up. He had never been popular, though many had sought his advice and assistance in the furthering of their own more or less dubious affairs. Once, in the third year after his coming to Vyônes, he had been stoned in public because of his bruited necromancies, and had been permanently lamed by a well-directed cobble. This injury, it was thought, he had never forgiven; and he was said to return the antagonism of the clergy with the hellish hatred of an Antichrist.

Apart from the sorcerous evils and abuses of which he was commonly suspected, he had long been looked upon as a corrupter of youth. Despite his minikin stature, his deformity and ugliness, he possessed a remarkable power, a mesmeric persuasion; and his pupils, whom he was said to have plunged into bottomless and ghoulish iniquities, were young men of the most brilliant promise. On the whole, his vanishment was regarded as a quite providential riddance.

Among the people of the city there was one man who took no part in the somber gossip and lurid speculation. This man was Gaspard du Nord, himself a student of the proscribed sciences, who had been numbered for a year among the pupils of Nathaire but had chosen to withdraw quietly from the master's household after learning the enormities that would attend his further initiation. He had, however, taken with him much rare and peculiar knowledge, together with a certain insight into the baleful powers and night-dark motives of the necromancer.

Because of this knowledge and insight, Gaspard preferred to remain silent when he heard of Nathaire's departure. Also, he did not think it well to revive the memory of his own past pupilage. Alone with his books, in a sparsely furnished attic, he frowned above a small, oblong mirror, framed with an arabesque of golden vipers, that had once been the property of Nathaire.

It was not the reflection of his own comely and youthful though subtly lined face that caused him to frown. Indeed, the mirror was of another kind than that which reflects the features of the gazer. In its depths, for a few instants, he had beheld a strange and ominous-looking scene, whose participants were known to him but whose location he could not recognize or orientate. Before he could study it closely, the mirror had clouded as if with the rising of alchemic fumes, and he had seen no more.

This clouding, he reflected, could mean only one thing: Nathaire had known himself watched and had put forth a counterspell that rendered the clairvoyant mirror useless. It was the realization of this fact, together with the brief, sinister glimpse of Nathaire's present activities, that troubled Gaspard and caused a chill horror to mount slowly in his mind: a horror that had not yet found a palpable form or a name.

2. The Gathering of the Dead

The departure of Nathaire and his pupils occurred in the late spring of 1281, during the interlunar dark. Afterwards a new moon waxed above the flowery fields and bright-leafed woods, and waned in ghostly silver. With its waning, people began to talk of other magicians and fresher mysteries.

Then, in the moon-deserted nights of early summer, there came a series of disappearances far more unnatural and inexplicable than that of the dwarfish, malignant necromancer.

It was found one day by grave-diggers, who had gone early to their toil in a cemetery outside the walls of Vyônes, that no less than six newly occupied graves had been opened, and the bodies, which were those of reputable citizens, removed. On closer examination, it became all too evident that this removal had not been effected by robbers. The coffins, which lay aslant or stood protruding upright from the mould, offered all the appearance of having been shattered from within as if by the use of extrahuman strength; and the fresh earth itself was up-heaved, as if the dead men, in some awful, untimely resurrection, had actually *dug* their way to the surface.

The corpses had vanished utterly, as if hell had swallowed them; and, as far as could be learned, there were no eyewitnesses of their fate. In those devil-ridden times, only one explanation of the happening seemed credible: demons had entered the graves and taken bodily possession of the dead, compelling them to arise and go forth.

To the dismay and horror of all Averoigne, the strange vanishment was followed with appalling promptness by many others of a like sort. It seemed as if an occult, resistless summons had been laid upon the dead. Nightly, for a period of two weeks, the cemeteries of Vyônes, and also those of other towns, of villages and hamlets, gave up a ghast-ly quota of their tenants. From brazen-bolted tombs, from common charnels, from shallow, unconsecrated trenches, from the marble-lidded vaults of churches and cathedrals, the weird exodus went on without cessation.

Worse than this, if possible, there were newly ceremented corpses that leapt from their biers or catafalques, and disregarding the horrified watchers, ran with great bounds of automatic frenzy into the night, never to be seen again by those who lamented them.

In every case, the missing bodies were those of young stalwart men who had died but recently and had met their death through violence or accident rather than wasting illness. Some were criminals who had paid the penalty of their misdeeds; others were men-at-arms or constables, slain in the execution of their duty. Knights who had died in tourney or personal combat were numbered among them; and many were the victims of the robber-bands who infested Averoigne at that time. There were monks, merchants, nobles, yeomen, pages, priests; but none, in any case, who had passed the prime of life. The old and in-firm, it seemed, were safe from the animating demons.

The situation was looked upon by the more superstitious as a veritable omening of the world's end. Satan was making war with his cohorts and was carrying the bodies of the holy dead into hellish captivity. The consternation increased a hundred-fold when it became plain that even the most liberal sprinkling of holy water, the performance of the most awful and cogent exorcisms, failed utterly to give protection against this diabolic ravishment. The Church owned itself powerless to cope with the strange evil; and the forces of secular law could do nothing to arraign or punish the intangible agency.

Because of the universal fear that prevailed, no effort was made to follow the missing cadavers. Ghastly tales, however, were told by late wayfarers who had met certain of these liches, striding alone or in companies along the roads of Averoigne. They gave the appearance of being deaf, dumb, totally insensate, and of hurrying with horrible speed and sureness toward a remote, predestined goal. The general direction of their flight, it seemed, was eastward; but only with the cessation of the exodus, which had numbered several hundred people, did anyone begin to suspect the actual destination of the dead.

This destination, it somehow became rumored, was the ruinous castle of Ylourgne, beyond the werewolf-haunted forest, in the outlying, semi-mountainous hills of Averoigne.

Ylourgne, a great, craggy pile that had been built by a line of evil and marauding barons now extinct, was a place that even the goatherds preferred to shun. The wrathful specters of its bloody lords were said to move turbulently in its crumbling halls; and its châtelaines were the Undead. No one cared to dwell in the shadow of its cliff-founded walls; and the nearest abode of living men was a small Cistercian monastery, more than a mile away on the opposite slope of the valley.

The monks of this austere brotherhood held little commerce with the world beyond the hills; and few were the visitors who sought admission at their high-perched portals. But, during that dreadful summer, following the disappearances of the dead, a weird and disquieting tale went forth from the monastery throughout Averoigne.

Beginning with late spring, the Cistercian monks were compelled to take cognizance of sundry odd phenomena in the old, long-deserted ruins of Ylourgne, which were visible from their windows. They had beheld flaring lights, where lights should not have been: flames of un-canny blue and crimson that shuddered behind the broken, weed-grown embrasures or rose starward above the jagged crenelations. Hideous noises had issued from the ruin by night together with the flames; and the monks had heard a clangor as of hellish anvils and hammers, a ringing of gigantic armor and maces, and had deemed that Ylourgne was become a mustering-ground of devils. Mephitic odors as of brimstone and burning flesh had floated across the valley; and even by day, when the noises were silent and the lights no longer flared, a thin haze of hell-blue vapor hung upon the battlements.

It was plain, the monks thought, that the place had been occupied from beneath by subterrestrial beings; for no one was seen to ap-proach it by way of the bare, open slopes and crags. Observing these signs of the Archfoe's activity in their neighborhood, they crossed themselves with new fervor and frequency, and said their Paters and Aves more interminably than before. Their toils and austerities, also, they redoubled. Otherwise, since the old castle was a place abandoned by men, they took no heed of the supposed occupation, deeming it well to mind their own affairs unless in case of overt Satanic hostility.

They kept a careful watch; but for several weeks they saw no one who actually entered Ylourgne or emerged therefrom. Except for the nocturnal lights and noises, and the hovering vapor by day, there was no proof of tenants either human or diabolic.

Then, one morning, in the valley below the terraced gardens of the monastery, two brothers, hoeing weeds in a carrot-patch, beheld the passing of a singular train of people who came from the direction of the great forest of Averoigne and went upward, climbing the steep, chasmy slope toward Ylourgne.

These people, the monks averred, were striding along in great haste, with stiff but flying steps; and all were strangely pale of feature and were habited in the garments of the grave. The shrouds of some were torn and ragged; and all were dusty with travel or grimed with the mould of interment. The people numbered a dozen or more; and after them, at intervals, there came several stragglers, attired like the rest. With marvellous agility and speed, they mounted the hill and disappeared at length amid the lowering walls of Ylourgne.

At this time, no rumor of the ravished graves and biers had reached the Cistercians. The tale was brought to them later, after they had beheld, on many successive mornings, the passing of small or great companies of the dead toward the devil-taken castle. Hundreds of these liches, they swore, had filed by beneath the monastery; and doubtless many others had gone past unnoted in the dark. None, however, were seen to come forth from Ylourgne, which had swallowed them up like the undisgorging Pit.

Though direly frightened and sorely scandalized, the brothers still thought it well to refrain from action. Some, the hardiest, irked by all these flagrant signs of evil, had desired to visit the ruins with holy water and lifted crucifixes. But their abbot, in his wisdom, enjoined them to wait. In the meanwhile, the nocturnal flames grew brighter, the noises louder.

Also, in the course of this waiting, while incessant prayers went up from the little monastery, a frightful thing occurred. One of the brothers, a stout fellow named Théophile, in violation of the rigorous discipline, had made over-frequent visits to the wine-casks. No doubt he had tried to drown his pious horror at these untoward happenings. At any rate, after his potations, he had the ill-luck to wander out among the precipices and break his neck.

Sorrowing for his death and dereliction, the brothers laid Théophile in the chapel and chanted their masses for his soul. These masses, in the dark hours before morning, were interrupted by the untimely resurrection of the dead monk, who, with his head lolling horribly on his broken neck, rushed as if fiend-ridden from the chapel and ran down the hill toward the demon flames and clamors of Ylourgne.

3. THE TESTIMONY OF THE MONKS

Following the above-related occurrence, two of the brothers who had previously desired to visit the haunted castle, again applied to the abbot for this permission, saying that God would surely aid them in avenging the abduction of Théophile's body as well as the taking of many others from consecrated ground. Marvelling at the hardihood of these lusty monks, who proposed to beard the Archenemy in his lair, the abbot permitted them to go forth, furnished with aspergillums and flasks of holy water; and bearing great crosses of hornbeam, such as would have served for maces with which to brain an armored knight.

The monks, whose names were Bernard and Stéphane, went boldly up at middle forenoon to assail the evil stronghold. It was an arduous climb, among overhanging boulders and along slippery scarps; but both were stout and agile, and, moreover, well accustomed to such climbing. Since the day was sultry and airless, their white robes were soon stained with sweat; but pausing only for brief prayer, they pressed on; and in good season they neared the castle, upon whose grey, time-eroded ramparts they could still descry no evidence of occupation or activity.

The deep moat that had once surrounded the place was now dry, and had been partly filled by crumbling earth and detritus from the walls. The drawbridge had rotted away; but the blocks of the barbican, collapsing into the moat, had made a sort of rough causey on which it was possible to cross. Not without trepidation, and lifting their crucifixes as warriors lift their weapons in the escalade of an armed fortress, the brothers climbed over the ruin of the barbican into the courtyard.

This too, like the battlements, was seemingly deserted. Overgrown nettles, rank grasses and sapling trees were rooted between its paving-stones. The high, massive donjon, the chapel, and that portion of the castellated structure containing the great hall, had preserved their main outlines after centuries of dilapidation. To the left of the broad bailey, a doorway yawned like the mouth of a dark cavern in the cliffy mass of the hall-building; and from this doorway there issued a thin, bluish vapor, writhing in phantom coils toward the unclouded heavens.

Approaching the doorway, the brothers beheld a gleaming of red fires within, like the eyes of dragons blinking through infernal murk. They felt sure that the place was an outpost of Erebus, an antechamber of the Pit; but nevertheless, they entered bravely, chanting loud exorcisms and brandishing their mighty crosses of hornbeam.

Passing through the cavernous doorway, they could see but indistinctly in the gloom, being somewhat blinded by the summer sunlight they had left. Then, with the gradual clearing of their vision, a monstrous scene was limned before them, with ever-growing details of crowding horror and grotesquery. Some of these details were obscure and mysteriously terrifying; others, all too plain, were branded as if with sudden, ineffaceable hell-fire on the minds of the monks.

They stood on the threshold of a colossal chamber, which seemed to have been made by the tearing down of upper floors and inner partitions adjacent to the castle hall, itself a room of huge extent. The chamber seemed to recede through interminable shadow, shafted with sunlight falling through the rents of ruin: sunlight that was powerless to dissipate the infernal gloom and mystery.

The monks averred, later, that they saw many people moving about the place, together with sundry demons, some of whom were shadowy and gigantic, and others barely to be distinguished from the men. These people, as well as their familiars, were occupied with the tending of reverberatory furnaces and immense pear-shaped and gourd-shaped vessels such as were used in alchemy. Some, also, were stooping above great fuming cauldrons, like sorcerers busy with the brewing of terrible drugs. Against the opposite wall, there were two enormous vats, built of stone and mortar, whose circular sides rose higher than a man's head, so that Bernard and Stéphane were unable to determine their contents. One of the vats gave forth a whitish glimmering; the other, a ruddy luminosity.

Near the vats, and somewhat between them, there stood a sort of low couch or litter, made of luxurious, weirdly figured fabrics such as the Saracens weave. On this the monks discerned a dwarfish being, pale and wizened, with eyes of chill flame that shone like evil beryls through the dusk. The dwarf, who had all the air of a feeble moribund, was supervising the toils of the men and their familiars.

The dazed eyes of the brothers began to comprehend other details. They saw that several corpses, among which they recognized that of Théophile, were lying on the middle floor, together with a heap of human bones that had been wrenched asunder at the joints, and great lumps of flesh piled like the carvings of butchers. One of the men was lifting the bones and dropping them into a cauldron beneath which there glowed a ruby-colored fire; and another was flinging the lumps of flesh into a tub filled with some hueless liquid that gave forth an evil hissing as of a thousand serpents.

Others had stripped the grave-clothes from one of the cadavers, and were starting to assail it with long knives. Others still were mounting rude flights of stone stairs along the walls of the immense vats, carrying vessels filled with semi-liquescent matters which they emptied over the high rims.

Appalled at this vision of human and Satanic turpitude, and feeling a more than righteous indignation, the monks resumed their chanting of sonorous exorcisms and rushed forward. Their entrance, it appeared, was not perceived by the heinously occupied crew of sorcerers and devils.

Bernard and Stéphane, filled with an ardor of godly wrath, were about to fling themselves upon the butchers who had started to assail the dead body. This corpse they recognized as being that of a notorious outlaw, named Jacques Le Loupgarou, who had been slain a few days previous in combat with the officers of the state. Le Loupgarou, noted for his brawn, his cunning and his ferocity, had long terrorized the woods and highways of Averoigne. His great body had been half eviscerated by the swords of the constabulary; and his beard was stiff and purple with the dried blood of a ghastly wound that had cloven his face from temple to mouth. He had died unshriven, but nevertheless, the monks were unwilling to see his helpless cadaver put to some unhallowed use beyond the surmise of Christians.

The pale, malignant-looking dwarf had now perceived the brothers. They heard him cry out in a shrill, imperatory tone that rose above the ominous hiss of the cauldrons and the hoarse mutter of men and demons. They knew not his words, which were those of some outlandish tongue and sounded like an incantation. Instantly, as if in response to an order, two of the men turned from their unholy chemistry, and lifting copper basins filled with an unknown, fetid liquor, hurled the contents of these vessels in the faces of Bernard and Stéphane.

The brothers were blinded by the stinging fluid, which bit their flesh as with many serpents' teeth; and they were overcome by the noxious fumes, so that their great crosses dropped from their hands and they both fell unconscious on the castle floor.

Recovering anon their sight and their other senses, they found that their hands had been tied with heavy thongs of gut, so that they were now helpless and could no longer wield their crucifixes or the sprinklers of holy water which they carried.

In this ignominious condition, they heard the voice of the evil dwarf, commanding them to arise. They obeyed, though clumsily and with difficulty, being denied the assistance of their hands. Bernard, who was still sick with the poisonous vapor he had inhaled, fell twice before he succeeded in standing erect; and his discomfiture was greeted with a cachinnation of foul, obscene laughter from the assembled sorcerers.

Now, standing, the monks were taunted by the dwarf, who mocked and reviled them, with appalling blasphemies such as could be uttered only by a bond-servant of Satan. At last, according to their sworn testimony, he said to them:

"Return to your kennel, ye whelps of Ialdabaoth, and take with you this message: *They that came here as many shall go forth as one.*"

Then, in obedience to a dreadful formula spoken by the dwarf, two of the familiars, who had the shape of enormous and shadowy beasts, approached the body of Le Loupgarou and that of Brother Théophile. One of the foul demons, like a vapor that sinks into a marsh, entered the bloody nostrils of Le Loupgarou, disappearing inch by inch, till its horned and bestial head was withdrawn from sight. The other, in like manner, went in through the nostrils of Brother Théophile, whose head lay wried athwart his shoulder on the broken neck.

Then, when the demons had completed their possession, the bodies, in a fashion horrible to behold, were raised up from the castle floor, the one with ravelled entrails hanging from its wide wounds, the other with a head that drooped forward loosely on its bosom. Then, animated by their devils, the cadavers took up the crosses of hornbeam that had been dropped by Stéphane and Bernard; and using the crosses for bludgeons, they drove the monks in ignominious flight from the castle, amid a loud, tempestuous howling of infernal laughter from the dwarf and his necromantic crew. And the nude corpse of Le Loupgarou and the robed cadaver of Théophile followed them far on the chasm-riven slopes below Ylourgne, striking great blows with the crosses, so that the backs of the two Cistercians were become a mass of bloody bruises.

After a defeat so signal and crushing, no more of the monks were emboldened to go up against Ylourgne. The whole monastery, thereafter, devoted itself to triple austerities, to quadrupled prayers; and awaiting the unknown will of God, and the equally obscure machinations of the Devil, maintained a pious faith that was somewhat tempered with trepidation.

In time, through goatherds who visited the monks, the tale of Sté-phane and Bernard went forth throughout Averoigne, adding to the grievous alarm that had been caused by the wholesale disappearance of the dead. No one knew what was really going on in the haunted castle or what disposition had been made of the hundreds of migratory corpses; for the light thrown on their fate by the monks' story, though lurid and frightful, was all too inconclusive; and the message sent by the dwarf was somewhat cabbalistic.

Everyone felt, however, that some gigantic menace, some black, infernal enchantment, was being brewed within the ruinous walls. The malignant, moribund dwarf was all too readily identified with the miss-ing sorcerer, Nathaire; and his underlings, it was plain, were Nathaire's pupils.

4. THE GOING-FORTH OF GASPARD DU NORD

Alone in his attic chamber, Gaspard du Nord, student of alchemy and sorcery and quondam pupil of Nathaire, sought repeatedly, but always in vain, to consult the viper-circled mirror. The glass remained obscure and cloudy, as with the risen fumes of Satanical alembics or baleful necromantic braziers. Haggard and weary with long nights of watching, Gaspard knew that Nathaire was even more vigilant than he.

Reading with anxious care the general configuration of the stars, he found the foretokening of a great evil that was to come upon Aver-oigne. But the nature of the evil was not clearly shown.

In the meanwhile, the hideous resurrection and migration of the dead were taking place. All Averoigne shuddered at the manifold enormity. Like the timeless night of a Memphian plague, terror settled everywhere; and people spoke of each new atrocity in bated whispers, without daring to voice the execrable tale aloud. To Gaspard, as to everyone, the whispers came; and likewise, after the horror had appar-ently ceased in early mid-summer, there came the appalling story of the Cistercian monks.

Now, at last, the long-baffled watcher found an inkling of that which he sought. The hiding-place of the fugitive necromancer and his apprentices, at least, had been uncovered; and the disappearing dead were clearly traced to their bourn. But still, even for the percipient Gaspard, there remained an undeclared enigma: the exact nature of the abominable brew, the hell-dark sorcery, that Nathaire was concocting in his remote den. Gaspard felt sure of one thing only: the dying, splenetic dwarf, knowing that his allotted time was short, and hating the people of Averoigne with a bottomless rancor, would prepare an enormous and maleficent magic without parallel.

Even with his knowledge of Nathaire's proclivities, and his awareness of the well-nigh inexhaustible arcanic science, the reserves of pit-deep wizardry possessed by the dwarf, he could form only vague, terrifical conjectures anent the incubated evil. But, as time went on, he felt an ever-deepening oppression, the adumbration of a monstrous menace crawling from the dark rim of the world. He could not shake off his disquietude; and finally he resolved, despite the obvious perils of such an excursion, to pay a secret visit to the neighborhood of Ylourgne.

Gaspard, though he came of a well-to-do family, was at that time in straitened circumstances; for his devotion to a somewhat doubtful science had been disapproved by his father. His sole income was a small pittance, purveyed secretly to the youth by his mother and sister. This sufficed for his meager food, the rent of his room, and a few books and instruments and chemicals; but it would not permit the purchase of a horse or even a humble mule for the proposed journey of more than forty miles.

Undaunted, he set forth on foot, carrying only a dagger and a wallet of food. He timed his wanderings so that he would reach Ylourgne at nightfall in the rising of a full moon. Much of his journey lay through the great, lowering forest, which approached the very walls of Vyônes on the eastern side and ran in a somber arc through Averoigne to the mouth of the rocky valley below Ylourgne. After a few miles, he emerged from the mighty wood of pines and oaks and larches; and thenceforward, for the first day, followed the river Isoile through an open, well-peopled plain. He spent the warm summer night beneath a beech tree, in the vicinity of a small village, not caring to sleep in the lonely woods where robbers and wolves—and creatures of a more baleful repute—were commonly supposed to dwell.

At evening of the second day, after passing through the wildest and oldest portion of the immemorial wood, he came to the steep, stony valley that led to his destination. This valley was the fountain-head of the Isoile, which had dwindled to a mere rivulet. In the brown twilight, between sunset and moonrise, he saw the lights of the Cistercian monastery; and opposite, on the piled, forbidding scarps, the grim and rugged mass of the ruinous stronghold of Ylourgne, with wan and wizard fires flickering behind its high embrasures. Apart from these fires, there was no sign of occupation; and he did not hear at any time the dismal noises reported by the monks.

Gaspard waited till the round moon, yellow as the eye of some immense nocturnal bird, had begun to peer above the darkling valley. Then, very cautiously, since the neighborhood was strange to him, he started to make his way toward the somber, brooding castle.

Even for one well-used to such climbing, the escalade would have offered enough difficulty and danger by moonlight. Several times, finding himself at the bottom of a sheer cliff, he was compelled to retrace his hard-won progress; and often he was saved from falling only by stunted shrubs and briars that had taken root in the niggard soil. Breathless, with torn raiment, and scored and bleeding hands, he gained at length the shoulder of the craggy height, below the walls.

Here he paused to recover breath and recuperate his flagging strength. He could see from his vantage the pale reflection as of hidden flames, that beat upward on the inner wall of the high-built donjon. He heard a low hum of confused noises, whose distance and direction were alike baffling. Sometimes they seemed to float downward from the black battlements, sometimes to issue from subterranean depths far in the hill.

Apart from this remote, ambiguous hum, the night was locked in a mortal stillness. The very winds appeared to shun the vicinity of the dread castle. An unseen, clammy cloud of paralyzing evil hung removeless upon all things; and the pale, swollen moon, the patroness of witches and sorcerers, distilled her green poison above the crumbling towers in a silence older than time.

Gaspard felt the obscenely clinging weight of a more burdenous thing than his own fatigue when he resumed his progress toward the barbican. Invisible webs of the waiting, ever-gathering evil seemed to impede him. The slow, noisome flapping of intangible wings was heavy in his face. He seemed to breathe a surging wind from unfathomable vaults and caverns of corruption. Inaudible howlings, derisive or minatory, thronged in his ears, and foul hands appeared to thrust him back. But, bowing his head as if against a blowing gale, he went on and climbed the mounded ruin of the barbican, into the weedy courtyard.

The place was deserted, to all seeming; and much of it was still deep in the shadows of the walls and turrets. Nearby in the black, silver-crenelated pile, Gaspard saw the open, cavernous doorway described by the monks. It was lit from within by a lurid glare, wannish and eerie as marsh-fires. The humming noise, now audible as a muttering of voices, issued from the doorway; and Gaspard thought that he could see dark, sooty figures moving rapidly in the lit interior.

Keeping in the further shadows, he stole along the courtyard, making a sort of circuit amid the ruins. He did not dare to approach the open entrance for fear of being seen; though, as far as he could tell, the place was unguarded.

He came to the donjon, on whose upper wall the wan light flickered obliquely through a sort of rift in the long building adjacent. This opening was at some distance from the ground; and Gaspard saw that it had been formerly the door to a stone balcony. A flight of broken steps led upward along the wall to the half-crumbled remnant of this balcony; and it occurred to the youth that he might climb the steps and peer unobserved into the interior of Ylourgne.

Some of the stairs were missing; and all were in heavy shadow. Gaspard found his way precariously to the balcony, pausing once in considerable alarm when a fragment of the worn stone, loosened by his footfall, dropped with a loud clattering on the courtyard flags below. Apparently it was unheard by the occupants of the castle; and after a little he resumed his climbing.

Cautiously he neared the large, ragged opening through which the light poured upward. Crouching on a narrow ledge, which was all that remained of the balcony, he peered in on a most astounding and terrific spectacle, whose details were so bewildering that he could barely comprehend their import till after many minutes.

It was plain that the story told by the monks—allowing for their religious bias—had been far from extravagant. Almost the whole interior of the half-ruined pile had been torn down and dismantled to afford room for the activities of Nathaire: in itself a superhuman task. This demolition in itself was a superhuman task for whose execution the sorcerer must have employed a legion of familiars as well as his ten pupils.

The vast chamber was fitfully illumed by the glare of athanors and braziers; and, above all, by the weird glimmering from the huge stone vats. Even from his high vantage, the watcher could not see the contents of these vats; but a white luminosity poured upward from the rim of one of them, and a flesh-tinted phosphorescence from the other.

Gaspard had seen certain of the experiments and evocations of Nathaire, and was all too familiar with the appurtenances of the dark arts. Within certain limits, he was not squeamish; nor was it likely that he would have been terrified overmuch by the shadowy, uncouth shapes of demons who toiled in the pit below him side by side with the black-clad pupils of the sorcerer. But a cold horror clutched his heart when he saw the incredible, enormous thing that occupied the central floor: the colossal human skeleton a hundred feet in length, stretching for more than the extent of the old castle hall; the skeleton whose bony right foot the group of men and devils, to all appearance, were busily clothing with human flesh!

The prodigious and macabre framework, complete in every part, with ribs like arches of some Satanic nave, shone as if it were still heated by the fires of an infernal welding. It seemed to shimmer and burn with unnatural life, to quiver with malign disquietude in the flickering glare and gloom. The great finger-bones, curving claw-like on the floor, appeared as if they were about to close upon some helpless prey. The tremendous teeth were set in an everlasting grin of sardonic cruelty and malice. The hollow eye-sockets, deep as Tartarean wells, appeared to seethe with myriad, mocking lights, like the eyes of elementals swimming upward in obscene shadow.

Gaspard was stunned by the shocking and stupendous phantasmagoria that yawned before him like a peopled hell. Afterwards, he was never wholly sure of certain things, and could remember very little of the actual manner in which the work of the men and their assistants was being carried on. Dim, dubious, bat-like creatures seemed to be flitting to and fro between one of the stone vats and the group that toiled like sculptors, clothing the bony foot with a reddish plasm which they applied and moulded like so much clay. Gaspard thought, but was not certain later, that this plasm, which gleamed as if with mingled blood and fire, was being brought from the rosy-litten vat in vessels borne by the claws of the shadowy flying creatures. None of them, however, approached the other vat, whose wannish light was momently enfeebled, as if it were dying down.

He looked for the minikin figure of Nathaire, whom he could not distinguish in the crowded scene. The sick necromancer—if he had not already succumbed to the little-known disease that had long wasted him like an inward flame—was no doubt hidden from view by the colossal skeleton and was perhaps directing the labors of the men and demons from his couch.

Spell-bound on that precarious ledge, the watcher failed to hear the furtive, cat-like feet that were climbing behind him on the ruinous stairs. Too late, he heard the clink of a loose fragment close upon his heels; and turning in startlement, he toppled into sheer oblivion beneath the impact of a cudgel-like blow, and did not even know that the beginning fall of his body toward the courtyard had been arrested by his assailant's arms.

5. The Horror of Ylourgne

Gaspard, returning from his dark plunge into Lethean emptiness, found himself gazing into the eyes of Nathaire: those eyes of liquid night and ebony, in which swam the chill, malignant fires of stars that had gone down to irremeable perdition. For some time, in the confusion of his senses, he could see nothing but the eyes, which seemed to have drawn him forth like baleful magnets from his swoon. Apparently disembodied, or set in a face too vast for human cognizance, they burned before him in chaotic murk. Then, by degrees, he saw the other features of the sorcerer, and the details of a lurid scene; and became aware of his own situation.

Trying to lift his hands to his aching head, he found that they were bound tightly together at the wrists. He was half-lying, half-leaning against an object with hard planes and edges that irked his back. This object he discovered to be a sort of alchemic furnace, or athanor, part of a litter of disused apparatus that stood or lay on the castle floor. Cupels, aludels, cucurbits, like enormous gourds and globes, were mingled in strange confusion with the piled, iron-clasped books and the sooty cauldrons and braziers of a darker science.

Nathaire, propped among Saracenic cushions with arabesques of sullen gold and fulgurant scarlet, was peering upon him from a kind of improvised couch, made with bales of Orient rugs and arrases, to whose luxury the rude walls of the castle, stained with mould and mottled with dead fungi, offered a grotesque foil. Dim lights and evilly swooping shadows flickered across the scene; and Gaspard could hear a guttural hum of voices behind him. Twisting his head a little, he saw one of the stone vats, whose rosy luminosity was blurred and blotted by vampire wings that went to and fro.

Gaspard and Nathaire, it seemed, were alone. The assailants of the youth, whoever or whatever they had been, had presumably returned to another task after bringing their bound, unconscious captive before the sorcerer.

"Welcome," said Nathaire, after an interval in which the student began to perceive the fatal progress of illness in the pain-pinched features before him. "So Gaspard du Nord has come to see his former master!" The harsh, imperatory voice, with demoniac volume, issued appallingly from the wizened frame.

"I have come," said Gaspard, in laconic echo. "Tell me, what devil's work is this in which I find you engaged? And what have you done with the dead bodies that were stolen by your accursed familiars?"

The frail, dying body of Nathaire, as if possessed by some sardonic fiend, rocked to and fro on the luxurious couch in a long, violent gust of laughter, without other reply.

"If your looks bear creditable witness," said Gaspard, when the baleful laughter had ceased, "you are mortally ill, and the time is short in which you can hope to atone for your deeds of malefice and make your peace with God—if indeed it still be possible for you to make peace. What foul and monstrous brew are you preparing, to insure the ultimate perdition of your soul?"

The dwarf was again seized by a spasm of diabolic mirth.

"Nay, nay, my good Gaspard," he said finally. "I have made another bond than the one with which puling cowards try to purchase the good will and forgiveness of the heavenly Tyrant. Hell may take me in the end, if it will; but Hell has paid, and will still pay, an ample and goodly price. I must die soon, it is true, for my doom is written in the stars: but in death, by the grace of Satan, I shall live again, and shall go forth endowed with the mighty thews of the Anakim, to visit vengeance on the people of Averoigne, who have long hated me for my necromantic wisdom and have held me in derision for my dwarf stature."

"What madness is this whereof you dream?" asked the youth, appalled by the more than human frenzy and malignity that seemed to dilate the shrunken frame of Nathaire and stream in Tartarean luster from his eyes.

"It is no madness, but a veritable thing: a miracle, mayhap, as life itself is a miracle. . . . From the fresh bodies of the dead, which otherwise would have rotted away in charnel foulness, my pupils and familiars are making for me, beneath my instruction, the giant form whose skeleton you have beheld. My soul, at the death of its present body, will pass into this colossal tenement through the working of certain spells of transmigration in which my faithful assistants have also been carefully instructed.

"If you had remained with me, Gaspard, and had not drawn back in your petty, pious squeamishness from the marvels and profundities that I should have unveiled for you, it would now be your privilege to share in the creation of this prodigy. . . . And if you had come to Ylourgne a little sooner in your presumptuous prying, I might have made a certain use of your stout bones and muscles . . . the same use I have made of other young men, who died through accident or violence. But it is too late even for this, since the building of the bones has been completed, and it remains only to invest them with human flesh. My good Gaspard, there is nothing whatever to be done with you—except to put you safely out of the way. Providentially, for this purpose, there is an oubliette beneath the castle: a somewhat dismal lodging place, no doubt, but one that was made strong and deep by the grim lords of Ylourgne."

Gaspard was unable to frame any reply to this sinister and extraordinary speech. Searching his horror-frozen brain for words, he felt
himself seized from behind by the hands of unseen beings who had
come, no doubt, in answer to some gesture of Nathaire: a gesture
which the captive had not perceived. He was blindfolded with some
heavy fabric, mouldy and musty as a grave-cloth, and was led stum-
bling through the litter of strange apparatus, and down a winding flight
of ruinous, narrow stairs from which the noisome breath of stagnating
water, mingled with the oily muskiness of serpents, arose to meet him.

He appeared to descend for a distance that would admit of no return. Slowly the stench grew stronger, more insupportable; the stairs
ended; a door clanged sullenly on rusty hinges; and Gaspard was thrust
forward on a damp, uneven floor that seemed to have been worn away
by myriad feet.

He heard the grating of a ponderous slab of stone. His wrists were
untied, the bandage was removed from his eyes, and he saw by the
light of flickering torches a round hole that yawned in the oozing floor
at his feet. Beside it was the lifted slab that had formed its lid. Before
he could turn to see the faces of his captors, to learn if they were men
or devils, he was seized rudely and thrust into the gaping hole. He fell
through Erebus-like darkness, for what seemed an immense distance,
before he struck bottom. Lying half-stunned in a shallow, fetid pool,
he heard the funereal thud of the heavy slab as it slid back into place
far above him.

6. THE VAULTS OF YLOURGNE

Gaspard was revived, after a while, by the chillness of the water in
which he lay. His garments were half-soaked; and the slimy, mephitic
pool, as he discovered by his first movement, was within an inch of his
mouth. He could hear a steady, monotonous dripping somewhere in
the rayless night of his dungeon. He staggered to his feet, finding that
his bones were still intact, and began a cautious exploration. Foul

drops fell upon his hair and lifted face as he moved; his feet slipped and splashed in the rotten water; there were angry, vehement hissings, and serpentine coils slithered coldly across his ankles.

He soon came to a rough wall of stone, and following the wall with his fingertips, he tried to determine the extent of the oubliette. The place was more or less circular, without corners, and he failed to form any just idea of its circuit. Somewhere in his wanderings, he found a shelving pile of rubble that rose above the water against the wall; and here, for the sake of comparative dryness and comfort, he ensconced himself, after dispossessing a number of outraged reptiles. These creatures, it seemed, were inoffensive, and probably belonged to some species of water-snake; but he shivered at the touch of their clammy scales.

Sitting on the rubble-heap, Gaspard reviewed in his mind the various horrors of a situation that was infinitely dismal and desperate. He had learned the incredible, soul-shaking secret of Ylourgne, the unimaginably monstrous and blasphemous project of Nathaire; but now, immured in this noisome hole as in a subterranean tomb, in depths beneath the devil-haunted pile, he could not even warn the world of the imminent menace.

The wallet of food, now more than half-empty, with which he started from Vyônes, was still hanging at his back; and he assured himself by investigation that his captors had not troubled to deprive him of his dagger. Gnawing a crust of stale bread in the darkness, and caressing with his hand the hilt of the precious weapon, he sought for some rift in the all-environing despair.

He had no means of measuring the black hours that went over him with the slowness of a slime-clogged river, crawling in blind silence to a subterrene sea. The ceaseless drip of water, probably from sunken hill-springs that had supplied the castle in former years, alone broke the stillness; but the sound became in time an equivocal monotone that suggested to his half-delirious mind the mirthless and perpetual chuckling of unseen imps. At last, from sheer bodily exhaustion, he fell into troubled nightmare-ridden slumber.

He could not tell if it were night or noon in the world without when he awakened; for the same stagnant darkness, unrelieved by ray or glimmer, brimmed the oubliette. Shivering, he became aware of a steady draft that blew upon him: a dank, unwholesome air, like the breath of unsunned vaults that had wakened into cryptic life and activity during his sleep. He had not noticed the draft heretofore; and his numb brain was startled into sudden hope by the intimation which it conveyed. Obviously there was some underground rift or channel through which the air entered; and this rift might somehow prove to be a place of egress from the oubliette.

Getting to his feet, he groped uncertainly forward in the direction of the draft. He stumbled over something that cracked and broke beneath his heels, and narrowly checked himself from falling on his face in the slimy, serpent-haunted pool. Before he could investigate the obstruction or resume his blind groping, he heard a harsh, grating noise above, and a wavering shaft of yellow light came down through the oubliette's opened mouth. Dazzled, he looked up and saw the round hole ten or twelve feet overhead, through which a dark hand had reached down with a flaring torch. A small basket, containing a loaf of coarse bread and a bottle of wine, was being lowered at the end of a cord.

Gaspard took the bread and wine, and the basket was drawn up. Before the withdrawal of the torch and the redepositing of the slab, he contrived to make a hasty but thorough survey of his dungeon.

The place was roughly circular, as he had surmised, and was perhaps fifteen feet in diameter. The thing over which he had stumbled was a human skeleton, lying half on the rubble-heap, half in the filthy water. It was brown and rotten with age, and its garments had long melted away in patches of liquid, running mould.

The walls were guttered and runneled by centuries of ooze, and their very stone, it seemed, was rotting slowly to decay. In the opposite side, at the bottom, he saw the opening he had suspected: a low mouth, not much bigger than a fox's hole, into which the sluggish water flowed. His heart sank at the sight; for, even if the water were deeper than it seemed, the hole was far too strait for the passage of a man's body. In a state of hopelessness that was like a veritable suffocation, he found his way back to the rubble-pile when the light had been withdrawn.

The loaf of bread and the bottle of wine were still in his hands. Mechanically, with dull, sodden hunger, he munched and drank. Afterwards he felt stronger; and the sour, common wine served to warm him and perhaps helped to inspire him with the idea which he presently conceived.

Finishing the bottle, he found his way across the dungeon to the low, burrow-like hole. The entering air-current had strengthened, and this he took for a good omen. Drawing his dagger, he started to pick with the point at the half-rotten, decomposing wall, in an effort to enlarge the opening. He was forced to kneel in noisome silt; and the writhing coils of water-snakes, hissing frightfully, crawled across his legs as he worked. Evidently the hole was their means of ingress and egress, to and from the oubliette.

The stone crumbled readily beneath his dagger, and Gaspard forgot the horror and ghastliness of his situation in the hope of escape. He had no means of knowing the thickness of the wall, or the nature and extent of the subterranes that lay beyond; but he felt sure that there was some channel of connection with the outer air.

For hours or days, it seemed, he toiled with his dagger, digging blindly at the soft wall and removing the debris that splashed in the water beside him. After a while, prone on his belly, he crept into the hole he had enlarged; and burrowing like some laborious mole, he made his way onward inch by inch.

At last, to his prodigious relief, the dagger-point went through into empty space. He broke away with his hands the thin shell of obstructing stone that remained; then, crawling on in the darkness, he found that he could stand upright on a sort of shelving floor.

Straightening his cramped limbs, he moved on very cautiously. He was in a narrow vault or tunnel, whose sides he could touch simultaneously with his outstretched fingertips. The floor was a downward incline; and the water deepened, rising to his knees and then to his waist. Probably the place had once been used as an underground exit from the castle; and the roof, falling in, had dammed the water.

More than a little dismayed, Gaspard began to wonder if he had exchanged the foul, skeleton-haunted oubliette for something even worse. The night around and before him was still untouched by any ray, and the air-current, though strong, was laden with a dankness and mouldiness as of interminable vaults.

Touching the tunnel-sides at intervals as he plunged hesitantly into the deepening water, he found a sharp angle, giving upon free space at his right. The space proved to be the mouth of an intersecting passage, whose flooded bottom was at least level and went no deeper into the stagnant foulness. Exploring it, he stumbled over the beginning of a flight of upward steps. Mounting these through the shoaling water, he soon found himself on dry stone.

The stairs, narrow, broken, irregular, without landings, appeared to wind in some eternal spiral that was coiled lightlessly about the bowels of Ylourgne. They were close and stifling as a tomb, and plainly they were not the source of the air current which Gaspard had started to follow. Whither they would lead he knew not; nor could he tell if they were the same stairs by which he had been conducted to his dungeon. But he climbed steadily, pausing only at long intervals to regain his breath as best he could in the dead, mephitis-burdened air.

At length, in the solid darkness, far above, he began to hear a mysterious, muffled sound: a dull but recurrent crash as of mighty blocks and masses of falling stone. The sound was unspeakably ominous and dismal, and it seemed to shake the unfathomable walls around Gaspard, and to thrill with a sinister vibration in the steps on which he trod.

He climbed now with redoubled caution and alertness, stopping ever and anon to listen. The recurrent crashing noise grew louder, more ominous, as if it were immediately above; and the listener crouched on the dark stairs for a time that might have been many minutes, without daring to go further. At last, with disconcerting suddenness, the sound came to an end, leaving a strained and fearful stillness.

With many baleful conjectures, not knowing what fresh enormity he should find, Gaspard ventured to resume his climbing. Again, in the blank and solid stillness, he was met by a sound: the dim, reverberant chanting of voices, as in some Satanic mass or liturgy with dirge-like cadences that turned to intolerably soaring paeans of evil triumph. Long before he could recognize the words, he shivered at the strong, malefic throbbing of the measured rhythm, whose fall and rise appeared somehow to correspond to the heartbeats of some colossal demon.

The stairs turned, for the hundredth time in their tortuous spiral; and coming forth from that long midnight, Gaspard blinked in the wan glimmering that streamed toward him from above. The choral voices met him in a more sonorous burst of infernal sound, and he knew the words for those of a rare and potent incantation, used by sorcerers for a supremely foul, supremely maleficent purpose. Affrightedly, as he climbed the last steps, he knew the thing that was taking place amid the ruins of Ylourgne.

Lifting his head warily above the castle floor, he saw that the stairs ended in a far corner of the vast room in which he had beheld Nathaire's unthinkable creation. The whole extent of the internally dismantled building lay before him, filled with a weird glare in which the beams of the slightly gibbous moon were mingled with the ruddy flames of dying athanors and the coiling, multi-colored tongues that rose from necromantic braziers.

Gaspard, for an instant, was puzzled by the flood of full moonlight amid the ruins. Then he saw that almost the whole inner wall of the castle, giving on the courtyard, had been removed. It was the tearing-down of the prodigious blocks, no doubt through an extrahuman labor levied by sorcery, that he had heard during his ascent from the subter-rene vaults. His blood curdled, he felt an actual horripilation, as he re-alized the purpose for which the wall had been demolished.

It was evident that a whole day and part of another night had gone by since his immurement; for the moon rode high in the pale sapphire welkin. Bathed in its chilly glare, the huge vats no longer emitted their eerie and electric phosphorescence. The couch of Saracen fabrics, on which Gaspard had beheld the dying dwarf, was now half-hidden from view by the mounting fumes of braziers and thuribles, amid which the sorcerer's ten pupils, clad in sable and scarlet, were performing their hideous and repugnant rite, with its malefically measured litany.

Fearfully, as one who confronts an apparition reared up from nether hell, Gaspard beheld the colossus that lay inert as if in Cyclope-an sleep on the castle flags. The thing was no longer a skeleton: the limbs were rounded into bossed, enormous thews, like the limbs of Biblical giants; the flanks were like an insuperable wall; the deltoids of the mighty chest were broad as platforms; the hands could have crushed the bodies of men like millstones. . . . *But the face of the stupen-dous monster, seen in profile athwart the pouring moon, was the face of the Satanic dwarf, Nathaire—remagnified a hundred times. but the same in its implacable madness and malevolence!*

The vast bosom seemed to rise and fall; and during a pause of the necromantic ritual, Gaspard heard the unmistakable sound of a mighty respiration. The eye in the profile was closed; but its lid appeared to tremble like a great curtain, as if the monster were about to awake; and the outflung hand, with fingers pale and bluish as a row of corpses, twitched unquietly on the castle flags.

An insupportable terror seized the watcher; but even this terror could not induce him to return to the noisome vaults he had left. With infinite hesitation and trepidation, he stole forth from the corner, keeping in a zone of ebon shadow that flanked the castle wall.

As he went, he saw for a moment, through bellying folds of vapor, the couch on which the shrunken form of Nathaire was lying pallid and motionless. It seemed that the dwarf was dead, or had fallen into a stupor preceding death. Then the choral voices, crying their dreadful incantation, rose higher in Satanic triumph; the vapors eddied like a hell-born cloud, coiling about the sorcerers in python-shaped volumes, and hiding again the Orient couch and its corpse-like occupant.

A thralldom of measureless evil oppressed the air. Gaspard felt that the awful transmigration, evoked and implored with ever-swelling, liturgic blasphemies, was about to take place—had perhaps already occurred. He thought that the breathing giant stirred, like one who tosses in light slumber.

Soon the towering, massively recumbent bulk was interposed between Gaspard and the chanting necromancers. They had not seen him; and he now dared to run swiftly, and gained the courtyard unpursued and unchallenged. Thence, without looking back, he fled like a devil-hunted thing upon the steep and chasm-riven slopes below Ylourgne.

7. THE COMING OF THE COLOSSUS

After the cessation of the exodus of liches, a universal terror still prevailed; a wide-flung shadow of apprehension, infernal and funereal, lay stagnantly on Averiogne. There were strange and disastrous portents in the aspect of the skies: flame-bearded meteors had been seen to fall beyond the eastern hills; a comet, far in the south had swept the stars with its luminous besom for a few nights, and had then faded, leaving among men the prophecy of bale and pestilence to come. By day the air was oppressed and sultry, and the blue heavens were heated as if by whitish fires. Clouds of thunder, darkling and withdrawn, shook their fulgurant lances on the far horizons, like some beleaguering Titan army. A murrain, such as would come from the working of wizard spells, was abroad among the cattle. All these signs and prodigies were an added heaviness on the burdened spirits of men, who went to and fro in daily fear of the hidden preparations and machinations of hell.

But, until the actual breaking-forth of the incubated menace, there was no one, save Gaspard du Nord, who had knowledge of its veritable form. And Gaspard, fleeing headlong beneath the gibbous moon toward Vyônes, and fearing to hear the tread of a colossal pursuer at any moment, had thought it more than useless to give warning in such towns and villages as lay upon his line of flight. Where, indeed—even if warned—could men hope to hide themselves from the awful thing, begotten by Hell on the ravished charnel, that would walk forth like the Anakim to visit its roaring wrath on a trampled world?

So, all that night, and throughout the day that followed, Gaspard du Nord, with the dried slime of the oubliette on his briar-shredded raiment, plunged like a madman through the towering woods that were haunted by robbers and werewolves. The westward-falling moon flickered in his eyes betwixt the gnarled, somber boles as he ran; and the dawn overtook him with the pale shafts of its searching arrows. The noon poured over him its white sultriness, like furnace-heated metal sublimed into light; and the clotted filth that clung to his tatters was again turned into slime by his own sweat. But still he pursued his nightmare-harried way, while a vague, seemingly hopeless plan took form in his mind.

In the interim, several monks of the Cistercian brotherhood, watching the grey walls of Ylourgne at early dawn with their habitual vigilance, were the first, after Gaspard, to behold the monstrous horror created by the necromancers. Their account of its epiphany may have been somewhat tinged by a pious exaggeration; but they swore that the giant rose abruptly, standing more than waist-high above the ruins of the barbican, amid a sudden leaping of long-tongued fires and a swirling of pitchy fumes erupted from Malebolge. The giant's head was level with the high top of the donjon, and his right arm, outthrust, lay like a bar of stormy cloud athwart the new-risen sun.

The monks fell grovelling to their knees, thinking that the Archfoe himself had come forth, using Ylourgne for his gateway from the Pit. Then, across the mile-wide valley, they heard a thunderous peal of demoniac laughter; and the giant, climbing over the mounded barbican at a single step, began to descend the scarped and craggy hill.

When he drew nearer, bounding from slope to slope, his features were manifestly those of some great devil animated with ire and malice toward the sons of Adam. His hair, in matted locks, streamed behind him like a mass of black pythons; his naked skin was livid and pale and cadaverous, like the skin of the dead; but beneath it, the stupendous thews of a Titan swelled and rippled. The eyes, wide and glaring, flamed like lidless cauldrons heated by the fires of the unplumbed Pit.

The rumor of his coming passed like a gale of terror through the monastery. Many of the brothers, deeming discretion the better part of religious fervor, hid themselves in the stone-hewn cellars and vaults. Others crouched in their cells, mumbling and shrieking incoherent pleas to all the Saints. Still others, the most courageous, repaired in a body to the chapel and knelt in solemn prayer before the wooden Christ on the great crucifix.

Bernard and Stéphane, now somewhat recovered from their grievous beating, alone dared to watch the advance of the giant. Their horror was inexpressibly increased when they began to recognize in the colossal features a magnified likeness to the lineaments of that evil dwarf who had presided over the dark, unhallowed activities of Ylourgne; and the laughter of the colossus, as he came down the valley, was like a tempest-borne echo of the damnable cachinnation that had followed their ignominious flight from the haunted stronghold. To Bernard and Stéphane, however, it seemed merely that the dwarf, who was no doubt an actual demon, had chosen to appear in his natural form.

Pausing in the valley-bottom, the giant stood opposite the monastery with his flame-filled eyes on a level with the window from which

Bernard and Stéphane were peering. He laughed again—an awful laugh, like a subterranean rumbling—and then, stooping, he picked up a handful of boulders as if they had been mere pebbles, and proceeded to pelt the monastery. The boulders crashed against the walls, as if hurled from great catapults or mangonels of war; but the stout building held, though shaken grievously.

Then, with both hands, the colossus tore loose an immense rock that was deeply embedded in the hill-side; and lifting this rock, he flung it at the stubborn walls. The tremendous mass broke in an entire side of the chapel; and those who had gathered therein were found later, crushed into bloody pulp amid the splinters of their carven Christ.

After that, as if disdaining to palter any further with a prey so insignificant, the colossus turned his back on the little monastery, and like some fiend-born Goliath, went roaring down the valley into Averoigne.

As he departed, Bernard and Stéphane, still watching from their window, saw a thing they had not perceived heretofore: a huge basket made of planking, that hung suspended by ropes between the giant's shoulders. In the basket, ten men—the pupils and assistants of Nathaire—were being carried like so many dolls or puppets in a peddler's pack.

Of the subsequent wanderings and depredations of the colossus, a hundred legends were long current throughout Averoigne: tales of an unexampled ghastliness, a wanton diabolism without parallel in all the histories of that demon-pestered land.

The goatherds of the hills below Ylourgne saw him coming, and fled with their nimble-footed flocks to the highest ridges. To these he paid little heed, merely trampling them down like beetles when they could not escape from his path. Following the hill-stream that was the source of the river Isoile, he came to the verge of the great forest; and here, it is related, he tore up a towering ancient pine by the roots, and snapping off the mighty boughs with his hands, shaped it into a cudgel which he carried henceforward.

With this cudgel, heavier than a battering-ram, he pounded into shapeless ruin a wayside shrine in the outer woods. A hamlet fell in his way, and he strode through it, beating in the roofs, toppling the walls, and crushing the inhabitants beneath his feet.

To and fro in a mad frenzy of destruction, like a death-drunken Cyclops, he wandered all that day. Even the fierce beasts of the woodland ran from him in fear. The wolves, in mid-hunt, abandoned their quarry and retired, howling dismally with terror, to their rocky dens. The black, savage hunting-dogs of the forest barons would not face him, and hid whimpering in their kennels.

Men heard his mighty laughter, his stormy bellowing; they saw his approach from a distance of many leagues, and fled or concealed themselves as best they could. The lords of moated castles called in their men-at-arms, drew up their drawbridges and prepared as if for the siege of an army. The peasants hid themselves in caverns, in cellars, in old wells, and even beneath hay-mounds, hoping that he would pass them by unnoticed. The churches were crammed with refugees who sought protection of the Cross, deeming that Satan himself, or one of his chief lieutenants, had risen to harry and lay waste the land.

In a voice like summer thunder, mad maledictions, unthinkable obscenities and blasphemies were uttered ceaselessly by the giant as he went to and fro. Men heard him address the litter of black-clad figures that he carried on his back, in tones of admonishment or demonstration such as a master would use to his pupils. People who had known Nathaire recognized the incredible likeness of the huge features, the similarity of the swollen voice, to his. A rumor went abroad that the dwarf sorcerer, through his loathly bond with the Adversary, had been permitted to transfer his hateful soul into this Titanic form; and, bearing his pupils with him, had returned to vent an insatiable ire, a bottomless rancor, on the world that had mocked him for his puny physique and reviled him for his sorcery. The charnel genesis of the monstrous avatar was also rumored; and, indeed, it was said that the colossus had openly proclaimed his identity.

It would be tedious to make explicit mention of all the enormities, all the atrocities, that were ascribed to the marauding giant. . . . There were people—mostly priests and women, it is told—whom he picked up as they fled, and pulled limb from limb as a child might quarter an insect. . . . And there were worse things, not to be named in this record. . . .

Many eye-witnesses told how he hunted Pierre, the Lord of La Frénaie, who had gone forth with his dogs and men to chase a noble stag in the nearby forest. Overtaking horse and rider, he caught them with one hand, and bearing them aloft as he strode over the tree-tops, he hurled them later against the granite walls of the Château of La Frénaie in passing. Then, catching the red stag that Pierre had hunted, he flung it after them; and the huge bloody blotches made by the impact of the pashed bodies remained long on the castle stone, and were never wholly washed away by the autumn rains and the winter snows.

Countless tales were told, also, of the deeds of obscene sacrilege and profanation committed by the colossus: of the wooden Virgin that he flung into the Isoile above Ximes, lashed with human gut to the rotting, mail-clad body of an infamous outlaw; of the wormy corpses that he dug with his hands from unconsecrated graves and hurled into the courtyard of the Benedictine abbey of Périgon; of the Church of Ste. Zénobie, which he buried with its priests and congregation beneath a mountain of ordure made by the gathering of all the dung-heaps from neighboring farms.

8. THE LAYING OF THE COLOSSUS

Back and forth, in an irregular, drunken, zig-zag course, from end to end and side to side of the harried realm, the giant strode without pause, like an energumen possessed by some implacable fiend of mischief and murder, leaving behind him, as a reaper leaves his swath, an ever-lengthening zone of havoc, of rapine and carnage. And when the sun, blackened by the smoke of burning villages, had set luridly beyond the forest, men still saw him moving in the dusk, and heard still the portentous rumbling of his mad, stormy cachinnation.

Nearing the gates of Vyônes at sunset, Gaspard du Nord saw behind him, through gaps in the ancient wood, the far-off head and shoulders of the terrible colossus, who moved along the Isoile, stooping from sight at intervals in some horrid deed.

Though numb with weariness and exhaustion, Gaspard quickened his flight. He did not believe, however, that the monster would try to invade Vyônes, the especial object of Nathaire's hatred and malice, before the following day. The evil soul of the sorcerous dwarf, exulting in its almost infinite capacity for harm and destruction, would defer the crowning act of vengeance, and would continue to terrorize, during the night, the outlying villages and rural districts.

In spite of his rags and filth, which rendered him practically unrecognizable and gave him a most disreputable air, Gaspard was admitted without question by the guards at the city gate. Vyônes was already thronged with people who had fled to the sanctuary of its stout walls from the adjacent country-side; and no one, not even of the most dubious character, was denied admittance. The walls were lined with archers and pike-bearers, gathered in readiness to dispute the entrance of the giant. Cross-bowmen were stationed above the gates, and mangonels were mounted at short intervals along the entire circuit of the ramparts. The city seethed and hummed like an agitated hive.

Hysteria and pandemonium prevailed in the streets. Pale, panic-stricken faces milled everywhere in an aimless stream. Hurrying torches flared dolorously in the twilight that deepened as if with the shadow of impending wings arisen from Erebus. The gloom was clogged with intangible fear, with webs of stifling oppression. Through all this rout of wild disorder and frenzy, Gaspard, like a spent but indomitable swimmer breasting some tide of eternal, viscid nightmare, made his way slowly to his attic lodgings.

Afterwards, he could scarcely remember eating and drinking. Overworn beyond the limit of bodily and spiritual endurance, he threw himself down on his pallet without removing his ooze-stiffened tatters, and slept soddenly till an hour halfway between midnight and dawn.

He awoke with the death-pale beams of the gibbous moon shining upon him through his window; and rising, spent the balance of the night in making certain occult preparations which, he felt, offered the only possibility of coping with the fiendish monster that had been created and animated by Nathaire.

Working feverishly by the light of the westering moon and a single dim taper, Gaspard assembled various ingredients of familiar alchemic use which he possessed, and compounded from these, through a long and somewhat cabbalistic process, a dark-grey powder which he had seen employed by Nathaire on numerous occasions. He had reasoned that the colossus, being formed from the bones and flesh of dead men unlawfully raised up, and energized only by the soul of a dead sorcerer, would be subject to the influence of this powder, which Nathaire had used for the laying of resurrected liches. The powder, if cast in the nostrils of such cadavers, would cause them to return peacefully to their tombs and lie down in a renewed slumber of death.

Gaspard made a considerable quantity of the mixture, arguing that no mere finger-pinch would suffice for the lulling of the gigantic charnel monstrosity. His guttering yellow candle was dimmed by the white dawn as he ended the Latin formula of fearsome verbal invocation from which the compound would derive much of its efficacy. The formula, which called for the cooperation of Alastor and other evil spirits, he used with unwillingness. But he knew that there was no alternative: sorcery could be fought only with sorcery.

Morning came with new terrors to Vyônes. Gaspard had felt, through a sort of intuition, that the vengeful colossus, who was said to have wandered with unhuman tirelessness and diabolic energy all night through Averoigne, would approach the hated city early in the day. His intuition was confirmed; for, scarcely had he finished his occult labors when he heard a mounting hubbub in the streets, and above the shrill, dismal clamor of frightened voices, the far-off roaring of the giant.

Gaspard knew that he must lose no time, if he were to post himself in a place of vantage from which he could throw his powder into the nostrils of the hundred-foot colossus. The city walls, and even most of the church spires, were not lofty enough for this purpose; and a brief reflection told him that the great cathedral, standing at the core of Vyônes, was the one place from whose roof he could front the invader with success. He felt sure that the men-at-arms on the walls could do little to prevent the monster from entering and wreaking his malevolent will. No earthly weapon could injure a being of such bulk and nature; for even a cadaver of normal size, reared up in this fashion, could be shot full of arrows or transfixed by a dozen pikes without retarding its progress.

Hastily he filled a huge leathern pouch with the powder; and carrying the pouch at his belt, he joined the agitated press of people in the street. Many were fleeing toward the cathedral, to seek the shelter of its august sanctity; and he had only to let himself be borne along by the frenzy-driven stream.

The cathedral nave was packed with worshippers, and solemn masses were being said by priests whose voices faltered at times with inward panic. Unheeded by the wan, despairing throng, Gaspard found a flight of coiling stairs that led tortuously to the gargoyle-warded roof of the high tower.

Here he posted himself, crouching behind the stone figure of a cat-headed griffin. From his vantage he could see, beyond the crowded spires and gables, the approaching giant, whose head and torso loomed above the city walls. A cloud of arrows, visible even at that distance, rose to meet the monster, who apparently did not even pause to pluck them from his hide. Great boulders hurled from mangonels were no more to him than a pelting of gravel; the heavy bolts of arbalests, embedded in his flesh, were mere slivers.

Nothing could stay his advance. The tiny figures of a company of pikemen, who opposed him with outthrust weapons, were swept from the wall above the eastern gate by a single sidelong blow of the seventy-foot pine that he bore for a cudgel. Then, having cleared the wall, the colossus climbed over it into Vyônes.

Roaring, chuckling, laughing like a maniacal Cyclops, he strode along the narrow streets between houses that rose only to his waist, trampling without mercy everyone who could not escape in time, and smashing in the roofs with stupendous blows of his bludgeon. With a push of his left hand he broke off the protruding gables, and overturned the church steeples with their bells clanging in dolorous alarm as they went down. A woeful shrieking and wailing of hysteria-laden voices accompanied his passing.

Straight toward the cathedral he came, as Gaspard had calculated, feeling that the high edifice would be made the special butt of his malevolence.

The streets were now emptied of people; but, as if to hunt them out and crush them in their hiding places, the giant thrust his cudgel like a battering-ram through walls and windows and roofs as he went by. The ruin and havoc that he left were indescribable.

Soon he loomed opposite the cathedral tower on which Gaspard waited behind the gargoyle. His head was level with the tower, and his eyes flamed like wells of burning brimstone as he drew near. His lips were parted over stalactitic fangs in a hateful snarl; and he cried out in a voice like the rumbling of articulate thunder:

"Ho! ye puling priests and devotees of a powerless God! *Come forth and bow to Nathaire the master, before he sweeps you into limbo!*"

It was then that Gaspard, with a hardihood beyond comparison, rose from his hiding place and stood in full view of the raging colossus.

"Draw nearer, Nathaire, if indeed it be you, foul robber of tombs and charnels," he taunted. "Come close, for I would hold speech with you."

A monstrous look of astonishment dimmed the diabolic rage on the colossal features. Peering at Gaspard as if in doubt or incredulity, the giant lowered his lifted cudgel and stepped close to the tower, till his face was only a few feet from the intrepid student. Then, when he had apparently convinced himself of Gaspard's identity, the look of maniacal wrath returned, flooding his eyes with Tartarean fire and twisting his lineaments into a mask of Apollyon-like malignity. His left arm came up in a prodigious arc, with twitching fingers that poised horribly above the head of the youth, casting upon him a vulture-black shadow in the full-risen sun. Gaspard saw the white, startled faces of the necromancer's pupils, peering over his shoulder from their plank-built basket.

"Is it you, Gaspard, my recreant pupil?" the colossus roared stormily. "I thought you were rotting in the oubliette beneath Ylourgne— and now I find you perched atop of this accursed cathedral which I am about to demolish! . . . You had been far wiser to remain where I left you, my good Gaspard."

His breath, as he spoke, blew like a charnel-polluted gale on the student. His vast fingers, with blackened nails like shovel-blades, hovered in ogreish menace. Gaspard had furtively loosened his leathern pouch that hung at his belt, and untied its mouth. Now, as the twitching fingers descended toward him, he emptied the contents of the pouch in the giant's face, and the fine powder, mounting in a dark-grey cloud, obscured the snarling lips and palpitating nostrils from his view.

Anxiously, he watched the effect, fearing that the powder might be useless after all, against the superior arts and Satanical resources of Nathaire. But miraculously, as it seemed, the evil lambence died in the pit-deep eyes, as the monster inhaled the flying cloud. His lifted hand, narrowly missing the crouching youth in its sweep, fell lifelessly at his side. The anger was erased from the mighty, contorted mask, as if from the face of a dead man; the great cudgel fell with a crash to the empty street; and then, with drowsy, lurching steps and listless, hanging arms, the giant turned his back to the cathedral and retraced his way through the devastated city.

He muttered dreamily to himself as he went; and people who heard him swore that the voice was no longer the awful, thunder-swollen voice of Nathaire, but the tones and accents of a multitude of men, amid which the voices of certain of the ravished dead were recognizable. And the voice of Nathaire himself, no louder now than in life, was heard at intervals through the manifold mutterings, as if protesting angrily.

Climbing the eastern wall as it had come, the colossus went to and fro for many hours, no longer wreaking a hellish wrath and rancor, but searching, as people thought, for the various tombs and graves from which the hundreds of bodies that composed it had been so foully reft. From charnel to charnel, from cemetery to cemetery it went, through all the land; but there was no grave anywhere in which the dead colossus could lie down.

Then, toward evening, men saw it from afar on the red rim of the sky, digging with its hands in the soft, loamy plain beside the river Isoile. There, in a monstrous and self-made grave, the colossus laid itself down, and did not rise again. The ten pupils of Nathaire, it was believed, unable to descend from their basket, were crushed beneath the mighty body; for none of them was ever seen thereafter.

For many days no one dared to approach the place where the corpse lay uncovered in its self-dug grave. And so the thing rotted prodigiously beneath the summer sun, breeding a mighty stench that wrought pestilence in that portion of Averoigne. And they who ventured to go near in the following autumn, when the stench had lessened greatly, swore that the voice of Nathaire, still protesting angrily, was heard by them to issue from the enormous, rook-haunted bulk.

Of Gaspard du Nord, who had been the savior of the province, it was related that he lived in much honor to a ripe age, being the one sorcerer of that region who at no time incurred the disapprobation of the Church.

NECROMANCY

My heart is made a necromancer's glass,
Where homeless forms and exile phantoms teem,
Where faces of forgotten sorrows gleam
And dead despairs archaic peer and pass:
Grey longings of some weary heart that was
Possess me, and the multiple, supreme,
Unwildered hope and star-emblazoned dream
Of questing armies. . . . Ancient queen and lass,
Risen vampire-like from out the wormy mould,
Deep in the magic mirror of my heart
Behold their perished beauty, and depart.
And now, from black aphelions far and cold,
Swimming in deathly light on charnel skies,
The enormous ghosts of bygone worlds arise.

THE ENCHANTRESS OF SYLAIRE

W hy, you big ninny! I could never marry you," declared the demoiselle Dorothée, only daughter of the Sieur des Flêches. Her lips pouted at Anselme like two ripe berries. Her voice was honey—but honey filled with bee-stings.

"You are not so ill-looking. And your manners are fair. But I wish I had a mirror that could show you to yourself for the fool that you really are."

"Why?" queried Anselme, hurt and puzzled.

"Because you are just an addle-headed dreamer, poring over books like a monk. You care for nothing but silly old romances and legends. People say that you even write verses. It is lucky that you are at least the second son of the Comte du Framboisier—for you will never be anything more than that."

"But you loved me a little yesterday," said Anselme, bitterly. "A woman finds nothing good in the man she has ceased to love."

"Dolt! Donkey!" cried Dorothée, tossing her blonde ringlets in pettish arrogance. "If you were not all that I have said, you would never remind me of yesterday. Go, idiot—and do not return."

Anselme, the hermit, had slept little, tossing distractedly on his hard, narrow pallet. His blood, it seemed, had been fevered by the sultriness of the summer night.

Then, too, the natural heat of youth had contributed to his unease. He had not wanted to think of women—a certain woman in particular. But, after thirteen months of solitude, in the heart of the wild woodland of Averoigne, he was still far from forgetting. Crueler even than

116

her taunts was the remembered beauty of Dorothée des Flèches: the full-ripened mouth, the round arms and slender waist, the breast and hips that had not yet acquired their amplest curves.

Dreams had thronged the few short intervals of slumber, bringing other visitants, fair but nameless, about his couch.

He arose at sundawn, weary but restless. Perhaps he would find refreshment by bathing, as he had often done, in a pool fed from the river Isoile and hidden among alder and willow thickets. The water, deliciously cool at that hour, would assuage his feverishness.

His eyes burned and smarted in the morning's gold glare when he emerged from the hut of wattled osier withes. His thoughts wandered, still full of the night's disorder. Had he been wise, after all, to quit the world, to leave his friends and family, and seclude himself because of a girl's unkindness? He could not deceive himself into thinking that he had become a hermit through any aspiration toward sainthood, such as had sustained the old anchorites. By dwelling so much alone, was he not merely aggravating the malady he had sought to cure?

Perhaps, it occurred to him belatedly, he was proving himself the ineffectual dreamer, the idle fool that Dorothée had accused him of being. It was weakness to let himself be soured by a disappointment.

Walking with downcast eyes, he came unaware to the thickets that fringed the pool. He parted the young willows without lifting his gaze, and was about to cast off his garments. But at that instant, the nearby sound of splashing water startled him from his abstraction.

With some dismay, Anselme realized that the pool was already occupied. To his further consternation, the occupant was a woman. Standing near to the center, where the pool deepened, she stirred the water with her hands till it rose and rippled against the base of her bosom. Her pale wet skin glistened like white rose petals dipped in dew.

Anselme's dismay turned to curiosity and then to unwilling delight. He told himself that he wanted to withdraw but feared to frighten the bather by a sudden movement. Stooping with her clear profile and her shapely left shoulder toward him, she had not perceived his presence.

A woman, young and beautiful, was the last sight he had wished to see. Nevertheless, he could not turn his eyes away. The woman was a stranger to him, and he felt sure that she was no girl of the village or countryside. She was lovely as any châtelaine of the great castles of Averoigne. And yet surely no lady or demoiselle would bathe unattended in a forest pool.

Thick-curling chestnut hair, bound by a light silver fillet, billowed over her shoulders and burned to red, living gold where the sun-rays searched it out through the foliage. Hung about her neck, a light golden chain seemed to reflect the lusters of her hair, dancing between her breasts as she played with the ripples.

The hermit stood watching her like a man caught in webs of sudden sorcery. His youth mounted within him, in response to her beauty's evocation.

Seeming to tire of her play, she turned her back and began to move toward the opposite shore, where, as Anselme now noticed, a pile of feminine garments lay in charming disorder on the grass. Step by step she rose up from the shoaling water, revealing hips and thighs like those of an antique Venus.

Then, beyond her, he saw that a huge wolf, appearing furtively as a shadow from the thicket, had stationed itself beside the heap of clothing. Anselme had never seen such a wolf before. He remembered the tales of werewolves, that were believed to infest that ancient wood, and his alarm was touched instantly with the fear which only preternatural things can arouse. The beast was strangely colored, its fur being a glossy bluish-black. It was far larger than the common grey wolves of the forest. Crouching inscrutably, half hidden in the sedges, it seemed to await the woman as she waded shoreward.

Another moment, thought Anselme, and she would perceive her danger, would scream and turn in terror. But still she went on, her head bent forward as if in serene meditation.

"Beware the wolf!" he shouted, his voice strangely loud and seeming to break a magic stillness. Even as the words left his lips, the wolf trotted away and disappeared behind the thickets toward the great elder forest of oaks and beeches. The woman smiled over her shoulder at Anselme, turning a short oval face with slightly slanted eyes and lips red as pomegranate flowers. Apparently she was neither frightened by the wolf nor embarrassed by Anselme's presence.

"There is nothing to fear," she said, in a voice like the pouring of warm honey. "One wolf, or two, will hardly attack me."

"But perhaps there are others lurking about," persisted Anselme. "And there are worse dangers than wolves for one who wanders alone and unattended through the forest of Averoigne. When you have dressed, with your permission I shall attend you safely to your home, whether it be near or far."

"My home lies near enough in one sense, and far enough in another," returned the lady, cryptically. "But you may accompany me there if you wish."

She turned to the pile of garments, and Anselme went a few paces away among the alders and busied himself by cutting a stout cudgel for weapon against wild beasts or other adversaries. A strange but delightful agitation possessed him, and he nearly nicked his fingers several times with the knife. The misogyny that had driven him to a woodland hermitage began to appear slightly immature, even juvenile. He had let himself be wounded too deeply and too long by the injustice of a pert child.

By the time Anselme finished cutting his cudgel, the lady had completed her toilet. She came to meet him, swaying like a lamia. A bodice of vernal green velvet, baring the upper slopes of her breasts, clung tightly about her as a lover's embrace. A purple velvet gown, flowered with pale azure and crimson, moulded itself to the sinuous outlines of her hips and legs. Her slender feet were enclosed in fine soft leather buskins, scarlet-dyed, with tips curling pertly upward. The fashion of her garments, though oddly antique, confirmed Anselme in his belief that she was a person of no common rank.

Her raiment revealed, rather than concealed, the attributes of her femininity. Her manner yielded—but it also withheld.

Anselme bowed before her with a courtly grace that belied his rough country garb.

"Ah! I can see that you have not always been a hermit," she said, with soft mockery in her voice.

"You know me, then," said Anselme.

"I know many things. I am Séphora, the enchantress. It is unlikely that you have heard of me, for I dwell apart, in a place that none can find—unless I permit them to find it."

"I know little of enchantment," admitted Anselme. "But I can believe that you are an enchantress."

For some minutes they had followed a little used path that serpentined through the antique wood. It was a path the hermit had never come upon before in all his wanderings. Lithe saplings and low-grown boughs of huge beeches pressed closely upon it. Anselme, holding them aside for his companion, came often in thrilling contact with her shoulder and arm. Often she swayed against him, as if losing her balance on the rough ground. Her weight was a delightful burden, too soon relinquished. His pulses coursed tumultuously and would not quiet themselves again.

Anselme had quite forgotten his eremitic resolves. His blood and his curiosity were excited more and more. He ventured various gallantries, to which Séphora gave provocative replies. His questions, however, she answered with elusive vagueness. He could learn nothing, could decide nothing, about her. Even her age puzzled him: at one moment he thought her a young girl, the next, a mature woman.

Several times, as they went on, he caught glimpses of black fur beneath the low, shadowy foliage. He felt sure that the strange black wolf he had seen by the pool was accompanying them with a furtive surveillance. But somehow his sense of alarm was dulled by the enchantment that had fallen upon him.

Now the path steepened, climbing a densely wooded hill. The trees thinned to straggly, stunted pines, encircling a brown, open moorland as the tonsure encircles a monk's crown. The moor was studded with Druidic monoliths, dating from ages prior to the Roman occupation of Averoigne. Almost at its center, there towered a massive cromlech, consisting of two upright slabs that supported a third like the lintel of a door. The path ran straight to the cromlech.

"This is the portal of my domain," said Séphora, as they neared it. "I grow faint with fatigue. You must take me in your arms and carry me through the ancient doorway."

Anselme obeyed very willingly. Her cheeks paled, her eyelids fluttered and fell as he lifted her. For a moment he thought that she had fainted; but her arms crept warm and clinging around his neck.

Dizzy with the sudden vehemence of his emotion, he carried her through the cromlech. As he went, his lips wandered across her eyelids and passed deliriously to the soft red flame of her lips and the rose pallor of her throat. Once more she seemed to faint, beneath his fervor.

His limbs melted and a fiery blindness filled his eyes. The earth seemed to yield beneath them like an elastic couch as he and Séphora sank down.

Lifting his head, Anselme looked about him with swiftly growing bewilderment. He had carried Séphora only a few paces—and yet the grass on which they lay was not the sparse and sun-dried grass of the moor, but was deep, verdant and filled with tiny vernal blossoms! Oaks and beeches, huger even than those of the familiar forest, loomed umbrageously on every hand with masses of new, golden-green leafage, where he had thought to see the open upland. Looking back, he saw that the grey, lichened slabs of the cromlech itself alone remained of that former landscape.

Even the sun had changed its position. It had hung at Anselme's left, still fairly low in the east, when he and Séphora had reached the moorland. But now, shining with amber rays through a rift in the forest, it had almost touched the horizon on his right.

He recalled that Séphora had told him she was an enchantress. Here, indeed, was proof of sorcery! He eyed her with curious doubts and misgivings.

"Be not alarmed," said Séphora, with a honeyed smile of reassurance. "I told you that the cromlech was the doorway to my domain. We are now in a land lying outside of time and space as you have hitherto known them. The very seasons are different here. But there is no sorcery involved, except that of the great ancient Druids, who knew the secret of this hidden realm and reared those mighty slabs for a portal between the worlds. If you should weary of me, you can pass back at any time through the doorway. —But I hope that you have not tired of me so soon."

Anselme, though still bewildered, was relieved by this information. He proceeded to prove that the hope expressed by Séphora was well-founded.

Indeed, he proved it so lengthily and in such detail that the sun had fallen below the horizon before Séphora could draw a full breath and speak again.

"The air grows chill," she said, pressing against him and shivering lightly. "But my home is close at hand."

They came in the twilight to a high round tower among trees and grass-grown mounds.

"Ages ago," announced Séphora, "there was a great castle here. Now the tower alone remains, and I am its châtelaine, the last of my family. The tower and the lands about it are named Sylaire."

Tall dim tapers lit the interior, which was hung with rich arrases, vaguely and strangely pictured. Aged, corpse-pale servants in antique garb went to and fro with the furtiveness of specters, setting wines and foods before the enchantress and her guest in a broad hall. The wines were of rare flavor and immense age, the foods were curiously spiced. Anselme ate and drank copiously. It was all like some fantastic dream, and he accepted his surroundings as a dreamer does, untroubled by their strangeness.

The wines were potent, drugging his senses into warm oblivion. Even stronger was the inebriation of Séphora's nearness.

However, Anselme was a little startled when the huge black wolf he had seen that morning entered the hall and fawned like a dog at the feet of his hostess.

"You see, he is quite tame," she said, tossing the wolf bits of meat from her plate. "Often I let him come and go in the tower; and sometimes he attends me when I go forth from Sylaire."

"He is a fierce-looking beast," Anselme observed doubtfully.

It seemed that the wolf understood the words, for he bared his teeth at Anselme, with a preternaturally deep growl. Spots of red fire glowed in his somber eyes, like coals fanned by devils in dark pits.

"Go away, Malachie," commanded the enchantress, sharply. The wolf obeyed her, slinking from the hall with a malign backward glance at Anselme.

"He does not like you," said Séphora. "That, however, is perhaps not surprising."

Anselme, bemused with wine and love, forgot to inquire the meaning of her last words.

Morning came too soon, with upward-slanting beams that fired the treetops around the tower.

"You must leave me for awhile," said Séphora, after they had breakfasted. "I have neglected my magic of late—and there are matters into which I should inquire."

Bending prettily, she kissed the palms of his hands. Then, with backward glances and smiles, she retired to a room at the tower's top beside her bedchamber. Here, she had told Anselme, her grimoires and potions and other appurtenances of magic were kept.

During her absence, Anselme decided to go out and explore the woodland about the tower. Mindful of the black wolf, whose tameness he did not trust despite Séphora's reassurances, he took with him the cudgel he had cut that previous day in the thickets near the Isoile.

There were paths everywhere, all leading to fresh loveliness. Truly, Sylaire was a region of enchantment. Drawn by the dreamy golden light, and the breeze laden with the freshness of spring flowers, Anselme wandered on from glade to glade.

He came to a grassy hollow, where a tiny spring bubbled from beneath mossed boulders. He seated himself on one of the boulders, musing on the strange happiness that had entered his life so unexpectedly. It was like one of the old romances, the tales of glamour and fantasy, that he had loved to read. Smiling, he remembered the gibes with which Dorothée des Flêches had expressed her disapproval of his taste for such reading matter. What, he wondered, would Dorothée think now? At any rate, she would hardly care—

His reflections were interrupted. There was a rustling of leaves, and the black wolf emerged from the boscage in front of him, whining as if to attract his attention. The beast had somehow lost his appearance of fierceness.

Curious, and a little alarmed, Anselme watched in wonder while the wolf began to uproot with his paws certain plants that somewhat resembled wild garlic. These he devoured with palpable eagerness.

Anselme's mouth gaped at the thing which ensued. One moment the wolf was before him. Then, where the wolf had been, there rose up the figure of a man, lean, powerful, with blue-black hair and beard, and darkly flaming eyes. The hair grew almost to his brows, the beard nearly to his lower eyelashes. His arms, legs, shoulders and chest were matted with bristles.

"Be assured that I mean you no harm," said the man. "I am Malachie du Marais, a sorcerer, and the one-time lover of Séphora. Tiring of me, and fearing my wizardry, she turned me into a werewolf by giving me secretly the waters of a certain pool that lies amid this enchanted domain of Sylaire. The pool is cursed from old time with the infection of lycanthropy—and Séphora has added her spells to its power. I can throw off the wolf shape for a little while during the dark of the moon. At other times I can regain my human form, though only for a few minutes, by eating the root that you saw me dig and devour. The root is very scarce."

Anselme felt that the sorceries of Sylaire were more complicated than he had hitherto imagined. But amid his bewilderment he was unable to trust the weird being before him. He had heard many tales of werewolves, who were reputedly common in medieval France. Their ferocity, people said, was that of demons rather than of mere brutes.

"Allow me to warn you of the grave danger in which you stand," continued Malachie du Marais. "You were rash to let yourself be enticed by Séphora. If you are wise, you will leave the purlieus of Sylaire with all possible dispatch. The land is old in evil and sorcery, and all who dwell within it are ancient as the land, and are equally accursed. The servants of Séphora, who waited upon you yestereve, are vampires that sleep by day in the tower vaults and come forth only by night. They go out through the Druid portal, to prey on the people of Averoigne."

He paused as if to emphasize the words that followed. His eyes glittered balefully, and his deep voice assumed a hissing undertone. "Séphora herself is an ancient lamia, well-nigh immortal, who feeds on the vital forces of young men. She has had many lovers throughout the ages—and I must deplore, even though I cannot specify, their ultimate fate. The youth and beauty that she retains are illusions. If you could see Séphora as she really is, you would recoil in revulsion, cured of your perilous love. You would see her—unthinkably old, and hideous with infamies."

"But how can such things be?" queried Anselme. "Truly, I cannot believe you."

Malachie shrugged his hairy shoulders. "At least I have warned you. But the wolf-change approaches, and I must go. If you will come to me later, in my abode which lies a mile to the westward of Séphora's tower, perhaps I can convince you that my statements are the truth. In the meanwhile, ask yourself if you have seen any mirrors, such as a beautiful young woman would use, in Séphora's chamber. Vampires and lamias are afraid of mirrors—for a good reason."

Anselme went back to the tower with a troubled mind. What Malachie had told him was incredible. Yet there was the matter of Séphora's servants. He had hardly noticed their absence that morning—and yet he had not seen them since the previous eve—and he could not remember any mirrors among Séphora's various feminine belongings.

He found Séphora awaiting him in the tower's lower hall. One glance at the utter sweetness of her womanhood, and he felt ashamed of the doubts with which Malachie had inspired him.

Séphora's blue-grey eyes questioned him, deep and tender as those of some pagan goddess of love. Reserving no detail, he told her of his meeting with the werewolf.

"Ah! I did well to trust my intuitions," she said. "Last night, when the black wolf growled and glowered at you, it occurred to me that he was perhaps becoming more dangerous than I had realized. This morning, in my chamber of magic, I made use of my clairvoyant powers—and I learned much. Indeed, I have been careless. Malachie has become a menace to my security. Also, he hates you, and would destroy our happiness."

"Is it true, then," questioned Anselme, "that he was your lover, and that you turned him into a werewolf?"

"He was my lover—long, long ago. But the werewolf form was his own choice, assumed out of evil curiosity by drinking from the pool of which he told you. He has regretted it since, for the wolf shape, while giving him certain powers of harm, in reality limits his actions and his sorceries. He wishes to return to human shape, and if he succeeds, will become doubly dangerous to us both.

"I should have watched him well—for now I find that he has stolen from me the recipe of antidote to the werewolf waters. My clairvoyance tells me that he has already brewed the antidote, in the brief intervals of humanity regained by chewing a certain root. When he drinks the potion, as I think that he means to do before long, he will regain human form—permanently. He waits only for the dark of the moon, when the werewolf spell is at its weakest."

"But why should Malachie hate me?" asked Anselme. "And how can I help you against him?"

"That first question is slightly stupid, my dear. Of course, he is jealous of you. As for helping me—well, I have thought of a good trick to play on Malachie."

She produced a small purple glass vial, triangular in shape, from the folds of her bodice.

"This vial," she told him, "is filled with the water of the werewolf pool. Through my clairvoyant vision, I learned that Malachie keeps his newly brewed potion in a vial of similar size, shape and color. If you can go to his den and substitute one vial for the other without detection, I believe that the results will be quite amusing."

"Indeed, I will go," Anselme assured her.

"The present should be a favorable time," said Séphora. "It is now within an hour of noon; and Malachie often hunts at this time. If you should find him in his den, or he should return while you are there, you can say that you came in response to his invitation."

She gave Anselme careful instructions that would enable him to find the werewolf's den without delay. Also, she gave him a sword, saying that the blade had been tempered to the chanting of magic spells that made it effective against such beings as Malachie. "The wolf's temper has grown uncertain," she warned. "If he should attack you, your alder stick would prove a poor weapon."

It was easy to locate the den, for well-used paths ran toward it with little deviation. The place was the mounded remnant of a tower that had crumbled down into grassy earth and mossy blocks. The entrance had once been a lofty doorway: now it was only a hole, such as a large animal would make in leaving and returning to its burrow.

Anselme hesitated before the hole. "Are you there, Malachie du Marais?" he shouted. There was no answer, no sound of movement from within. Anselme shouted once more. At last, stooping on hands and knees, he entered the den.

Light poured through several apertures, latticed with wandering tree-roots, where the mound had fallen in from above. The place was a cavern rather than a room. It stank with carrion remnants into whose nature Anselme did not inquire too closely. The ground was littered with bones, broken stems and leaves of plants, and shattered or rusted vessels of alchemic use. A verdigris-eaten kettle hung from a tripod above ashes and ends of charred fagots. Rain-sodden grimoires lay mouldering in rusty metal covers. The three-legged ruin of a table was propped against the wall. It was covered with a medley of oddments, among which Anselme discerned a purple vial resembling the one given him by Séphora.

In one corner was a litter of dead grass. The strong, rank odor of a wild beast mingled with the carrion stench.

Anselme looked about and listened cautiously. Then, without delay, he substituted Séphora's vial for the one on Malachie's table. The stolen vial he placed under his jerkin.

There was a padding of feet at the cavern's entrance. Anselme turned—to confront the black wolf. The beast came toward him, crouching tensely as if about to spring, with eyes glaring like crimson coals of Avernus. Anselme's fingers dropped to the hilt of the enchanted sword that Séphora had given him.

The wolf's eyes followed his fingers. It seemed that he recognized the sword. He turned from Anselme, and began to chew some roots of the garlic-like plant, which he had doubtless collected to make possible those operations which he could hardly have carried on in wolfish form.

This time, the transformation was not complete. The head, arms and body of Malachie du Marais rose up again before Anselme; but the legs were the hind legs of a monstrous wolf. He was like some bestial hybrid of antique legend.

"Your visit honors me," he said, half snarling, with suspicion in his eyes and voice. "Few have cared to enter my poor abode, and I am grateful to you. In recognition of your kindness, I shall make you a present."

With the padding movements of a wolf, he went over to the ruinous table and groped amid the confused oddments with which it was covered. He drew out an oblong silver mirror, brightly burnished, with jewelled handle, such as a great lady or damsel might own. This he offered to Anselme.

"I give you the mirror of Reality," he announced. "In it, all things are reflected according to their true nature. The illusions of enchantment cannot deceive it. You disbelieved me when I warned you against Séphora. But if you hold this mirror to her face and observe the reflection, you will see that her beauty, like everything else in Sylaire, is a hollow lie—the mask of ancient horror and corruption. If you doubt me, hold the mirror to my face—now: for I, too, am part of the land's immemorial evil."

Anselme took the silver oblong and obeyed Malachie's injunction. A moment, and his nerveless fingers almost dropped the mirror. He had seen reflected within it a face that the sepulcher should have hidden long ago. . . .

The horror of that sight had shaken him so deeply that he could not afterwards recall the circumstances of his departure from the werewolf's lair. He had kept the werewolf's gift; but more than once he had been prompted to throw it away. He tried to tell himself that what he had seen was merely the result of some wizard trick. He refused to believe that any mirror would reveal Séphora as anything but the young and lovely sweetheart whose kisses were still warm on his lips.

All such matters, however, were driven from Anselme's mind by the situation that he found when he re-entered the tower hall. Three visitors had arrived during his absence. They stood fronting Séphora, who, with a tranquil smile on her lips, was apparently trying to explain something to them. Anselme recognized the visitors with much amazement, not untouched with consternation.

One of them was Dorothée des Flêches, clad in a trim travelling habit. The others were two serving men of her father, armed with longbows, quivers of arrows, broadswords and daggers. In spite of this array of weapons, they did not look any too comfortable or at home. But Dorothée seemed to have retained her usual matter-of-fact assurance.

"What are you doing in this queer place, Anselme?" she cried. "And who is this woman, this châtelaine of Sylaire, as she calls herself?"

Anselme felt that she would hardly understand any answer that he could give to either query. He looked at Séphora, then back at Dorothée. Séphora was the essence of all the beauty and romance that he had ever craved. How could he have fancied himself in love with Dorothée, how could he have spent thirteen months in a hermitage because of her coldness and changeability? She was pretty enough, with the common bodily charms of youth. But she was stupid, wanting in imagination—prosy already in the flush of her girlhood as a middle-aged housewife. Small wonder that she had failed to understand him.

"What brings you here?" he countered. "I had not thought to see you again."

"I missed you, Anselme," she sighed. "People said that you had left the world because of your love for me, and had become a hermit.

At last I came to seek you. But you had disappeared. Some hunters had seen you pass yesterday with a strange woman, across the moor of Druid stones. They said you had both vanished beyond the cromlech, fading as if in air. Today I followed you with my father's serving men. We found ourselves in this strange region, of which no one has ever heard. And now this woman—"

The sentence was interrupted by a mad howling that filled the room with eldritch echoes. The black wolf, with jaws foaming and slavering, broke in through the door that had been opened to admit Séphora's visitors. Dorothée des Flêches began to scream as he dashed straight toward her, seeming to single her out for the first victim of his rabid fury.

Something, it was plain, had maddened him. Perhaps the water of the werewolf pool, substituted for the antidote, had served to redouble the original curse of lycanthropy.

The two serving men, bristling with their arsenal of weapons, stood like effigies. Anselme drew the sword given him by the enchantress, and leaped forward between Dorothée and the wolf. He raised his weapon, which was straight-bladed, and suitable for stabbing. The mad werewolf sprang as if hurled from a catapult, and his red, open gorge was spitted on the outthrust point. Anselme's hand was jarred on the sword-hilt, and the shock drove him backward. The wolf fell threshing at Anselme's feet. His jaws had clenched on the blade. The point protruded beyond the stiff bristles of his neck.

Anselme tugged vainly at the sword. Then the black-furred body ceased to thresh—and the blade came easily. It had been withdrawn from the sagging mouth of the dead ancient sorcerer, Malachie du Marais, which lay before Anselme on the flagstones. The sorcerer's face was now the face that Anselme had seen in the mirror, when he had held it up at Malachie's injunction.

"You have saved me! How wonderful!" cried Dorothée. Anselme saw that she had started toward him with outthrust arms. A moment more, and the situation would become embarrassing.

He recalled the mirror, which he had kept under his jerkin, together with the vial he had stolen from Malachie du Marais. What, he wondered, would Dorothée see in its burnished depths?

He drew the mirror forth swiftly and held it to her face as she advanced upon him. What she beheld in the mirror he never knew but the effect was startling. Dorothée gasped, and her eyes dilated in manifest horror. Then, covering her eyes with her hands, as if to shut out some ghastly vision, she ran shrieking from the hall. The serving men followed her. The celerity of their movements made it plain that they were not sorry to leave this dubious lair of wizards and witches.

Séphora began to laugh softly. Anselme found himself chuckling. For awhile they abandoned themselves to uproarious mirth. Then Séphora sobered.

"I know why Malachie gave you the mirror," she said. "Do you not wish to see my reflection in it?"

Anselme realized that he still held the mirror in his hand. Without answering Séphora, he went over to the nearest window, which looked down on a deep pit lined with bushes, that had been part of an ancient, half-filled moat. He hurled the silver oblong into the pit.

"I am content with what my eyes tell me, without the aid of any mirror," he declared. "Now let us pass to other matters, which have been interrupted too long."

Again the clinging deliciousness of Séphora was in his arms, and her fruit-soft mouth was crushed beneath his hungry lips.

The strongest of all enchantments held them in its golden circle.

AMITHAINE

Who has seen the towers of Amithaine
Swan-throated rising from the main
Whose tides to some remoter moon
Flow in a fadeless afternoon? . . .
Who has seen the towers of Amithaine
Shall sleep, and dream of them again.

On falcon banners never furled,
Beyond the marches of the world,
They blazon forth the heraldries
Of dream-established sovereignties
Whose princes wage immortal wars
For beauty with the bale-red stars.

Amid the courts of Amithaine
The broken iris rears again
Restored from gardens youth has known;
And strains from ruinous viols flown
The legends tell in Amithaine
Of her that is its châtelaine.

Dreamer, beware! in her wild eyes
Full many a sunken sunset lies,
And gazing, you shall find perchance
The fallen kingdoms of romance,
And past the bourns of north and south
Follow the roses of her mouth.

The trumpets blare in Amithaine
For paladins that once again
Ride forth to ghostly, glamorous wars
Against the doom-preparing stars.
Dreamer, awake! . . . but I remain
To ride with them in Amithaine.

THE BEAST OF AVEROIGNE

1. THE DEPOSITION OF BROTHER GÉRÔME

I, a poor scrivener and the humblest monk of the Benedictine Abbey of Périgon, have been asked by our abbot Théophile to write down this record of a strange evil that is still rampant, still unquelled. And, ere I have done writing, it may be that the evil shall come forth again from its lurking-place, and again be manifest.

We, the friars of Périgon, and all others who have knowledge of this thing, agree that its advent was coeval with the first rising of the red comet which still burns nightly, a flying balefire, above the moonless hills. Like Satan's rutilant hair, trailing on the wind of Gehenna as he hastens worldward, it rose below the Dragon in early summer; and now it follows the Scorpion toward the western woods. Some say that the horror came from the comet, flying without wings to earth across the stars. And truly, before this summer of 1369, and the lifting of that red, disastrous scourge upon the heavens, there was no rumor or legend of such a thing in all Averoigne.

As for me, I must deem that the beast is a spawn of the seventh hell, a foulness born of the bubbling, flame-blent ooze; for it has no likeness to the beasts of earth, to the creatures of air and water. And the comet may well have been the fiery vehicle of its coming.

To me, for my sins and unworthiness, was it first given to behold the beast. Surely the sight thereof was a warning of those ways which lead to perdition: for on that occasion I had broken the rule of St. Benedict which forbids eating during a one-day's errand away from the monastery. I had tarried late, after bearing a letter from Théophile to

the good priest of Ste. Zénobie, though I should have been back well
before evensong. And also, apart from eating, I had drunk the mellow
white wine of Ste. Zénobie with its kindly people. Doubtless because I
had done these things, I met the nameless, night-born terror in the
woods behind the abbey when I returned.

The day had vanished, fading unaware; and the long summer eve,
without moon, had thickened to a still and eldritch darkness ere I approached the abbey postern. And hurrying along the forest path, I felt
an eerie fear of the gnarled, hunchback oaks and their pit-deep shadows. And when I saw between their antic boughs the vengefully
streaming fire of the new comet, which seemed to pursue me as I
went, the goodly warmth of the wine died out and I began to regret my
truancy. For I knew that the comet was a harbinger of ill, an omen of
death and Satanry to come.

Now, as I passed among the ancient trees that tower thickly, growing toward the postern, I thought that I beheld a light from one of the
abbey windows and was much cheered thereby. But, going on, I saw
that the light was near at hand, beneath a lowering bough beside my
path; and moreover, it moved as with the flitting of a restless fenfire,
and was wholly dissimilar to the honest glow of a lamp, lantern or taper. And the light was of changeable color, being pale as a corposant,
or ruddy as new-spilled blood, or green as the poisonous distillation
that surrounds the moon.

Then, with ineffable terror, I beheld the thing to which the light
clung like a hellish nimbus, moving as it moved, and revealing dimly
the black abomination of head and limbs that were not those of any
creature wrought by God. The horror stood erect, rising to the height
of a tall man, and it moved with the swaying of a great serpent, and its
members undulated as if they were boneless. The round black head,
having no visible ears or hair, was thrust forward on a neck of snakish
length. Two eyes, small and lidless, glowing hotly as coals from a wizard's brazier, were set low and near together in the noseless face above

the serrate gleaming of bat-like teeth.

This much I saw, and no more, ere the thing went past me with the strange nimbus flaring from venomous green to a wrathful red. Of its actual shape, and the number of its limbs, I could form no just notion. It uttered no sound, and its motion was altogether silent. Running and slithering rapidly, it disappeared in the bough-black night, among the antique oaks; and I saw the hellish light no more.

I was nigh dead with fear when I reached the abbey and sought admittance at the postern. And the porter who came at last to admit me, after I had knocked many times, forbore to chide me for my tardiness when I told him of that which I had seen in the moonless wood.

On the morrow, I was called before Théophile, who rebuked me sternly for my breach of discipline, and imposed a penance of daylong solitude. Being forbidden to hold speech with the others, I did not hear till the second morn of the thing that was found before nones in the wood behind Périgon, where I had met the nameless beast.

The thing was a great stag which had been slain in some ungodly fashion, not by wolf or hunter or poacher. It was unmarked by any wound, other than a wide gash that had laid bare the spine from neck to tail; and the spine itself had been shattered and the white marrow sucked therefrom; but no other portion of the stag had been devoured. None could surmise the nature of the beast that slew and ravened in such a manner; but many, for the first time, began to credit my tale, which the abbot and the brothers had hitherto looked upon as a sort of drunken dream. Verily, they said, a creature from the Pit was abroad, and this creature had killed the stag and had sucked the marrow from its broken spine. And I, aghast with the recollection of that loathly vision, marvelled at the mercy of God, which had permitted me to escape the doom of the stag.

None other, it seemed, had beheld the monster on that occasion; for all the monks, save me, had been asleep in the dormitory; and Théophile had retired early to his cell. But, during the nights that followed the slaying of the stag, the presence of this baleful thing was made manifest to all.

Now, night by night, the comet greatened, burning like an evil mist of blood and fire, while the stars blenched before it and terror shadowed the thoughts of men. And in our prayers, from prime to evensong, we sought to deprecate the unknown ills which the comet would bring in its train. And day by day, from peasants, priests, woodcutters and others who came to visit the abbey, we heard the tale of fearsome and mysterious depredations, similar in all ways to the killing of the stag.

Dead wolves were found with their chines laid open and the spinal marrow gone; and an ox and a horse were treated in like fashion. Then, it would seem, the beast grew bolder—or else it wearied of such humble prey as deer and wolves, horses and oxen.

At first, it did not strike at living men, but assailed the helpless dead like some foul eater of carrion. Two freshly buried corpses were found lying in the cemetery at Ste. Zénobie, where the thing had dug them from their graves and had laid open their vertebrae. In each case, only a little of the marrow had been eaten; but as if in rage or disappointment, the cadavers had been torn into shreds from crown to heel, and the tatters of their flesh were mixed inextricably with the rags of their cerements. From this, it would seem that only the spinal marrow of creatures newly killed was pleasing to the monster.

Thereafter the dead were not molested; but a grievous toll was taken from the living. On the night following the desecration of the graves, two charcoal-burners, who plied their trade in the forest at a distance of no more than a mile from Périgon, were slain foully in their hut. Other charcoal-burners, dwelling nearby, heard the shrill screams that fell to sudden silence; and peering fearfully through the chinks of their bolted doors, they saw anon in the grey starlight the departure of a black, obscenely glowing shape that issued from the hut. Not till dawn did they dare to verify the fate of their hapless fellows, who, they then discovered, had been served in the same manner as the wolves and other victims of the beast.

When the tale of this happening was brought to the abbey, Théophile called me before him and questioned me closely anent the apparition which I had encountered. He, like the others, had doubted me at first, deeming that I was frightened by a shadow or by some furtive creature of the wood. But, after the series of atrocious maraudings, it was plain to all that a fiendish thing such as had never been fabled in Averoigne, was abroad and ravening through the summer woods. And moreover it was plain that this thing was the same which I had beheld on the eve of my return from Ste. Zénobie.

Our good abbot was greatly exercised over this evil, which had chosen to manifest itself in the neighborhood of the abbey, and whose depredations were all committed within a five-hours' journey of Périgon. Pale from his over-strict austerities and vigils, with hollow cheeks and burning eyes, Théophile called me before him and made me tell my story over and over, listening as one who flagellates himself for a fancied sin. And though I, like all others, was deeply sensible of this hellish horror and the scandal of its presence, I marvelled somewhat at the godly wrath and indignation of our abbot, in whom blazed a martial ardor against the minions of Asmodai.

"Truly," he said, "there is a great devil among us, that has risen with the comet from Malebolge. We, the monks of Périgon, must go forth with cross and holy water to hunt the devil in its hidden lair, which lies haply at our very portals."

So, on the afternoon of that same day, Théophile, together with myself and six others chosen for their hardihood, sallied forth from the abbey and made search of the mighty forest for miles around, entering with lifted crosses, by torchlight, the deep caves to which we came, but finding no fiercer thing than wolf or badger. Also, we searched the vaults of the ruined castle of Faussesflammes, which is said to be haunted by vampires. But nowhere could we trace the sable monster, or find any sign of its lairing.

Since then, the middle summer has gone by with nightly deeds of terror, beneath the blasting of the comet. Beasts, men, children, women, have been done to death by the monster, which, though seeming to haunt mainly the environs of the abbey, has ranged afield even to the shores of the river Isoile and the gates of La Frênaie and Ximes. And some have beheld the monster at night, a black and slithering foulness clad in changeable luminescence; but no man has ever beheld it by day.

Thrice has the horror been seen in the woods behind the abbey; and once, by full moonlight, a brother peering from his window descried it in the abbey garden, as it glided between the rows of peas and turnips, going toward the forest. And all agree that the thing is silent, uttering no sound, and is swifter in its motion than the weaving viper.

Much have these occurrences preyed on our abbot, who keeps to his cell in unremitting prayer and vigil, and comes forth no longer, as was his wont, to dine and hold converse with the guests of the abbey. Pale and meager as a dying saint he grows, and a strange illness devours him as if with perpetual fever; and he mortifies the flesh till he totters with weakness. And we others, living in the fear of God, and abhorring the deeds of Satan, can only pray that the unknown scourge be lifted from the land, and pass with the passing of the comet.

2. THE LETTER OF THÉOPHILE TO SISTER THERÈSE

...To you, my sister in God as well as by consanguinity, I must ease my mind (if this be possible) by writing again of the dread thing that harbors close to Périgon: for this thing has struck once more within the abbey walls, coming in darkness and without sound or other ostent than the Phlegethonian luster that surrounds its body and members.

I have told you of the death of Brother Gérôme, slain at evening in his cell, while he was copying an Alexandrian manuscript. Now the fiend has become even bolder; for last night it entered the dormitory, where the brothers sleep in their robes, girded and ready to arise instantly. And without waking the others, on whom it must have cast a

Lethean spell, it took Brother Augustin, slumbering on his pallet at the end of the row. And the fell deed was not discovered till daybreak, when the monk who slept nearest to Augustin awakened and saw his body, which lay face downward with the back of the robe and the flesh beneath a mass of bloody tatters.

On this occasion, the Beast was not beheld by anyone; but at other times, full often, it has been seen around the abbey; and its craftiness and hardihood are beyond belief, except as those of an archdevil. And I know not where the horror will end; for exorcisms and the sprinkling of holy water at all doors and windows have failed to prevent the intrusion of the Beast; and God and Christ and all the holy Saints are deaf to our prayers.

Of the terror laid upon Averoigne by this thing, and the bale and mischief it has wrought outside the abbey, I need not tell, since all this will have come to you as a matter of common report. But here, at Périgon, there is much that I would not have rumored publicly, lest the good fame of the abbey should suffer. I deem it an humiliating thing, and a derogation and pollution of our sanctity, that a foul fiend should have ingress to our halls unhindered and at will.

There are strange whispers among the brothers, who believe that Satan himself has risen to haunt us. Several have met the Beast even in the chapel, where it has left an unspeakably blasphemous sign of its presence. Bolts and locks are vain against it; and vain is the lifted cross to drive it away. It comes and goes at its own choosing; and they who behold it flee in irrestrainable terror. None knows where it will strike next; and there are those among the brothers who believe it menaces me, the elected abbot of Périgon; since many have seen it gliding along the hall outside my cell. And Brother Constantin, the cellarer, who returned late from a visit to Vyônes not long ago, swears that he saw it by moonlight as it climbed the wall toward that window of my cell which faces the great forest. And seeing Constantin, the thing dropped to the ground like a huge ape and vanished among the trees.

All, it would seem, save me, have beheld the monster. And now, my sister, I must confess a strange thing, which above all else would attest the influential power of Hell in this matter, and the hovering of the wings of Asmodai about Périgon.

Each night since the coming of the comet and the Beast, I have retired early to my cell, with the intention of spending the nocturnal hours in vigil and prayer, as I am universally believed to do. And each night a stupor falls upon me as I kneel before the Christ on the silver crucifix; and oblivion steeps my senses in its poppy; and I lie without dreams on the cold floor till dawn. Of that which goes on in the abbey I know nothing; and all the brothers might be done to death by the Beast, and their spines broken and sucked as is its invariable fashion, without my knowledge.

Haircloth have I worn; and thorns and thistle-burs have I strewn on the floor, to awake me from this evil and ineluctable slumber that is like the working of some Orient drug. But the thorns and thistles are as a couch of paradisal ease, and I feel them not till dawn. And dim and confused are my senses when I awaken; and deep languor thralls my limbs. And day by day a lethal weakness grows upon me, which all ascribe to saintly pernoctations of prayer and austerity.

Surely I have become the victim of a spell, and am holden by a baleful enchantment while the Beast is abroad with its hellish doings. Heaven, in its inscrutable wisdom, punishing me for what sin I know not, has delivered me utterly to this bondage and has thrust me down to the sloughs of a Stygian despair.

Ever I am haunted by an eerie notion, that the Beast comes nightly to earth from the red comet which passes like a fiery wain above Averoigne; and by day it returns to the comet, having eaten its fill of that provender for which it seeks. And only with the comet's fading will the horror cease to harry the land and infest Périgon. But I know not if this thought is madness, or a whisper from the Pit.

Pray for me, Thérèse, in my bewitchment and my despair: for God has abandoned me, and the yoke of hell has somehow fallen upon me; and naught can I do to defend the abbey from this evil. And I, in my turn, pray that such things may touch you not nor approach you in the quiet cloisters of the convent at Ximes. . . .

3. THE STORY OF LUC LE CHAUDRONNIER

Old age, like a moth in some fading arras, will gnaw my memories oversoon, as it gnaws the memories of all men. Therefore I write this record of the true origin and slaying of that creature known as the Beast of Averoigne. And when I have ended the writing, the record shall be sealed in a brazen box, and that box be set in a secret chamber of my house at Ximes, so that no man shall learn the dreadful verity of this matter till many years and decades have gone by. Indeed, it were not well for such evil prodigies to be divulged while any who took part in the happening are still on the earthward side of Purgatory. And at present the truth is known only to me and to certain others who are sworn to maintain secrecy.

The ravages of the Beast, however, are common knowledge, and have become a tale with which to frighten children. Men say that it slew fifty people, night by night, in the summer of 1369, devouring in each case the spinal marrow. It ranged mostly about the abbey of Périgon and to Ximes and Ste. Zénobie and La Frênaie. Its nativity and lairing-place were mysteries that none could unravel; and church and state were alike powerless to curb its maraudings, so that a dire terror fell upon the land and people went to and fro as in the shadow of death.

From the very beginning, because of my own commerce with occult things and with the spirits of darkness, the baleful Beast was the subject of my concern. I knew that it was no creature of earth or of the terrene hells, but had come with the flaming comet from ulterior space; but regarding its character and attributes and genesis, I could learn no more at first than any other. Vainly I consulted the stars and made use of geomancy and necromancy; and the familiars whom I interrogated professed themselves ignorant, saying that the Beast was altogether alien and beyond the ken of sublunar devils.

Then I bethought me of the ring of Eibon, which I had inherited from my fathers, who were also wizards. The ring had come down, it was said, from ancient Hyperborea; and it was made of a redder gold than any that the earth yields in latter cycles, and was set with a great purple gem, somber and smouldering, whose like is no longer to be found. And in the gem an antique demon was held captive, a spirit from pre-human worlds and ages, which would answer the interrogation of sorcerers.

So, from a rarely opened casket, I brought out the ring of Eibon and made such preparations as were needful for the questioning of the demon. And when the purple stone was held inverted above a small brazier filled with hotly burning amber, the demon made answer, speaking in a voice that was like the shrill singing of fire. It told me the origin of the Beast, which belonged to a race of stellar devils that had not visited the earth since the foundering of Atlantis; and it told me the attributes of the Beast, which, in its own proper form, was invisible and intangible to men, and could manifest itself only in a fashion supremely abominable. Moreover, it informed me of the one method by which the Beast could be banished, if overtaken in a tangible shape. Even to me, the student of darkness, these revelations were a source of horror and surprise. And for many reasons, I deemed the mode of exorcism a doubtful and perilous thing. But the demon had sworn that there was no other way.

Musing on these dark matters, I waited among my books and braziers and alembics, for the stars had warned me that my intervention would be required in good time.

Toward the end of August, when the great comet was beginning to decline a little, there occurred the lamentable death of Sister Thérèse, killed by the Beast in her cell at the Benedictine convent of Ximes. On this occasion, the Beast was plainly seen by late passers as it ran down the convent wall by moonlight from a window; and others met it in the shadowy streets or watched it climb the city ramparts, running like a monstrous beetle or spider on the sheer stone as it fled from Ximes to regain its hidden lair.

To me, following the death of Thérèse, there came privily the town marshal, together with the abbot Théophile, in whose worn features and bowed form I descried the ravages of mortal sorrow and horror and humiliation. And the two, albeit with palpable hesitation, begged my advice and assistance in the laying of the Beast.

"You, Messire le Chaudronnier," said the marshal, "are reputed to know the arcanic arts of sorcery, and the spells that summon or dismiss evil demons and other spirits. Therefore, in dealing with this devil, it may be that you shall succeed where all others have failed. Not willingly do we employ you in the matter, since it is not seemly for the church and the law to ally themselves with wizardry. But the need is desperate, lest the demon should take other victims. In return for your aid, we can promise you a goodly reward of gold and a guarantee of lifelong immunity from all inquisition and prosecution which your doings might otherwise invite. The Bishop of Ximes, and the Archbishop of Vyônes, are privy to this offer, which must be kept secret."

"I ask no reward," I replied, "if it be in my power to rid Averoigne of this scourge. But you have set me a difficult task, and one that is haply attended by strange perils."

"All assistance that can be given you shall be yours to command," said the marshal. "Men-at-arms shall attend you, if need be."

Then Théophile, speaking in a low, broken voice, assured me that all doors, including those of the abbey of Périgon, would be opened at my request, and that everything possible would be done to further the laying of the fiend.

I reflected briefly, and said:

"Go now, but send to me, an hour before sunset, two men-at-arms, mounted, and with a third steed. And let the men be chosen for their valor and discretion: for this very night I shall visit Périgon, where the horror seems to center."

Remembering the advice of the gem-imprisoned demon, I made no preparation for the journey, except to place upon my index finger the ring of Eibon, and to arm myself with a small hammer, which I placed at my girdle in lieu of a sword. Then I awaited the set hour, when the men and the horses came to my house, as had been stipulated.

The men were stout and tested warriors, clad in chain-mail, and carrying swords and halberds. I mounted the third horse, a black and spirited mare, and we rode forth from Ximes toward Périgon, taking a direct and little-used way which ran for many miles through the were-wolf-haunted forest.

My companions were taciturn, speaking only in answer to some question, and then briefly. This pleased me; for I knew that they would maintain a discreet silence regarding that which might occur before dawn. Swiftly we rode, while the sun sank in a redness as of welling blood among the tall trees; and soon the darkness wove its thickening webs from bough to bough, closing upon us like some inexorable net of evil. Deeper we went, into the brooding woods; and even I, the master of sorceries, trembled a little at the knowledge of all that was abroad in the darkness.

Undelayed and unmolested, however, we came to the abbey at late moonrise, when all the monks, except the aged porter, had retired to their dormitory. The abbot, returning at sunset from Ximes, had given word to the porter of our coming, and he would have admitted us; but this, as it happened, was no part of my plan. Saying I had reason to believe the Beast would re-enter the abbey that very night, I told the porter my intention of waiting outside the walls to intercept it, and merely asked him to accompany us in a tour of the building's exterior, so that he could point out the various rooms. This he did, and during the course of the tour, he indicated a certain window in the second story as being that of Théophile's chamber. The window faced the forest, and I remarked the abbot's rashness in leaving it open. This, the porter told me, was his invariable custom, in spite of the oft-repeated demoniac invasions of the monastery. Behind the window we saw the glimmering of a taper, as if the abbot were keeping late vigil.

We had committed our horses to the porter's care. After he had conducted us around the abbey and had left us, we returned to the space before Théophile's window and began our long watch in silence.

Pale and hollow as the face of a corpse, the moon rose higher, swimming above the somber oaks and pines, and pouring a spectral silver on the grey stone of the abbey walls. In the west the comet flared among the lusterless signs, veiling the lifted sting of the Scorpion as it sank.

We waited hour by hour in the shortening shadow of a tall oak, where none could see us from the windows. When the moon had passed over, sloping westward, the shadow began to lengthen toward the wall. All was mortally still, and we saw no movement, apart from the slow shifting of the light and shade. Half-way between midnight and dawn, the taper went out in Théophile's cell, as if it had burned to the socket; and thereafter the room remained dark.

Unquestioning, with ready weapons, the two men-at-arms companioned me in that vigil. Well they knew the demonian terror which they might face before dawn; but there was no trace of trepidation in their bearing. And knowing much that they could not know, I drew the ring of Eibon from my finger, and made ready for that which the demon had directed me to do.

The men stood nearer than I to the forest, facing it perpetually according to a strict order that I had given. But nothing stirred in the fretted gloom; and the slow night ebbed; and the skies grew paler, as if with morning twilight. Then, an hour before sunrise, when the shadow of the great oak had reached the wall and was climbing toward Théophile's window, there came the thing I had anticipated. Very suddenly it came, and without forewarning of its nearness, a horror of hellish red light, swift as a kindling, windblown flame, that leapt from the forest gloom and sprang upon us where we stood stiff and weary from our night-long vigil.

One of the men-at-arms was borne to the ground, and I saw above him, in a floating redness as of ghostly blood, the black and semi-serpentine form of the Beast. A flat and snakish head, without ears or nose, was tearing at the man's armor with sharp serrate teeth, and I heard the teeth clash and grate on the linked iron. Swiftly I laid the ring of Eibon on a stone I had placed in readiness, and broke the dark jewel with a blow of the hammer that I carried.

From the pieces of the lightly shattered gem, the disemprisoned demon rose in the form of a smoky fire, small as a candle-flame at first, and greatening like the conflagration of piled faggots. And, hissing softly with the voice of fire, and brightening to a wrathful, terrible gold, the demon leapt forward to do battle with the Beast, even as it had promised me, in return for its freedom after cycles of captivity.

It closed upon the Beast with a vengeful flaring, tall as the flame of an *auto-da-fé*, and the Beast relinquished the man-at-arms on the ground beneath it, and writhed back like a burnt serpent. The body and members of the Beast were loathfully convulsed, and they seemed to melt in the manner of wax and to change dimly and horribly beneath the flame, undergoing an incredible metamorphosis. Moment by moment, like a werewolf that returns from its beasthood, the thing took on the wavering similitude of man. The unclean blackness flowed and swirled, assuming the weft of cloth amid its changes, and becoming the folds of a dark robe and cowl such as are worn by the Benedictines. Then, from the cowl, a face began to peer, and the face, though shadowy and distorted, was that of the abbot Théophile.

This prodigy I beheld for an instant; and the men also beheld it. But still the fire-shaped demon assailed the abhorrently transfigured thing, and the face melted again into waxy blackness, and a great column of sooty smoke arose, followed by an odor as of burning flesh commingled with some mighty foulness. And out of the volumed smoke, above the hissing of the demon, there came a single cry in the voice of Théophile. But the smoke thickened, hiding both the assailant and that which it assailed; and there was no sound, other than the singing of fed fire.

At last, the sable fumes began to lift, ascending and disappearing amid the boughs, and a dancing golden light, in the shape of a will-o'-the-wisp, went soaring over the dark trees toward the stars. And I knew that the demon of the ring had fulfilled its promise, and had now gone back to those remote and ultramundane deeps from which the sorcerer Eibon had drawn it down in Hyperborea to become the captive of the purple gem.

The stench of burning passed from the air, together with the mighty foulness; and of that which had been the Beast there was no longer any trace. So I knew that the horror born of the red comet had been driven away by the fiery demon. The fallen man-at-arms had risen, unharmed beneath his mail, and he and his fellow stood beside me, saying naught. But I knew that they had seen the changes of the Beast, and had divined something of the truth. So, while the moon grew grey with the nearness of dawn, I made them swear an awful oath of secrecy, and enjoined them to bear witness to the statement I must make before the monks of Périgon.

Then, having settled this matter, so that the good renown of the holy Théophile should suffer no calumny, we aroused the porter. We averred that the Beast had come upon us unaware, and had gained the abbot's cell before we could prevent it, and had come forth again, carrying Théophile with its snakish members as if to bear him away to the sunken comet. I had exorcised the unclean devil, which had vanished in a cloud of sulphurous fire and vapor; and, most unluckily, the abbot had been consumed by the fire. His death, I said, was a true martyrdom, and would not be in vain: the Beast would no longer plague the country or bedevil Périgon, since the exorcism I had used was infallible.

This tale was accepted without question by the Brothers, who grieved mightily for their good abbot. Indeed, the tale was true enough, for Théophile had been innocent, and was wholly ignorant of the foul change that came upon him nightly in his cell, and the deeds that were done by the Beast through his loathfully transfigured body. Each night the thing had come down from the passing comet to assuage its hellish hunger; and being otherwise impalpable and powerless, it had used the abbot for its energumen, moulding his flesh in the image of some obscene monster from beyond the stars.

It had slain a peasant girl in Ste. Zénobie on that night while we waited behind the abbey. But thereafter the Beast was seen no more in Averoigne; and the murderous deeds were not repeated.

In time the comet passed to other heavens, fading slowly; and the black terror it had wrought became a varying legend, even as all other bygone things. The abbot Théophile was canonized for his strange martyrdom; and they who read this record in future ages will believe it not, saying that no demon or malign spirit could have prevailed thus upon true holiness. Indeed, it were well that none should believe the story: for thin is the veil betwixt man and the godless deep. The skies are haunted by that which it were madness to know; and strange abominations pass evermore between earth and moon and athwart the galaxies. Unnamable things have come to us in alien horror and will come again. And the evil of the stars is not as the evil of earth.

SONG OF THE NECROMANCER

I will repeat a subtle rune—
And thronging suns of Otherwhere
Shall blaze upon the blinded air,
And spectres terrible and fair
Shall walk the riven world at noon.

The star that was mine empery
Is dust upon unwinnowed skies:
But primal dreams have made me wise,
And soon the shattered years shall rise
To my remembered sorcery.

To mantic mutterings, brief and low,
My palaces shall lift amain,
My bowers bloom; I will regain
The lips whereon my lips have lain
In rose-red twilights long ago.

Before my murmured exorcism,
The world, a wispy wraith, shall flee:
A stranger earth, a weirder sea,
Peopled with shapes of Faëry,
Shall swell upon the waste abysm.

The pantheons of darkened stars
Shall file athwart the crocus dawn;
Goddess and Gorgon, Lar and faun,
Shall tread the amaranthine lawn,
And giants fight their thunderous wars.

Like graven mountains of basalt,
Dark idols of my demons there
Shall tower through bright zones of air,
Fronting the sun with level stare;
And hell shall pave my deepest vault.

Phantom and fiend and sorcerer
Shall serve me . . . till my term shall pass,
And I become no more, alas!
Than a frail shadow on the glass
Before some latter conjurer.

MOTHER OF TOADS

"Why must you always hurry away, my little one?"
The voice of Mère Antoinette, the witch, was an amorous croaking. She ogled Pierre, the apothecary's young apprentice, with eyes fullorbed and unblinking as those of a toad. The folds beneath her chin swelled like the throat of some great batrachian. Her huge breasts, pale as frog-bellies, bulged from her torn gown as she leaned toward him.

Pierre Baudin, as usual, gave no answer; and she came closer, till he saw in the hollow of those breasts a moisture glistening like the dew of marshes . . . like the slime of some amphibian . . . a moisture that seemed always to linger there.

Her voice, raucously coaxing, persisted. "Stay awhile tonight, my pretty orphan. No one will miss you in the village. And your master will not mind." She pressed against him with shuddering folds of fat. With her short flat fingers, which gave almost the appearance of being webbed, she seized his hand and drew it to her bosom.

Pierre wrenched the hand away and drew back discreetly. Repelled, rather than abashed, he averted his eyes. The witch was more than twice his age, and her charms were too uncouth and unsavory to tempt him for an instant. Also, her repute was such as to have nullified the attractions of a younger and fairer sorceress. Her witchcraft had made her feared among the peasantry of that remote province, where belief in spells and philters was still common. The people of Averoigne called her *La Mère des Crapauds*, Mother of Toads, a name given for more than one reason. Toads swarmed innumerably about her hut; they were said to be her familiars, and dark tales were told concerning their relationship to the sorceress, and the duties they performed at her

153

bidding. Such tales were all the more readily believed because of those batrachian features that had always been remarked in her aspect.

The youth disliked her, even as he disliked the sluggish, abnormally large toads on which he had sometimes trodden in the dusk, upon the path between her hut and the village of Les Hiboux. He could hear some of these creatures croaking now; and it seemed, weirdly, that they uttered half-articulate echoes of the witch's words.

It would be dark soon, he reflected. The path along the marshes was not pleasant by night, and he felt doubly anxious to depart. Still without replying to Mère Antoinette's invitation, he reached for the black triangular vial she had set before him on her greasy table. The vial contained a philter of curious potency which his master, Alain le Dindon, had sent him to procure. Le Dindon, the village apothecary, was wont to deal surreptitiously in certain dubious medicaments supplied by the witch; and Pierre had often gone on such errands to her osier-hidden hut.

The old apothecary, whose humor was rough and ribald, had sometimes rallied Pierre concerning Mère Antoinette's preference for him. "Some night, my lad, you will remain with her," he had said. "Be careful, or the big toad will crush you." Remembering this gibe, the boy flushed angrily as he turned to go.

"Stay," insisted Mère Antoinette."The fog is cold on the marshes; and it thickens apace. I knew that you were coming, and I have mulled for you a goodly measure of the red wine of Ximes."

She removed the lid from an earthen pitcher and poured its steaming contents into a large cup. The purplish-red wine creamed delectably, and an odor of hot, delicious spices filled the hut, overpowering the less agreeable odors from the simmering cauldron, the half-dried newts, vipers, bat-wings and evil, nauseous herbs hanging on the walls, and the reek of the black candles of pitch and corpse-tallow that burned always, by noon or night, in that murky interior.

"I'll drink it," said Pierre, a little grudgingly. "That is, if it contains nothing of your own concoction."

"'Tis naught but sound wine, four seasons old, with spices of Arabia," the sorceress croaked ingratiatingly. "'Twill warm your stomach . . . and . . ." She added something inaudible as Pierre accepted the cup.

Before drinking, he inhaled the fumes of the beverage with some caution but was reassured by its pleasant smell. Surely it was innocent of any drug, any philter brewed by the witch: for, to his knowledge, her preparations were all evil-smelling.

Still, as if warned by some premonition, he hesitated. Then he remembered that the sunset air was indeed chill; that mists had gathered furtively behind him as he came to Mère Antoinette's dwelling. The wine would fortify him for the dismal return walk to Les Hiboux. He quaffed it quickly and set down the cup.

"Truly, it is good wine," he declared. "But I must go now."

Even as he spoke, he felt in his stomach and veins the spreading warmth of the alcohol, of the spices . . . of something more ardent than these. It seemed that his voice was unreal and strange, falling as if from a height above him. The warmth grew, mounting within him like a golden flame fed by magic oils. His blood, a seething torrent, poured tumultuously and more tumultuously through his members.

There was a deep soft thundering in his ears, a rosy dazzlement in his eyes. Somehow the hut appeared to expand, to change luminously about him. He hardly recognized its squalid furnishings, its litter of baleful oddments, on which a torrid splendor was shed by the black candles, tipped with ruddy fire, that towered and swelled gigantically into the soft gloom. His blood burned as with the throbbing flame of the candles.

It came to him, for an instant, that all this was a questionable enchantment, a glamour wrought by the witch's wine. Fear was upon him and he wished to flee. Then, close beside him, he saw Mère Antoinette.

Briefly he marvelled at the change that had befallen her. Then fear and wonder were alike forgotten, together with his old repulsion. He knew why the magic warmth mounted ever higher and hotter within him; why his flesh glowed like the ruddy tapers.

The soiled skirt she had worn lay at her feet, and she stood naked as Lilith, the first witch. The lumpish limbs and body had grown voluptuous; the pale, thick-lipped mouth enticed him with a promise of ampler kisses than other mouths could yield. The pits of her short round arms, the concave of her ponderously drooping breasts, the heavy creases and swollen rondures of flanks and thighs, all were fraught with luxurious allurement.

"Do you like me now, my little one?" she questioned.

This time he did not draw away but met her with hot, questing hands when she pressed heavily against him. Her limbs were cool and moist; her breasts yielded like the turf-mounds above a bog. Her body was white and wholly hairless; but here and there he found curious roughnesses . . . like those on the skin of a toad . . . that somehow sharpened his desire instead of repelling it.

She was so huge that his fingers barely joined behind her. His two hands, together, were equal only to the cupping of a single breast. But the wine had filled his blood with a philterous ardor.

She led him to her couch beside the hearth where a great cauldron boiled mysteriously, sending up its fumes in strange-twining coils that suggested vague and obscene figures. The couch was rude and bare. But the flesh of the sorceress was like deep, luxurious cushions. . . .

Pierre awoke in the ashy dawn, when the tall black tapers had dwindled down and had melted limply in their sockets. Sick and confused, he sought vainly to remember where he was or what he had done. Then, turning a little, he saw beside him on the couch a thing that was like some impossible monster of ill dreams: a toad-like form, large as a fat woman. Its limbs were somehow like a woman's arms and legs. Its pale, warty body pressed and bulged against him, and he felt the rounded softness of something that resembled a breast.

Nausea rose within him as memory of that delirious night returned. Most foully he had been beguiled by the witch, and had succumbed to her evil enchantments.

It seemed that an incubus smothered him, weighing upon all his limbs and body. He shut his eyes, that he might no longer behold the loathsome thing that was Mère Antoinette in her true semblance. Slowly, with prodigious effort, he drew himself away from the crushing nightmare shape. It did not stir or appear to waken; and he slid quickly from the couch.

Again, compelled by a noisome fascination, he peered at the thing on the couch—and saw only the gross form of Mère Antoinette. Perhaps his impression of a great toad beside him had been but an illusion, a half-dream that lingered after slumber. He lost something of his nightmarish horror; but his gorge still rose in a sick disgust, remembering the lewdness to which he had yielded.

Fearing that the witch might awaken at any moment and seek to detain him, he stole noiselessly from the hut. It was broad daylight, but a cold, hueless mist lay everywhere, shrouding the reedy marshes, and hanging like a ghostly curtain on the path he must follow to Les Hiboux. Moving and seething always, the mist seemed to reach toward him with intercepting fingers as he started homeward. He shivered at its touch, he bowed his head and drew his cloak closer around him.

Thicker and thicker the mist swirled, coiling, writhing endlessly, as if to bar Pierre's progress. He could discern the twisting, narrow path for only a few paces in advance. It was hard to find the familiar landmarks, hard to recognize the osiers and willows that loomed suddenly before him like grey phantoms and faded again into the white nothingness as he went onward. Never had he seen such a fog: it was like the blinding, stifling fumes of a thousand witch-stirred cauldrons.

Though he was not altogether sure of his surroundings, Pierre thought that he had covered half the distance to the village. Then, all at once, he began to meet the toads. They were hidden by the mist till he came close upon them. Misshapen, unnaturally big and bloated, they squatted in his way on the little footpath or hopped sluggishly before him from the pallid gloom on either hand.

Several struck against his feet with a horrible and heavy flopping. He stepped unaware upon one of them, and slipped in the squashy noisomeness it had made, barely saving himself from a headlong fall on the bog's rim. Black, miry water loomed close beside him as he staggered there.

Turning to regain his path, he crushed others of the toads to an abhorrent pulp under his feet. The marshy soil was alive with them. They flopped against him from the mist, striking his legs, his bosom, his very face with their clammy bodies. They rose up by scores like a devil-driven legion. It seemed that there was a malignance, an evil purpose in their movements, in the buffeting of their violent impact. He could make no progress on the swarming path, but lurched to and fro, slipping blindly, and shielding his face with lifted hands. He felt an eery consternation, an eldritch horror. It was as if the nightmare of his awakening in the witch's hut had somehow returned upon him.

The toads came always from the direction of Les Hiboux, as if to drive him back toward Mère Antoinette's dwelling. They bounded against him like a monstrous hail, like missiles flung by unseen demons. The ground was covered by them, the air was filled with their hurtling bodies. Once, he nearly went down beneath them.

Their number seemed to increase, they pelted him in a noxious storm. He gave way before them, his courage broke, and he started to run at random, without knowing that he had left the safe path. Losing all thought of direction, in his frantic desire to escape from those impossible myriads, he plunged on amid the dim reeds and sedges, over ground that quivered gelatinously beneath him. Always at his heels he heard the soft, heavy flopping of the toads; and sometimes they rose up like a sudden wall to bar his way and turn him aside. More than once, they drove him back from the verge of hidden quagmires into which he would otherwise have fallen. It was as if they were herding him deliberately and concertedly to a destined goal.

Now, like the lifting of a dense curtain, the mist rolled away, and Pierre saw before him in a golden dazzle of morning sunshine the green, thick-growing osiers that surrounded Mère Antoinette's hut. The toads had all disappeared, though he could have sworn that hundreds of them were hopping close about him an instant previously. With a feeling of helpless fright and panic, he knew that he was still within the witch's toils; that the toads were indeed her familiars, as so many people believed them to be. They had prevented his escape, and had brought him back to the foul creature . . . whether woman, batrachian, or both . . . who was known as The Mother of Toads.

Pierre's sensations were those of one who sinks momently deeper into some black and bottomless quicksand. He saw the witch emerge from the hut and come toward him. Her thick fingers, with pale folds of skin between them like the beginnings of a web, were stretched and flattened on the steaming cup that she carried. A sudden gust of wind arose as if from nowhere, lifting the scanty skirts of Mère Antoinette about her fat thighs, and bearing to Pierre's nostrils the hot, familiar spices of the drugged wine.

"Why did you leave so hastily, my little one?" There was an amorous wheedling in the very tone of the witch's question. "I should not have let you go without another cup of the good red wine, mulled and spiced for the warming of your stomach. . . . See, I have prepared it for you . . . knowing that you would return."

She came very close to him as she spoke, leering and sidling, and held the cup toward his lips. Pierre grew dizzy with the strange fumes and turned his head away. It seemed that a paralyzing spell had seized his muscles, for the simple movement required an immense effort.

His mind, however, was still clear, and the sick revulsion of that nightmare dawn returned upon him. He saw again the great toad that had lain at his side when he awakened.

"I will not drink your wine," he said firmly. "You are a foul witch, and I loathe you. Let me go."

"Why do you loathe me?" croaked Mère Antoinette. "You loved me yesternight. I can give you all that other women give . . . and more."

"You are not a woman," said Pierre. "You are a big toad. I saw you in your true shape this morning. I'd rather drown in the marshwaters than sleep with you again."

An indescribable change came upon the sorceress before Pierre had finished speaking. The leer slid from her thick and pallid features, leaving them blankly inhuman for an instant. Then her eyes bulged and goggled horribly, and her whole body appeared to swell as if inflated with venom.

"Go, then!" she spat with a guttural virulence. "But you will soon wish that you had stayed. . . ."

The queer paralysis had lifted from Pierre's muscles. It was as if the injunction of the angry witch had served to revoke an insidious, half-woven spell. With no parting glance or word, Pierre turned from her and fled with long, hasty steps, almost running, on the path to Les Hiboux.

He had gone little more than a hundred paces when the fog began to return. It coiled shoreward in vast volumes from the marshes, it poured like smoke from the very ground at his feet. Almost instantly, the sun dimmed to a wan silver disk and disappeared. The blue heavens were lost in the pale and seething voidness overhead. The path before Pierre was blotted out till he seemed to walk on the sheer rim of a white abyss, that moved with him as he went.

Like the clammy arms of specters, with death-chill fingers that clutched and caressed, the weird mists drew closer still about Pierre. Then, thickened in his nostrils and throat, they dripped in a heavy dew from his garments. They choked him with the fetor of rank waters and putrescent ooze . . . and a stench as of liquefying corpses that had risen somewhere to the surface amid the fen.

Then, from the blank whiteness, the toads assailed Pierre in a surging, solid wave that towered above his head and swept him from the dim path with the force of falling seas as it descended. He went down, splashing and floundering, into water that swarmed with the numberless batrachians. Thick slime was in his mouth and nose as he struggled to regain his footing. The water, however, was only knee-deep, and the bottom, though slippery and oozy, supported him with little yielding when he stood erect.

He discerned indistinctly through the mist the nearby margin from which he had fallen. But his steps were weirdly and horribly hampered by the toad-seething waters when he strove to reach it. Inch by inch, with a hopeless panic deepening upon him, he fought toward the solid shore. The toads leaped and tumbled about him with a dizzying eddy-like motion. They swirled like a viscid undertow around his feet and shins. They swept and swelled in great loathsome undulations against his retarded knees.

However, he made slow and painful progress, till his outstretched fingers could almost grasp the wiry sedges that trailed from the low bank. Then, from that mist-bound shore, there fell and broke upon him a second deluge of those demoniac toads; and Pierre was borne helplessly backward into the filthy waters.

Held down by the piling and crawling masses, and drowning in nauseous darkness at the thick-oozed bottom, he clawed feebly at his assailants. For a moment, ere oblivion came, his fingers found among them the outlines of a monstrous form that was somehow toadlike . . . but large and heavy as a fat woman. At the last, it seemed to him that two enormous breasts were crushed closely down upon his face.

THE WITCH WITH EYES OF AMBER

I met a witch with amber eyes
Who slowly sang a scarlet rune,
Shifting to an icy laughter
Like the laughter of the moon.

Red as a wanton's was her mouth,
And fair the breast she bade me take
With a word that clove and clung
Burning like a furnace-flake.

But from her bright and lifted bosom,
When I touched it with my hand,
Came the many-needled coldness
Of a glacier-taken land.

And, lo! the witch with eyes of amber
Vanished like a blown-out flame,
Leaving but the lichen-eaten
Stone that bore a blotted name.

A Rendezvous in Averoigne

Gérard de l'Automne was meditating the rhymes of a new ballade in honor of Fleurette, as he followed the leaf-arrassed pathway toward Vyônes through the woodland of Averoigne. Since he was on his way to meet Fleurette, who had promised to keep a rendezvous among the oaks and beeches like any peasant girl, Gérard himself made better progress than the ballade. His love was at that stage which, even for a professional troubadour, is more productive of distraction than inspiration; and he was recurrently absorbed in a meditation upon other than merely verbal felicities.

The grass and trees had assumed the fresh enamel of a medieval May; the turf was figured with little blossoms of azure and white and yellow, like an ornate broidery; and there was a pebbly stream that murmured beside the way, as if the voices of undines were parleying deliciously beneath its waters. The sun-lulled air was laden with a wafture of youth and romance; and the longing that welled from the heart of Gérard seemed to mingle mystically with the balsams of the wood.

Gérard was a *trouvère* whose scant years and many wanderings had brought him a certain renown. After the fashion of his kind he had roamed from court to court, from château to château; and he was now the guest of the Comte de la Frênaie, whose high castle held dominion over half the surrounding forest. Visiting one day that quaint cathedral town, Vyônes, which lies so near to the ancient wood of Averoigne, Gérard had seen Fleurette, the daughter of a well-to-do mercer named. Guillaume Cochin; and had become more sincerely enamored of her blonde piquancy than was to be expected from one who had been so frequently susceptible in such matters. He had managed to make his feelings known to her; and, after a month of billets-doux, ballades and stolen interviews contrived by the help of a complaisant waiting-woman, she had made this woodland tryst with him in the absence of her father from Vyônes. Accompanied by her maid and a man-servant, she was to leave the town early that afternoon and meet Gérard under a certain beech-tree of enormous age and size. The servants would then withdraw discreetly; and the lovers, to all intents and purposes, would be alone. It was not likely that they would be seen or interrupt-ed; for the gnarled and immemorial wood possessed an ill-repute among the peasantry. Somewhere in this wood there was the ruinous and haunted Château des Faussesflammes; and, also, there was a dou-ble tomb, within which the Sieur Hugh du Malinbois and his châ-telaine, who were notorious for sorcery in their time, had lain unconsecrated for more than two hundred years. Of these, and their phantoms, there were grisly tales; and there were stories of loups-garous and goblins, of fays and devils and vampires that infested Av-eroigne. But to these tales Gérard had given little heed, considering it improbable that such creatures would fare abroad in open daylight. The madcap Fleurette had professed herself unafraid also; but it had been necessary to promise the servants a substantial *pourboire*, since they shared fully the local superstitions.

Gérard had wholly forgotten the legendry of Averoigne, as he has-tened along the sun-flecked path. He was nearing the appointed beech-tree, which a turn of the path would soon reveal; and his pulses quick-ened and became tremulous, as he wondered if Fleurette had already reached the trysting-place. He abandoned all effort to continue his bal-lade, which, in the three miles he had walked from La Frênaie, had not progressed beyond the middle of a tentative first stanza.

His thoughts were such as would befit an ardent and impatient lover. They were now interrupted by a shrill scream that rose to an un-endurable pitch of fear and horror, issuing from the green stillness of the pines beside the way. Startled, he peered at the thick branches; and as the scream fell back to silence, he heard the sound of dull and hurrying footfalls, and a scuffling as of several bodies. Again the scream arose. It was plainly the voice of a woman in some distressful peril. Loosening his dagger in its sheath, and clutching more firmly a long hornbeam staff which he had brought with him as a protection against the vipers which were said to lurk in Averoigne, he plunged without hesitation or premeditation among the low-hanging boughs from which the voice had seemed to emerge.

In a small open space beyond the trees, he saw a woman who was struggling with three ruffians of exceptionally brutal and evil aspect. Even in the haste and vehemence of the moment, Gérard realized that he had never before seen such men or such a woman. The woman was clad in a gown of emerald green that matched her eyes; in her face was the pallor of dead things, together with a faëry beauty; and her lips were dyed as with the scarlet of newly flowing blood. The men were dark as Moors, and their eyes were red slits of flame beneath oblique brows with animal-like bristles. There was something very peculiar in the shape of their feet; but Gérard did not realize the exact nature of the peculiarity till long afterwards. Then he remembered that all of them were seemingly club-footed, though they were able to move with surpassing agility. Somehow, he could never recall what sort of clothing they had worn.

The woman turned a beseeching gaze upon Gérard as he sprang forth from amid the boughs. The men, however, did not seem to heed his coming; though one of them caught in a hairy clutch the hands which the woman sought to reach toward her rescuer.

Lifting his staff, Gérard rushed upon the ruffians. He struck a tremendous blow at the head of the nearest one—a blow that should have levelled the fellow to earth. But the staff came down on unresisting air, and Gérard staggered and almost fell headlong in trying to recover his equilibrium. Dazed and uncomprehending, he saw that the knot of struggling figures had vanished utterly. At least, the three men had vanished; but from the middle branches of a tall pine beyond the open space, the death-white features of the woman smiled upon him for a moment with faint, inscrutable guile ere they melted among the needles.

Gérard understood now; and he shivered as he crossed himself. He had been deluded by phantoms or demons, doubtless for no good purpose; he had been the gull of a questionable enchantment. Plainly there was something after all in the legends he had heard, in the ill-renown of the forest of Averoigne.

He retraced his way toward the path he had been following. But when he thought to reach again the spot from which he had heard that shrill unearthly scream, he saw that there was no longer a path; nor, indeed, any feature of the forest which he could remember or recognize. The foliage about him no longer displayed a brilliant verdure; it was sad and funereal, and the trees themselves were either cypress-like, or were already sere with autumn or decay. In lieu of the purling brook there lay before him a tarn of waters that were dark and dull as clotting blood, and which gave back no reflection of the brown autumnal sedges that trailed therein like the hair of suicides, and the skeletons of rotting osiers that writhed above them.

Now, beyond all question, Gérard knew that he was the victim of an evil enchantment. In answering that beguileful cry for succor, he had exposed himself to the spell, had been lured within the circle of its power. He could not know what forces of wizardry or demonry had willed to draw him thus; but he knew that his situation was fraught with supernatural menace. He gripped the hornbeam staff more tightly in his hand, and prayed to all the saints he could remember, as he peered about for some tangible bodily presence of ill.

The scene was utterly desolate and lifeless, like a place where cadavers might keep their tryst with demons. Nothing stirred, not even a dead leaf; and there was no whisper of dry grass or foliage, no song of birds nor murmuring of bees, no sigh nor chuckle of water. The corpse-grey heavens above seemed never to have held a sun; and the chill, unchanging light was without source or destination, without beams or shadows.

Gérard surveyed his environment with a cautious eye; and the more he looked the less he liked it: for some new and disagreeable detail was manifest at every glance. There were moving lights in the wood that vanished if he eyed them intently; there were drowned faces in the tarn that came and went like livid bubbles before he could discern their features. And, peering across the lake, he wondered why he had not seen the many-turreted castle of hoary stone whose nearer walls were based in the dead waters. It was so grey and still and vasty, that it seemed to have stood for incomputable ages between the stagnant tarn and the equally stagnant heavens. It was ancienter than the world, it was older than the light: it was coeval with fear and darkness; and a horror dwelt upon it and crept unseen but palpable along its bastions.

There was no sign of life about the castle; and no banners flew above its turrets or its donjon. But Gérard knew, as surely as if a voice had spoken aloud to warn him, that here was the fountain-head of the sorcery by which he had been beguiled. A growing panic whispered in his brain, he seemed to hear the rustle of malignant plumes, the mutter of demonian threats and plottings. He turned, and fled among the funereal trees.

Amid his dismay and wilderment, even as he fled, he thought of Fleurette and wondered if she were awaiting him at their place of rendezvous, or if she and her companions had also been enticed and led astray in a realm of damnable unrealities. He renewed his prayers, and implored the saints for her safety as well as his own.

The forest through which he ran was a maze of bafflement and eeriness. There were no landmarks, there were no tracks of animals or men; and the swart cypresses and sere autumnal trees grew thicker and thicker as if some malevolent will were marshalling them against his progress. The boughs were like implacable arms that strove to retard him; he could have sworn that he felt them twine about him with the strength and suppleness of living things. He fought them, insanely, desperately, and seemed to hear a crackling of infernal laughter in their twigs as he fought. At last, with a sob of relief, he broke through into a sort of trail. Along this trail, in the mad hope of eventual escape, he ran like one whom a fiend pursues; and after a short interval he came again to the shores of the tarn, above whose motionless waters the high and hoary turrets of that time-forgotten castle were still dominant. Again he turned and fled; and once more, after similar wanderings and like struggles, he came back to the inevitable tarn.

With a leaden sinking of his heart, as into some ultimate slough of despair and terror, he resigned himself and made no further effort to escape. His very will was benumbed, was crushed down as by the incumbence of a superior volition that would no longer permit his puny recalcitrance. He was unable to resist when a strong and hateful compulsion drew his footsteps along the margent of the tarn toward the looming castle.

When he came nearer, he saw that the edifice was surrounded by a moat whose waters were as stagnant as those of the lake, and were mantled with the iridescent scum of corruption. The drawbridge was down and the gates were open, as if to receive an expected guest. But still there was no sign of human occupancy; and the walls of the great grey building were silent as those of a sepulcher. And more tomb-like even than the rest was the square and overtowering bulk of the mighty donjon.

Impelled by the same power that had drawn him along the lakeshore, Gérard crossed the drawbridge and passed beneath the frowning barbican into a vacant courtyard. Barred windows looked blankly down; and at the opposite end of the court a door stood mysteriously open, revealing a dark hall. As he approached the doorway, he saw that a man was standing on the threshold; though a moment previous he could have sworn that it was untenanted by any visible form.

Gérard had retained his hornbeam staff; and though his reason told him that such a weapon was futile against any supernatural foe, some obscure instinct prompted him to clasp it valiantly as he neared the waiting figure on the sill.

The man was inordinately tall and cadaverous, and was dressed in black garments of a superannuate mode. His lips were strangely red, amid his bluish beard and the mortuary whiteness of his face. They were like the lips of the woman who, with her assailants, had disappeared in a manner so dubious when Gérard had approached them. His eyes were pale and luminous as marsh-lights; and Gérard shuddered at his gaze and at the cold, ironic smile of his scarlet lips, that seemed to reserve a world of secrets all too dreadful and hideous to be disclosed.

"I am the Sieur du Malinbois," the man announced. His tones were both unctuous and hollow, and served to increase the repugnance felt by the young troubadour. And when his lips parted, Gérard had a glimpse of teeth that were unnaturally small and were pointed like the fangs of some fierce animal.

"Fortune has willed that you should become my guest," the man went on. "The hospitality which I can proffer you is rough and inadequate, and it may be that you will find my abode a trifle dismal. But at least I can assure you of a welcome no less ready than sincere."

"I thank you for your kind offer," said Gérard. "But I have an appointment with a friend; and I seem in some unaccountable manner to have lost my way. I should be profoundly grateful if you would direct me toward Vyônes. There should be a path not far from here; and I have been so stupid as to stray from it."

The words rang empty and hopeless in his own ears even as he uttered them; and the name that his strange host had given—the Sieur du Malinbois—was haunting his mind like the funereal accents of a knell; though he could not recall at that moment the macabre and spectral ideas which the name tended to evoke.

"Unfortunately, there are no paths from my château to Vyônes," the stranger replied. "As for your rendezvous, it will be kept in another manner, at another place, than the one appointed. I must therefore insist that you accept my hospitality. Enter, I pray; but leave your hornbeam staff at the door. You will have no need of it any longer."

Gérard thought that he made a moué of distaste and aversion with his over-red lips as he spoke the last sentences; and that his eyes lingered on the staff with an obscure apprehensiveness. And the strange emphasis of his words and demeanor served to awaken other phantasmal and macabre thoughts in Gérard's brain; though he could not formulate them fully till afterwards. And somehow he was prompted to retain the weapon, no matter how useless it might be against an enemy of spectral or diabolic nature. So he said:

"I must crave your indulgence if I retain the staff. I have made a vow to carry it with me, in my right hand or never beyond arm's reach, till I have slain two vipers."

"That is a queer vow," rejoined his host. "However, bring it with you if you like. It is of no matter to me if you choose to encumber yourself with a wooden stick."

He turned abruptly, motioning Gérard to follow him. The troubadour obeyed unwillingly, with one rearward glance at the vacant heavens and the empty courtyard. He saw with no great surprise that a sudden and furtive darkness had closed in upon the château without moon or star, as if it had been merely waiting for him to enter before it descended. It was thick as the folds of a serecloth, it was airless and stifling like the gloom of a sepulcher that has been sealed for ages; and Gérard was aware of a veritable oppression, a corporeal and psychic difficulty in breathing, as he crossed the threshold.

He saw that cressets were now burning in the dim hall to which his host had admitted him; though he had not perceived the time and agency of their lighting. The illumination they afforded was singularly vague and indistinct, and the thronging shadows of the hall were unexplainably numerous, and moved with a mysterious disquiet; though the flames themselves were still as tapers that burn for the dead in a windless vault.

At the end of the passage, the Sieur du Malinbois flung open a heavy door of dark and somber wood. Beyond, in what was plainly the eating-room of the château, several people were seated about a long table by the light of cressets no less dreary and dismal than those in the hall. In the strange, uncertain glow, their faces were touched with a gloomy dubiety, with a lurid distortion; and it seemed to Gérard that shadows hardly distinguishable from the figures were gathered around the board. But nevertheless he recognized the assembled company at a glance, with an overpowering shock of astonishment.

At one end of the board, there sat the woman in emerald green who had vanished in so doubtful a fashion amid the pines when Gérard answered her call for succor. At one side, looking very pale and forlorn and frightened, was Fleurette Cochin. At the lower end reserved for retainers and inferiors, there sat the maid and the man-servant who had accompanied Fleurette to her rendezvous with Gérard.

The Sieur du Malinbois turned to the troubadour with a smile of sardonic amusement.

"I believe you have already met everyone assembled," he observed "But you have not yet been formally presented to my wife, Agathe, who is presiding over the board. Agathe, I bring to you Gérard de l'Automne, a young troubadour of much note and merit."

The woman nodded slightly, without speaking, and pointed to a chair opposite Fleurette. Gérard seated himself, and the Sieur du Malinbois assumed according to feudal custom a place at the head of the table beside his wife.

Now, for the first time, Gérard noticed that there were servitors who came and went in the room, setting upon the table various wines and viands. The servitors were preternaturally swift and noiseless, and somehow it was very difficult to be sure of their precise features or their costumes. They seemed to walk in an adumbration of sinister insoluble twilight. But the troubadour was disturbed by a feeling that they resembled the swart demoniac ruffians who had disappeared together with the woman in green when he approached them.

The meal that ensued was a weird and funereal affair. A sense of insuperable constraint, of smothering horror and hideous oppression, was upon Gérard; and though he wanted to ask Fleurette a hundred questions, and also demand an explanation of sundry matters from his host and hostess, he was totally unable to frame the words or to utter them. He could only look at Fleurette, and read in her eyes a duplication of his own helpless bewilderment and nightmare thralldom. Nothing was said by the Sieur du Malinbois and his lady, who were exchanging glances of a secret and baleful intelligence all through the meal; and Fleurette's maid and man-servant were obviously paralyzed by terror, like birds beneath the hypnotic gaze of deadly serpents.

The foods were rich and of strange savor; and the wines were fabulously old, and seemed to retain in their topaz or violet depths the unextinguished fire of buried centuries. But Gérard and Fleurette could barely touch them; and they saw that the Sieur du Malinbois and his lady did not eat or drink at all. The gloom of the chamber deepened; the servitors became more furtive and spectral in their movements; the stifling air was laden with unformulable menace, was constrained by the spell of a black and lethal necromancy. Above the aromas of the rare foods, the bouquets of the antique wines, there crept forth the choking mustiness of hidden vaults and embalmed centurial corruption, together with the ghostly spice of a strange perfume that seemed to emanate from the person of the châtelaine. And now Gérard was remembering many tales from the legendry of Averoigne, which he had heard and disregarded; was recalling the story of a Sieur du Malinbois and his lady, the last of the name and the most evil, who had been buried somewhere in this forest hundreds of years ago; and whose tomb was shunned by the peasantry, since they were said to continue their sorceries even in death. He wondered what influence had bedrugged his memory, that he had not recalled it wholly when he had first heard the name. And he was remembering other things and other stories, all of which confirmed his instinctive belief regarding the nature of the people into whose hands he had fallen. Also, he recalled a folklore superstition concerning the use to which a wooden stake can be put; and realized why the Sieur du Malinbois had shown a peculiar interest in the hornbeam staff. Gérard had laid the staff beside his chair when he sat down; and he was reassured to find that it had not vanished. Very quietly and unobtrusively, he placed his foot upon it.

The uncanny meal came to an end; and the host and his châtelaine arose.

"I shall now conduct you to your rooms," said the Sieur du Malinbois, including all of his guests in a dark, inscrutable glance. "Each of you can have a separate chamber, if you so desire; or Fleurette Cochin and her maid Angélique can remain together; and the man-servant Raoul can sleep in the same room with Messire Gérard."

A preference for the latter procedure was voiced by Fleurette and the troubadour. The thought of uncompanioned solitude in that castle of timeless midnight and nameless mystery was abhorrent to an insupportable degree.

The four were now led to their respective chambers, on opposite sides of a hall whose length was but indeterminately revealed by the dismal lights. Fleurette and Gérard bade each other a dismayed and reluctant good-night beneath the constraining eye of their host. Their rendezvous was hardly the one which they had thought to keep; and both were overwhelmed by the supernatural situation amid whose dubious horrors and ineluctable sorceries they had somehow become involved. And no sooner had Gérard left Fleurette than he began to curse himself for a poltroon because he had not refused to part from her side; and he marvelled at the spell of drug-like involition that had bedrowsed all his faculties. It seemed that his will was not his own, but had been thrust down and throttled by an alien power.

The room assigned to Gérard and Raoul was furnished with a couch, and a great bed whose curtains were of antique fashion and fabric. It was lighted with tapers that had a funereal suggestion in their form, and which burned dully in an air that was stagnant with the mustiness of dead years.

"May you sleep soundly," said the Sieur du Malinbois. The smile that accompanied and followed the words was no less unpleasant than the oily and sepulchral tone in which they were uttered. The troubadour and the servant were conscious of profound relief when he went out and closed the leaden-clanging door. And their relief was hardly diminished even when they heard the click of a key in the lock.

Gérard was now inspecting the room; and he went to the one window, through whose small and deep-set panes he could see only the pressing darkness of a night that was veritably solid, as if the whole place were buried beneath the earth and were closed in by clinging mould. Then, with an access of unsmothered rage at his separation from Fleurette, he ran to the door and hurled himself against it, he beat upon it with his clenched fists, but in vain. Realizing his folly, and desisting at last, he turned to Raoul.

"Well, Raoul," he said, "what do you think of all this?"

Raoul crossed himself before he answered; and his face had assumed the vizard of a mortal fear.

"I think, Messire," he finally replied, "that we have all been decoyed by a malefic sorcery; and that you, myself, the demoiselle Fleurette, and the maid Angélique, are all in deadly peril of both soul and body."

"That, also, is my thought," said Gérard. "And I believe it would be well that you and I should sleep only by turns; and that he who keeps vigil should retain in his hands my hornbeam staff, whose end I shall now sharpen with my dagger. I am sure that you know the manner in which it should be employed if there are any intruders; for if such should come, there would be no doubt as to their character and their intentions. We are in a castle which has no legitimate existence, as the guests of people who have been dead, or supposedly dead, for more than two hundred years. And such people, when they stir abroad, are prone to habits which I need not specify."

"Yes, Messire." Raoul shuddered; but he watched the sharpening of the staff with considerable interest. Gérard whittled the hard wood to a lance-like point, and hid the shavings carefully. He even carved the outline of a little cross near the middle of the staff, thinking that this might increase its efficacy or save it from molestation. Then, with the staff in his hand, he sat down upon the bed, where he could survey the litten room from between the curtains.

"You can sleep first, Raoul." He indicated the couch, which was near the door.

The two conversed in a fitful manner for some minutes. After hearing Raoul's tale of how Fleurette, Angélique and himself had been led astray by the sobbing of a woman amid the pines, and had been unable to retrace their way, the troubadour changed the theme. And henceforth he spoke idly and of matters remote from his real preoccupations, to fight down his torturing concern for the safety of Fleurette. Suddenly he became aware that Raoul had ceased to reply; and saw that the servant had fallen asleep on the couch. At the same time an irresistible drowsiness surged upon Gérard himself in spite of all his volition, in spite of the eldritch terrors and forebodings that still murmured in his brain. He heard through his growing hebetude a whisper as of shadowy wings in the castle halls; he caught the sibilation of ominous voices, like those of familiars that respond to the summoning of wizards; and he seemed to hear, even in the vaults and towers and remote chambers, the tread of feet that were hurrying on malign and secret errands. But oblivion was around him like the meshes of a sable net; and it closed in relentlessly upon his troubled mind, and drowned the alarms of his agitated senses.

When Gérard awoke at length, the tapers had burned to their

sockets; and a sad and sunless daylight was filtering through the window. The staff was still in his hand; and though his senses were still dull with the strange slumber that had drugged them, he felt that he was unharmed. But peering between the curtains, he saw that Raoul was lying mortally pale and lifeless on the couch, with the air and look of an exhausted moribund.

He crossed the room, and stooped above the servant. There was a small red wound on Raoul's neck; and his pulses were slow and feeble, like those of one who has lost a great amount of blood. His very appearance was withered and vein-drawn. And a phantom spice arose from the couch—a lingering wraith of the perfume worn by the châtelaine Agathe.

Gérard succeeded at last in arousing the man; but Raoul was very weak and drowsy. He could remember nothing of what had happened during the night; and his horror was pitiful to behold when he realized the truth.

"It will be your turn next, Messire," he cried. "These vampires mean to hold us here amid their unhallowed necromancies till they have drained us of our last drop of blood. Their spells are like mandragora or the sleepy syrups of Cathay; and no man can keep awake in their despite."

Gérard was trying the door; and somewhat to his surprise he found it unlocked. The departing vampire had been careless, in the lethargy of her repletion. The castle was very still; and it seemed to Gérard that the animating spirit of evil was now quiescent; that the shadowy wings of horror and malignity, the feet that had sped on baleful errands, the summoning sorcerers, the responding familiars, were all lulled in a temporary slumber.

He opened the door, he tip-toed along the deserted hall, and knocked at the portal of the chamber allotted to Fleurette and her maid. Fleurette, fully dressed, answered his knock immediately; and he caught her in his arms without a word, searching her wan face with a tender anxiety. Over her shoulder he could see the maid Angélique, who was sitting listlessly on the bed with a mark on her white neck similar to the wound that had been suffered by Raoul. He knew, even before Fleurette began to speak, that the nocturnal experiences of the demoiselle and her maid had been identical with those of himself and the man-servant.

While he tried to comfort Fleurette and reassure her, his thoughts were now busy with a rather curious problem. No one was abroad in the castle; and it was more than probable that the Sieur du Malinbois and his lady were both asleep after the nocturnal feast which they had undoubtedly enjoyed. Gérard pictured to himself the place and the fashion of their slumber; and he grew even more reflective as certain possibilities occurred to him.

"Be of good cheer, sweetheart," he said to Fleurette. "It is in my mind that we may soon escape from this abominable mesh of enchantments. But I must leave you for a little and speak again with Raoul, whose help I shall require in a certain matter."

He went back to his own chamber. The man-servant was sitting on the couch and was crossing himself feebly and muttering prayers with a faint, hollow voice.

"Raoul," said the troubadour a little sternly, "you must gather all your strength and come with me. Amid the gloomy walls that surround us, the somber ancient halls, the high towers and the heavy bastions, there is but one thing that veritably exists; and all the rest is a fabric of illusion. We must find the reality whereof I speak, and deal with it like true and valiant Christians. Come, we will now search the castle ere the lord and châtelaine shall awaken from their vampire lethargy."

He led the way along the devious corridors with a swiftness that betokened much forethought. He had reconstructed in his mind the hoary pile of battlements and turrets as he had seen them on the previous day; and he felt that the great donjon, being the center and stronghold of the edifice, might well be the place which he sought.

With the sharpened staff in his hand, with Raoul lagging bloodlessly at his heels, he passed the doors of many secret rooms, the many windows that gave on the blindness of an inner court, and came at last to the lower story of the donjon-keep.

It was a large, bare room, entirely built of stone, and illumined only by narrow slits high up in the wall, that had been designed for the use of archers. The place was very dim; but Gérard could see the glimmering outlines of an object not ordinarily to be looked for in such a situation, that arose from the middle of the floor. It was a tomb of marble; and stepping nearer, he saw that it was strangely weather-worn and was blotched by lichens of grey and yellow, such as flourish only within access of the sun. The slab that covered it was doubly broad and massive, and would require the full strength of two men to lift.

Raoul was staring stupidly at the tomb. "What now, Messire?" he queried.

"You and I, Raoul, are about to intrude upon the bedchamber of our host and hostess."

At his direction, Raoul seized one end of the slab; and he himself took the other. With a mighty effort that strained their bones and sinews to the cracking-point, they sought to remove it; but the slab hardly stirred. At length, by grasping the same end in unison, they were able to tilt the slab; and it slid away and dropped to the floor with a thunderous crash. Within, there were two open coffins, one of which contained the Sieur Hugh du Malinbois and the other his lady Agathe. Both of them appeared to be slumbering peacefully as infants; a look of tranquil evil, of pacified malignity, was imprinted upon their features; and their lips were dyed with a fresher scarlet than before.

Without hesitation or delay, Gérard plunged the lance-like end of his staff into the bosom of the Sieur du Malinbois. The body crumbled as if it were wrought of ashes kneaded and painted to human semblance; and a slight odor as of age-old corruption arose to the nostrils of Gérard. Then the troubadour pierced in like manner the bosom of the châtelaine. And simultaneously with her dissolution, the walls and floor of the donjon seemed to dissolve like a sullen vapor, they rolled away on every side with a shock as of unheard thunder. With a sense of weird vertigo and confusion Gérard and Raoul saw that the whole château had vanished like the towers and battlements of a bygone storm; that the dead lake and its rotting shores no longer offered their malefical illusions to the eye. They were standing in a forest-glade, in the full unshadowed light of the afternoon sun; and all that remained of the dismal castle was the lichen-mantled tomb that stood open beside them. Fleurette and her maid were a little distance away; and Gérard ran to the mercer's daughter and took her in his arms. She was dazed with wonderment, like one who emerges from the night-long labyrinth of an evil dream, and finds that all is well.

"I think, sweetheart," said Gérard, "that our next rendezvous will not be interrupted by the Sieur du Malinbois and his châtelaine."

But Fleurette was still bemused with wonder, and could only respond to his words with a kiss.

THE DARK CHÂTEAU

The mysteries of your former dust,
Your lives declined from solar light—
These would you know, or these surmise?
Beneath a swathed and mummied sun,
Descend where dayless dials rust,
Where the void hourglass fills with night;
And seeing with still-living eyes
Dim Acherontic waters run,

Follow where shrouded barges float
And fall, in regions of the dead,
Into the sable-foaming depths.
Then over ghostland mountains go
To find, beyond a bridgeless moat,
What stairs with shadow carpeted
Crumble behind the climber's steps
In some foreknown forlorn château.

Where exiled ghosts of gales that blew
At eve from vintages antique
Still stir the blurring tapestries,
And empty armor guards the rooms
By rotting portraits that were you,
Pass on. From airless cupboards bleak
Startle memorial spiceries
And plagues adrowse in attared glooms.

By oriels charged with stifled stains,
With night-blent purples, gules embrowned,
And spring's lost verdure, graver now
Than cypress at the set of day,
Pause, and look forth: no ghost remains
Save you to gaze on that dim ground
Where once the budding almond-bough
Waved, and the oleander-spray.

Hoar silence is the seneschal
Of court and keep, of niche and coigne.
With drumless ear no lute annoys,
Nor clang from jarring jambarts drawn,
Death, with dulled arrasses for pall,
Waits whitely there; and none will join
Your quest, nor ever any voice
Speak from the chambered epochs gone:

Till from the vaults with shadows brimmed
Shall come a cowled lampadephore,
Holding his lamp, by no breath blown,
To mirrors moony-clear and still
Where never living face is limned,
But wan reflections fixed of yore—
Long-mouldered shapes that were your own—
Graven in glass, unchanged and chill.

THE MANDRAKES

Gilles Grenier the sorcerer and his wife Sabine, coming into lower Averoigne from parts unknown or at least unverified, had selected the location of their hut with a careful forethought.

The hut was close to those marshes through which the slackening waters of the river Isoile, after leaving the great forest, had overflowed in sluggish, reed-clogged channels and sedge-hidden pools mantled with scum like witches' oils. It stood among osiers and alders on a low, mound-shaped elevation; and in front, toward the marshes, there was a loamy meadow-bottom where the short fat stems and tufted leaves of the mandrake grew in lush abundance, being more plentiful and of greater size than elsewhere through all that sorcery-ridden province. The fleshy, bifurcated roots of this plant, held by many to resemble the human body, were used by Gilles and Sabine in the brewing of love-philters. Their potions, being compounded with much care and cunning, soon acquired a marvellous renown among the peasants and villagers, and were even in request among people of a loftier station, who came privily to the wizard's hut. They would rouse, people said, a kindly warmth in the coldest and most prudent bosom, would melt the armor of the most obdurate virtue. As a result, the demand for these sovereign magistrals became enormous.

The couple dealt also in other drugs and simples, in charms and divination; and Gilles, according to common belief, could read infallibly the dictates of the stars. Oddly enough, considering the temper of the Fifteenth Century, when magic and witchcraft were still so widely reprobated, he and his wife enjoyed a repute by no means ill or unsavory. No charges of malefice were brought against them; and because of the number of honest marriages promoted by the philters, the local clergy were content to disregard the many illicit amours that had come to a successful issue through the same agency.

It is true, there were those who looked askance at Gilles in the beginning, and who whispered fearfully that he had been driven out of Blois, where all persons bearing the name Grenier were popularly believed to be werewolves. They called attention to the excessive hairiness of the wizard, whose hands were black with bristles and whose beard grew almost to his eyes. Such insinuations, however, were generally considered as lacking proof, insomuch as no other signs or marks of lycanthropy were ever displayed by Gilles. And in time, for reasons that have been sufficiently indicated, the few detractors of Gilles were wholly overborne by a secret but widespread sentiment of public favor.

Even by their patrons, very little was known regarding the strange couple, who maintained the reserve proper to those who dealt in mystery and enchantment. Sabine, a comely woman with blue-grey eyes and wheat-colored hair, and no trace of the traditional witch in her appearance, was obviously much younger than Gilles, whose sable mane and beard were already touched with the white warp of time. It was rumored by visitors that she had oftentimes been overheard in sharp dispute with her husband; and people soon made a jest of this, remarking that the philters might well be put to a domestic use by those who purveyed them. But aside from such rumors and ribaldries, little was thought of the matter. The connubial infelicities of Gilles and his wife, whether grave or trivial, in no wise impaired the renown of their love-potions.

Also, little was thought of Sabine's presence, when, five years after the coming of the pair into Averoigne, it became remarked by neighbors and customers that Gilles was alone. In reply to queries, the sorcerer merely said that his spouse had departed on a long journey, to visit relatives in a remote province. The explanation was accepted without debate, and it did not occur to anyone that there had been no eye-witnesses of Sabine's departure.

It was then mid-autumn; and Gilles told the inquirers, in a somewhat vague and indirect fashion, that his wife would not return before spring. Winter came early that year and tarried late, with deeply crusted snows in the forest and on the uplands, and a heavy armor of fretted ice on the marshes. It was a winter of much hardship and privation. When the tardy spring had broken the silver buds of the willows and covered the alders with a foliage of chrysolite, few thought to ask Gilles regarding Sabine's return. And later, when the purple bells of the mandrake were succeeded by small orange-colored apples, her prolonged absence was taken for granted.

Gilles, living tranquilly with his books and cauldrons, and gathering the roots and herbs for his magical medicaments, was well enough pleased to have it taken for granted. He did not believe that Sabine would ever return; and his unbelief, it would seem, was far from irrational. He had killed her one eve in autumn, during a dispute of unbearable acrimony, slitting her soft, pale throat in self-defense with a knife which he had wrested from her fingers when she lifted it against him. Afterward he had buried her by the late rays of a gibbous moon beneath the mandrakes in the meadow-bottom, replacing the leafy sods with much care, so that there was no evidence of their having been disturbed other than by the digging of a few roots in the way of daily business.

After the melting of the long snows from the meadow, he himself could scarcely have been altogether sure of the spot in which he had interred her body. He noticed, however, as the season drew on, that there was a place where the mandrakes grew with even more than their wonted exuberance; and this place, he believed, was the very site of her grave. Visiting it often, he smiled with a secret irony, and was pleased rather than troubled by the thought of that charnel nourishment which might have contributed to the lushness of the dark, glossy leaves. In fact, it may well have been a similar irony that had led him to choose the mandrake-meadow as a place of burial for the murdered witch-wife.

Gilles Grenier was not sorry that he had killed Sabine. They had been ill-mated from the beginning, and the woman had shown toward him in their quotidian quarrels the venomous spitefulness of a very hell-cat. He had not loved the vixen; and it was far pleasanter to be alone, with his somewhat sober temper unruffled by her acrid speeches, and his sallow face and grizzling beard untorn by her sharp finger-nails.

With the renewal of spring, as the sorcerer had expected, there was much demand for his love-philters among the smitten swains and lasses of the neighborhood. There came to him, also, the gallants who sought to overcome a stubborn chastity, and the wives who wished to recall a wandering fancy or allure the forbidden desires of young men. Anon, it became necessary for Gilles to replenish his stock of mandrake potions; and with this purpose in mind, he went forth at midnight beneath the full May moon, to dig the newly grown roots from which he would brew his amatory enchantments.

Smiling darkly beneath his beard, he began to cull the great, moon-pale plants which flourished on Sabine's grave, digging out the homunculus-like taproots very carefully with a curious trowel made from the femur of a witch.

Though he was well used to the weird and often vaguely human forms assumed by the mandrake, Gilles was somewhat surprised by the appearance of the first root. It seemed inordinately large, unnaturally white; and, eyeing it more closely, he saw that it bore the exact likeness of a woman's body and lower limbs, being cloven to the middle and clearly formed even to the ten toes! There were no arms, however, and the bosom ended in the large tuft of ovate leaves.

Gilles was more than startled by the fashion in which the root seemed to turn and writhe when he lifted it from the ground. He dropped it hastily, and the minikin limbs lay quivering on the grass. But, after a little reflection, he took the prodigy as a possible mark of Satanic favor, and continued his digging. To his amazement, the next root was formed in much the same manner as the first. A half-dozen

more, which he proceeded to dig, were shaped in miniature mockery
of a woman from breasts to heels; and amid the superstitious awe and
wonder with which he regarded them, he became aware of their singularly intimate resemblance to Sabine.

At this discovery, Gilles was deeply perturbed, for the thing was
beyond his comprehension. The miracle, whether divine or demoniac,
began to assume a sinister and doubtful aspect. It was as if the slain
woman herself had returned, or had somehow wrought her unholy
simulacrum in the mandrakes.

His hand trembled as he started to dig up another plant; and working with less than his usual care, he failed to remove the whole of the
bifurcated root, cutting into it clumsily with the trowel of sharp bone.

He saw that he had severed one of the tiny ankles. At the same instant, a shrill, reproachful cry, like the voice of Sabine herself in mingled pain and anger, seemed to pierce his ears with intolerable acuity,
though the volume was strangely lessened, as if the voice had come
from a distance. The cry ceased, and was not repeated. Gilles, sorely
terrified, found himself staring at the trowel, on which there was a
dark, blood-like stain. Trembling, he pulled out the severed root, and
saw that it was dripping with a sanguine fluid.

At first, in his dark fear and half-guilty apprehension he thought of
burying the roots which lay palely before him with their eldritch and
obscene similitude to the dead sorceress. He would hide them deeply
from his own sight and the ken of others, lest the murder he had done
should somehow be suspected.

Presently, however, his alarm began to lessen. It occurred to him
that, even if seen by others, the roots would be looked upon merely as
a freak of nature and would in no manner serve to betray his crime,
since their actual resemblance to the person of Sabine was a thing
which none but he could rightfully know.

Also, he thought, the roots might well possess an extraordinary
virtue, and from them, perhaps, he would brew philters of never-

equalled power and efficacy. Overcoming entirely his initial dread and repulsion, he filled a small osier basket with the quivering, leaf-headed figurines. Then he went back to his hut, seeing in the bizarre phenomenon merely the curious advantage to which it might be turned, and wholly oblivious to any darker meaning, such as might have been read by others in his place.

In his callous hardihood, he was not disquieted overmuch by the profuse bleeding of a sanguine matter from the mandrakes when he came to prepare them for his cauldron. The ungodly, furious hissing, the mad foaming and boiling of the brew, like a devil's broth, he ascribed to the unique potency of its ingredients. He even dared to choose the most shapely and perfect of the woman-like plants, and hung it up in his hut amid other roots and dried herbs and simples, intending to consult it as an oracle in the future, according to the custom of wizards.

The new philters which he had concocted were bought by eager customers, and Gilles ventured to recommend them for their surpassing virtue, which would kindle amorous warmth in a bosom of marble or enflame the very dead.

Now, in the old legend of Averoigne which I recount herewith, it is told that the impious and audacious wizard, fearing neither God nor devil nor witch-woman, dared to dig again in the earth of Sabine's grave, removing many more of the white, female-shapen roots, which cried aloud in shrill complaint to the waning moon or turned like living limbs at his violence. And all those which he dug were formed alike, in the miniature image of the dead Sabine, from breasts to toes. And from them, it is said, he compounded other philters, which he meant to sell in time when such should be requested.

As it happened, however, these latter potions were never dispensed; and only a few of the first were sold, owing to the frightful and calamitous consequences that followed their use. For those to whom the potions had been administered privily, whether men or

women, were not moved by the genial fury of desire, as was the wonted result, but were driven by a darker rage, by a woeful and Satanic
madness, irresistibly impelling them to harm or even slay the persons
who had sought to attract their love.

Husbands were turned against wives, lasses against their lovers,
with speeches of bitter hate and scatheful deeds. A certain young gal-
lant who had gone to the promised rendezvous was met by a vengeful
madwoman, who tore his face into bleeding shreds with her nails. A
mistress who had thought to win back her recreant knight was mis-
treated foully and done to death by him who had hitherto been impec-
cably gentle, even if faithless.

The scandal of these untoward happenings was such as would attend an invasion of demons. The crazed men and women, it was
thought at first, were veritably possessed by devils. But when the use
of the potions became rumored, and their provenance was clearly established, the burden of the blame fell upon Gilles Grenier, who, by
the law of both church and state, was now charged with sorcery.

The constables who went to arrest Gilles found him at evening in
his hut of raddled osiers, stooping and muttering above a cauldron that
foamed and hissed and boiled as if it had been filled with the spate of
Phlegethon. They entered and took him unaware. He submitted calmly,
but expressed surprise when told of the lamentable effect of the love-
philters; and he neither affirmed nor denied the charge of wizardry.

As they were about to leave with their prisoner, the officers heard
a shrill, tiny, shrewish voice that cried from the shadows of the hut,
where bunches of dried simples and other sorcerous ingredients were
hanging. It appeared to issue from a strange, half-withered root, cloven
in the very likeness of a woman's body and legs—a root that was partly
pale, and partly black with cauldron-smoke. One of the constables
thought that he recognized the voice as being that of Sabine, the sorcerer's wife. All swore that they heard the voice clearly, and were able
to distinguish these words:

"Dig deeply in the meadow, where the mandrakes grow the thickliest."

The officers were sorely frightened, both by this uncanny voice and the obscene likeness of the root, which they regarded as a work of Satan. Also, there was much doubt anent the wisdom of obeying the oracular injunction. Gilles, who was questioned narrowly as to its meaning, refused to offer any interpretation; but certain marks of perturbation in his manner finally led the officers to examine the mandrake meadow below the hut.

Digging by lantern-light in the specified spot, they found many more of the roots, which seemed to crowd the ground; and beneath, they came to the rotting corpse of a woman, which was still recognizable as that of Sabine. As a result of this discovery, Gilles Grenier was arraigned not only for sorcery but also for the murder of his wife. He was readily convicted of both crimes, though he denied stoutly the imputation of intentional malefice, and claimed to the very last that he had killed Sabine only in defense of his own life against her termagant fury. He was hanged on the gibbet in company with other murderers, and his dead body was then burned at the stake.

CANTICLE

In my heart a wizard book,
Only love shall ever look:
Darling, when thou readest there,
Wisely falter and forebear
Ere thou turn'st the pages olden,
Deeply writ and deeply folden,
Where the legends of lost moons
Lie in chill unchanging runes.
Trifle not with charm or spell,
Heptagram or pentacle,
Leave in silence, long unsaid,
All the words that wake the dead.

Darling, in my heart withholden,
Letters rubrical and golden
Tell the secret of our love
And the philtred spells thereof;
There, my memories of thee,
Half of all the gramarie,
Are a firm unfading lore:
Read but these . . . and read no more . . .
Shall it profit thee to find
Loves that went with snow and wind?
Leave in silence, long unsaid,
All the words that wake the dead.

THE SATYR

Raoul, Comte de la Frênaie, was by nature the most unsuspicious of husbands. His lack of suspicion, perhaps, was partly lack of imagination; and, for the rest, was doubtless due to the dulling of his observational faculties by the heavy wines of Averoigne. At any rate, he had seen nothing amiss in the friendship of his wife, Adèle, with Olivier du Montoir, a young poet who might in time have rivaled Ronsard as one of the most brilliant luminaries of the Pleiade, if it had not been for an unforeseen but fatal circumstance. Indeed, M. le Comte had been rather proud than otherwise, because of the interest shown in Mme. la Comtesse by this erudite and comely youth, who had already moistened his lips at the fount of Helicon and was becoming known throughout other provinces than Averoigne for his melodious villanelles and graceful ballades. Nor was Raoul disturbed by the fact that many of these same villanelles and ballades were patently written in celebration of Adèle's visible charms, and made liberal mention of her wine-dark tresses, her golden eyes, and sundry other details no less alluring, and equally essential to feminine perfection. M. le Comte did not pretend to understand poetry: like many others, he considered it something apart from all common sense or mundane relevancy; and his mental powers became totally paralyzed whenever they were confronted by anything in rhyme and meter. In the meanwhile the ballades and their author were gradually waxing in boldness.

That year, the snows of an austere winter had melted away in a week of halcyon warmth; and the land was filled suddenly with the tender green and chrysolite and chrysoprase of early spring. Olivier came oftener and oftener to the château de la Frênaie, and he and

Adèle were often alone, since they had so much to discuss that was beyond the interests or the comprehension of M. le Comte. And now, sometimes, they walked abroad in the forest that rolled a sea of vernal verdure almost to the grey walls and barbican, and within whose sun-warm glades the perfume of the first wild flowers was tinging delicately the quiet air. If people gossiped, they did so discreetly, and beyond hearing of Raoul, or of Adèle and Olivier.

All things being as they were, it is hard to know just why M. le Comte became suddenly troubled concerning the integrity of his marital honor. Perhaps, in some interim of the hunting and drinking between which he divided nearly all his time, he had noticed that his wife was growing younger and fairer and was blooming as a woman never blooms except to the magical sunlight of love. Perhaps he had caught some glance of ardent or affectionate understanding between Adèle and Olivier; or, perhaps, it was the influence of the premature spring, which had pierced the vinous muddlement of his brain with an obscure stirring of forgotten thoughts and emotions, and thus had given him a flash of insight. At any rate he was troubled when, on this afternoon of earliest April, he returned to the château from Vyônes, where he had gone on business, and learned from his servitors that Mme. la Comtesse and Olivier du Montoir had left a few minutes previously for a promenade in the forest. His dull face, however, betrayed little. He seemed to reflect for a moment. Then:

"Which way did they go? I have reason to see Mme. la Comtesse at once."

His servants gave him the desired direction, and he went out, following slowly the footpath they had indicated, till he was beyond sight of the château. Then he quickened his pace, and began to finger the hilt of his rapier as he went on through the thickening woods.

"I am a little afraid, Olivier. Shall we go any farther?"

The couple had wandered beyond the limits of their customary stroll, and were nearing a portion of the forest of Averoigne where the trees were older and taller than all others. Here, some of the huge oaks were said to date back to pagan days. Few people ever passed beneath them; and queer beliefs and legends had been attached to them by the peasantry for ages. Things had been seen within these precincts whose very existence was an affront to science and a blasphemy to religion; and evil influences were said to attend those who dared to intrude upon the sullen umbrage of the immemorial glades and thickets. The beliefs varied, and the legends were far from explicit; but all agreed that the wood was haunted by some entity inimical to man, some primordial spirit of ill that was ancienter than Christ or Satan. Panic, madness, demoniac possession, or baleful, unreasoning passions that led them to doom, were the lot of all who had trodden the demesnes of this entity. There were those who whispered what the spirit was, who told incredible tales regarding its true nature, and described its true aspect; but such tales were not meet for the ear of devout Christians.

"Prithee, let us go on," said Olivier. "Look you, Madame, and see how the ancient trees have put on the emerald freshness of April, how innocently they rejoice in the sun's return."

"But the stories people tell, Olivier."

"They are stories to frighten babes and beldames. Let us go on. There is enchantment here, but only the enchantment of beauty."

Indeed, as he had said, the great-limbed oaks and venerable beeches were fresh with their new-born foliage. The forest wore an aspect of blitheness and vertumnal gaiety, and it was hard to believe the old superstitions and legends. The day was one of those days when hearts that feel the urgency of an unavowed love are fain to wander indefinitely. So, after certain feminine demurs, and many reassurances, Adèle allowed Olivier to persuade her, and they went on.

The feet of animals, if not of men, had continued the path they were following, and had made an easy way into the wood of fabulous evil. The drooping boughs enfolded them with arms of soft verdure, and seemed to draw them in; and shafts of yellow sunshine rifted the high trees to aureole the lovely secret lilies that bloomed about the darkly writhing coils of enormous roots. The trees were twisted and knotted, were heavy with centurial incrustations of bark, were humped and misshapen with the growth of unremembered years; but there was an air of antique wisdom about them, together with a tranquil friendliness. Adèle exclaimed with delight; and neither she nor Olivier was aware of anything sinister or doubtful in the unison of exquisite beauty and gnarled quaintness which the old forest offered to them.

"Was I not right?" Olivier queried. "Is there ought to fear in harmless trees and flowers?"

Adèle smiled, but made no other answer. In the circle of bright sunlight where they were now standing, she and Olivier looked at each other with a new and pervasive intimacy. There was a strange perfume on the windless air, coming in slow wafts from an undiscernible source—a perfume that seemed to speak insidiously of love and languor and amorous yielding. Neither knew the flower from which it issued, for all at once there were many unfamiliar blossoms around their feet, with heavy bells of carnal white or pink, or curled and twining petals, or hearts like a rosy wound. Looking, they saw each other as in a sudden dazzle of flame; and each felt a violent quickening of the blood, as if they had drunk a sovereign philter. The same thought was manifest in the bold fervor of Olivier's eyes, and the modest flush upon the cheeks of Mme. la Comtesse. The long-cherished love, which neither had openly declared up to this hour, was clamoring importunately in the veins of both. They resumed their onward walk; and both were now silent through the self-same constraint and embarrassment.

They dared not look at each other; and neither of them had eyes for the changing wood through which they wandered, and neither saw the foul, obscene deformity of the grey boles that gathered on each hand, or the shameful and monstrous fungi that reared their spotted pallor in the shade, or the red, venerous flowers flaunting in the sun.

The spell of their desire was upon the lovers; they were drugged with the mandragora of passion; and everything beyond their own bodies, their own hearts, the throbbing of their own delirious blood, was vaguer than a dream.

The wood thickened and the arching boughs above were a weft of manifold gloom. The eyes of ferine animals peered from their hidden burrows, with gleams of crafty crimson or chill, ferocious beryl; and the dank smell of stagnant waters, choked with the leaves of bygone autumn, arose to greet the lovers, and to break a little the perilous charm that possessed them.

They paused on the edge of a rock-encircled pool, above which the ancient alders twined their decaying tops as if to maintain for ever the mad posture of a superannuate frenzy. And there, between the nether boughs of the alders in a frame of new leaves, they saw the face that leered upon them.

The apparition was incredible; and, for the space of a long breath, they could not believe they had really seen it. There were two horns in a matted mass of coarse, animal-like hair above the semi-human face with its obliquely slitted eyes and fang-revealing mouth and beard of wild-boar bristles. The face was old—incomputably old, and its lines and wrinkles were those of unreckoned years of lust; and its look was filled with the slow, unceasing increment of all the malignity and corruption and cruelty of elder ages. It was the face of Pan, as he glared from his secret wood upon travelers taken unaware.

Adèle and Olivier were seized by a nightmare terror, as they recalled the old legends. The charm of their passionate obsession was broken, and the drug of desire relinquished its hold on their senses. Like people awakened from a heavy sleep, they saw the face, and heard through the tumult of their blood the cachinnation of a wild and evil and panic laughter as the apparition vanished among the boughs.

Shuddering, Adèle flung herself for the first time into the arms of her lover.

"Did you see it?" she whispered, as she clung to him. Olivier drew her close. In that delicious nearness, the horrible thing he had seen and heard became somehow improbable and unreal. There must have been a double sorcery abroad, to lull his horror thus; but he knew not whether the thing had been a momentary hallucination, a fantasy wrought by the sun amid the alder-leaves, or the demon that was fabled to dwell in Averoigne; and the startlement he had felt was somehow without meaning or reason. He could even thank the apparition, whatever it was, because it had thrown Adèle into his embrace. He could think of nothing now but the proximity of that warm, delectable mouth, for which he had hungered so long. He began to reassure her, to make light of her fears, to pretend that she could have seen nothing; and his reassurances merged into ardent protestations of love. He kissed her . . . and they both forgot the vision of the satyr. . . .

They were lying on a patch of golden moss, where the sun-rays fell through a single cleft in the high foliage, when Raoul found them. They did not see or hear him; and their first intimation of his coming, as well as their last, was the rapier which he drove through Olivier's body till it pierced the bosom of Adèle.

Adèle screamed and twisted in a brief agony, and the corpse of Olivier moved in a limp unison with her twisting. Raoul drew the rapier out and made sure of the woman with a second thrust. Then, with a vague feeling that he had avenged his honor in the proper fashion, and a sense of dull, unhappy confusion, of muddled and bleary wonder as to what it was all about, he stood looking down at his victims.

They were both very quiet now, as beseems a couple who have been slain in open adultery. And there was no movement, no sign of life, in the lonely forest where so few people ever came. Therefore, M. le Comte was startled beyond all measure when he heard the wild, malign, unhuman laughter, the mad and diabolical cachination which issued from the alder boughs.

He raised his bloody rapier, and peered at the boughs, but he could see nothing. The laughter ceased, and was not followed by any other sound. He crossed himself, and began hurriedly to retrace the path by which he had entered the wood.

CAMBION

I am that spawn of witch and demon
By time's mad prophets long foretold:
The unnamed fear of king and freeman,
I roam the lawless outland wold,
Crouching amid the weeds and mould
With dire Alecto for my leman.

I am that hidden piper, playing
The Pan-like strains of malefice
That lure the lonely wanderer, straying
Upon the crumbling precipice:
To filmed morass or blind abyss
His feet must follow, never staying.

I am that swart, unseen pursuer
Whose lust begets a changeling breed:
All women know me for their wooer:
Mine is the whisper maidens heed
At twilight; mine the spells that lead
The matron to the nighted moor.

I am that messenger whose call
Convenes dark mage and banished lord
And branded witch and whip-flayed thrall,
To plot, amid the madness poured
On the black Sabbat's frothing horde,
The bale of realms, the planet's fall.

THE DISINTERMENT OF VENUS

I

Prior to certain highly deplorable and scandalous happenings in the year 1550, the vegetable garden of Périgon was situated on the southeast side of the abbey. After these events, it was removed to the northwest side, where it has remained ever since; and the former garden-site was given to weeds and briars which, by strict order of the successive abbots, no one has ever tried to eradicate or curb.

The happenings which compelled this removal of the Benedictine's turnip and carrot patches became a popular tale in Averoigne, to the lasting shame of the good Brothers. It is hard to say how much or how little of the legend is apocryphal.

One April morning, three monks were spading lustily in the garden. Their names were Paul, Pierre and Hughues. The first was a man of ripe years, hale and robust; the second was in his early prime; the third was little more than a boy, and had but recently taken his final vows.

Being moved with an especial ardor, in which the vernal stirring of youthful sap may have played its part, Hughues proceeded to dig the loamy soil even more diligently and deeply than his comrades. The ground was almost free of stones, owing to the careful and industrious tillage of many generations of monks; but anon, through the muscular zeal with which it was wielded, the spade of Hughues encountered a well-buried object of indeterminate size but unquestionable hardness.

Hughues felt that this obstruction, which in all likelihood was a small boulder, should be removed for the honor of the monastery and

199

the glory of God. Bending busily, he shoveled away the moist, blackish loam in an effort to uncover it.

The task was more arduous than he had expected; and the supposed boulder began to reveal an amazing length and a quite singular formation as he bared it by degrees. Leaving their own toil, Pierre and Paul came to his assistance. Soon, through the zealous endeavors of the three, the nature of the buried object became all too manifest.

In the large pit they had now dug, the monks beheld the grimy head and torso of what was plainly a marble woman or goddess from antique years. The pale stone of shoulders and arms, tinged faintly as if with a living rose, had been scraped clean in places by their delving shovels; but the face and breasts were still black with the heavily caked loam.

The figure stood erect, as if on a hidden pedestal or altar. One arm was raised, caressing with a shapely hand the ripe contour of the bosom; the other, hanging idly, was still plunged in the earth. Digging deeper, the monks began to uncover the full voluptuous hips and rounded thighs; and finally, taking turns in the pit, whose rim was now higher than their heads, they came to the sunken pedestal, which stood on a pavement of granite.

During the course of their excavations, as the nature of their find began to disclose itself unmistakably, the Brothers had felt a strange, powerful excitement whose cause they could hardly have explained, but which seemed to arise, like some obscure contagion, from the long-buried arms and bosom of the image. Mingled with a pious horror due to the infamous nudity and paganry of the feminine statue, there was an unacknowledged pleasure which the three would have rebuked in themselves as vile and shameful if they had recognized it.

Oddly fearful of chipping or scratching the marble, they wielded their spades with much chariness; and when the digging was completed and the comely feet were uncovered on their pedestal, Paul, the oldest, standing beside the image in the pit, began to wipe away with a handful of weeds and grass the maculations of dark loam that still clung to its lovely body. This task he performed with great thoroughness; and he ended by polishing the marble with the hem and sleeves of his black robe.

He felt an unwonted but delicious fever as he touched the smooth marble; and he lingered so long over his self-imposed task, and the movements of his rough hands were so lover-like and caressing, that they aroused the unspoken disapproval of Pierre and Hughues; who, nevertheless, were half conscious of a covert desire to follow his example.

At length, Paul emerged reluctantly from the pit. He and his fellows, who were not without classic learning, now saw that the figure was evidently a statue of Venus, dating no doubt from the Roman occupation of Averoigne, when certain altars to this divinity had been established by the invaders.

The vicissitudes of half-legendary time, the long dark years of inhumation, had harmed the Venus little if at all. The slight mutilation of an ear-tip half-hidden by rippling curls, and the partial fracture of a shapely middle toe, merely served to add, if possible, a keener seduction to her languorously sensual beauty.

She was exquisite as the succubi of youthful dreams, but her perfection was touched with inenarrable evil. The lines of the mature figure were fraught with a maddening luxuriousness; the eyelids were drooped in a pretended coyness of false virtue; the lips of the full, Circean face were half-pouting, half-smiling with ambiguous allure. It was the masterpiece of an unknown, decadent sculptor; not the noble, maternal Venus of heroic times, but the sly and cruelly voluptuous Cotytto, the Cytherean of dark orgies, ready for her descent into the Hollow Hill.

Staring at the fully revealed image, the good monks became forcibly aware of certain unhallowed emotions which they would never have been willing to avow. A sensuous enchantment, an amorous thralldom, seemed to flow from the flesh-pale marble and to weave itself like invisible hair about the hearts of the Brothers. They felt the prompting of forbidden thoughts and reveries, of rebel desires which they had supposedly put away with the assuming of their monkhood.

With a sudden, mutual feeling of shame, that caused them to avoid each other's eyes, they began to debate what should be done with the Venus, which, in a monastery garden, was somewhat misplaced, and would become a source of embarrassment. Since their combined efforts would barely have sufficed to elevate the heavy image from the pit, they sent Hughues, as the youngest, to report their find to the abbot and await his decision regarding its disposal. In the meanwhile, Paul and Pierre resumed their garden labors, stealing covert glances at the fair head of the goddess, which was all that they could see in the deep hole at a little distance.

II

The discovery of the Venus was destined to become a cause of much excitement, perturbation, and even dissension amid the quiet Brotherhood at Périgon. Augustin, the abbot, came out in person to inspect the find, accompanied by many monks who were not engaged at that hour in some special task.

Even the saintly abbot, in spite of his reverend age and rigorous temper, was somewhat discomfited by the peculiar witchery which seemed to emanate from the marble. Sternly he repressed his agitation and gave no sign, other than a deepening of the natural austerity of his demeanor. Curtly he ordered the bringing of ropes, and directed the raising of the Venus from her loamy bed to a standing position on the garden ground beside the hole. In this task, Paul, Pierre and Hughues were assisted by two others.

After making sure that their lovely burden had been set firmly on her pedestal, the five brothers showed a singular inclination to tarry about the Venus. Many others now pressed forward to examine the figure closely; and several were even prompted to touch it, till rebuked for this unseemly action by their superior, who, if he felt a similar impulse, would not sacrifice his holy dignity by yielding to it.

Certain of the elder and more severe Benedictines urged the immediate destruction of the image, which, they argued, was a heathen abomination that defiled the abbey garden by its presence, and therefore should not be countenanced. Others, moved by the evil beauty of the Venus in a manner impossible for them to admit, pleaded furtively and shamefacedly for her preservation. Still others, the most practical, pointed out that the Venus, being a rare and beautiful example of Roman sculpture, might well be sold at a goodly price to some rich and impious art-lover.

Augustin, though he felt that the Venus should be indubitably destroyed as an impure pagan idol, was filled with a queer and unaccountable hesitation which led him to defer the necessary orders for her demolishment. It was as if the subtly wanton loveliness of the marble were pleading for clemency like a living form, with a voice half-human, half-divine. Averting his eyes from the white bosom, he spoke harshly, bidding the Brothers to return to their labors and devotions, and saying that the Venus could remain in the garden till arrangements were made for her ultimate disposition and removal. Pending this, he instructed one of the Brothers to bring sackcloth and drape therewith the unseemly nudity of the goddess.

Even at the time, Augustin was criticized for his peculiar delay and laxness in this matter by some of the deans. During the few years that remained to him, he was to regret bitterly the flash of carnal weakness that had prompted him to defer the destruction of the image.

Contenting himself for the nonce with a severe injunction to the effect that no one should approach the Venus other than those whose labors in the garden should compel an involuntary proximity, Augustin retired with the various Brothers, some of whom, as they went, gave many a backward glance at the life-like charms of the naked goddess. Later, there was much peeping from the cell windows that looked up-on the garden; and more than one Brother, caught in this indecorous occupation, was reprimanded austerely by the deans.

However, such peccadillos were trivial indeed, compared with the grave scandal involving a number of the monks, which ensued shortly. Those concerned were Paul, Pierre and Hughues, together with the two who had helped in raising the Venus from her pit, and three oth-ers who had also touched the limbs or body of the statue with their fingers.

These eight, it was found, had absented themselves without leave from the monastery during the night that followed the discovery of the Venus. Covertly and shamefastly, several of them returned the next morning; and their fellow-truants straggled in during the day, or were apprehended through rumors and charges that had been brought against them.

All, it was learned, had been guilty of open or furtive lechery. Some had annoyed the peasant women of the neighborhood with sa-tyr-like advances; others had played the incubus with village girls at Ste. Zénobie, or had been seen in houses of ill-fame, many miles away in Ximes.

Summoned before their indignant abbot, these piacular culprits could offer no explanation or defense, other than the plea that they had been driven by an irresistible carnal compulsion. They attributed their downfall to the antique Venus, saying that they had been haunted by lubric thoughts and goaded by lascivious desires such as had tor-mented Anthony during his desert vigil, ever since the hour when they had touched the flesh-white marble of the statue.

Many of those who had beheld the evil image but had not touched it, now confessed that they had been conscious of like thoughts and impulses; and all agreed that a foul enchantment had been exerted by the Venus. Since only those who had laid hands on the marble were actually driven beyond the bounds of decorum or decency, it was plain that the full power of the diabolic pagan charm was inherent in such contact; and that anyone who dared to handle the Venus henceforth would be in grave danger of perdition.

The whole situation, though supremely scandalous, was so unusual that it could not be dealt with in any ordinary fashion. In view of their sorcerous temptation and demoniac compulsion, the eight offending monks were not expelled from the order, as their heinous lecheries might well have merited, but were merely sentenced to severe and protracted penance.

In the meanwhile, nothing was done with the Venus; for obviously, anyone who ventured to touch it—even, perhaps, with the motive of demolition—would court the baleful witchcraft that had already brought a profound and far-reaching evil on Périgon. It was suggested that some layman (to whom the penalty of heathen madness would be a less serious matter than to those who had taken vows of chastity) should be hired to shatter the idol and remove and bury its fragments. This, no doubt, would have been accomplished in good time, if it had not been for the hasty and fanatic zeal of Brother Louis.

III

This Brother, a youth of good family, was conspicuous among the Benedictines both for his comely face and his austere piety. Handsome as Adonis, he was given to ascetic vigils and prolonged devotions, outdoing in this regard the abbot and the deans.

At the hour of the statue's disinterment, he was busily engaged in copying a Latin Testament; and neither then nor at any later time had he cared to inspect a find which he considered more than dubious. He had expressed disapprobation on hearing from his fellows the details of the discovery; and feeling that the abbey garden was polluted by the presence of an obscene image, he had purposely avoided all windows through which the womanly nakedness of the antique marble might have been visible to his chaste eyes.

Therefore it was with supreme horror and indignation that he learned of the downfall of the eight Benedictines who had touched the image. It seemed to him an insupportable thing that these virtuous, god-fearing monks should be brought to shame through the operation of some carnal pagan spell. He reprobated openly the hesitation of Augustin and his delay in destroying the idol. More mischief, he felt, would ensue if it were suffered to remain intact and were left to contaminate the beholders with its unchaste nudity. The act of demolition should be accomplished at once.

Secure in his own consciousness of sanctity and virtue, and fearless of any temptation or baleful influence that might be exerted by the Venus, Brother Louis, after long and painful reflection, resolved that he would take the matter into his own hands. Though this action would involve a nominal disobedience to the abbot's order, he would go forth that very evening, armed with a heavy hammer, and would smash the idol into many fragments. Thus the honor of Périgon would be vindicated, and his insubordination become a justifiable thing.

Brooding deeply as he went about his daily toils and devotions, Louis confided this intention to no one. Wild whispers were circulating among the monks; and it was said that several others besides the eight culprits had been drawn to touch the sorcerous marble in secret, and would succumb anon to the overpowering nympholepsy which they had incurred. It was said also that the image was no mere lifeless lump of stone, but had sought to entice with wanton smiles and harlot gestures those who had labored in the garden after Paul, Pierre and Hughues. Hearing these whispers, Louis was confirmed in his resolution.

Visiting on some pretext or other the workshop of the abbey at twilight, he concealed an iron hammer beneath his robe and carried it away with him to his cell. Then, toiling patiently at the Latin manuscript by candle-light, while a holy wrath and ardor mounted within him, he waited till most of the Brothers had retired to their dormitory.

A rosy-tinted moon that was slightly past the full had climbed above the neighboring forest when Louis stole forth into the garden by a postern door. The blackish clods of freshly-spaded loam were topped with an eerie silver; and Louis had not gone far on the open ground when he discerned the Venus, whose nude limbs and bosom startled him as if they had been those of a living woman.

Indeed, as he went nearer, he could not persuade himself that the figure was a mere statue. The full, wan breasts appeared to quiver in the moonlight as with the rise and fall of a breathing bosom; the drooping eyelids seemed to lift in a captious coquetry; the doubtfully smiling lips assumed a more seductive curve; the delicate fingers stirred a little, as if to beckon him. Aware, however, that this illusion might well be part of the baneful enchantment whose cause he had come forth to destroy, Louis strove to resist the insidious impressions that troubled him more and more.

Sinking into the soft and thoroughly spaded soil at each step, he went boldly forward till he stood face to face with the Venus on the verge of the dark hole from which she had been exhumed. Without delay, with a feeling of imperative haste, he tried to lift the ponderous hammer; but it seemed that his arm, though sustained by a righteous anger, a holy indignation, would no longer obey him.

He knew not how the change had been wrought, nor how the spell had fallen; but he felt the impotence of a dreamer, helpless in the thrall of some strange dream. A subtly clinging web was upon his senses. Wildly, with dying horror and rebellion, he stared at the immemorial temptress who seemed to proffer her divine beauty; and staring, he forgot his wrath, his purpose, his fear and horror—and his cenobitic vows.

The hammer fell unheeded from his fingers. Bathed in a perilous light, and swathed with alluring shadows, the Venus appeared to live and palpitate—to lift comely hands that implored his mercy—to open fair eyes and delicious lips that claimed his love.

An unleashed delirium, sudden and irresistible, sang triumphantly in his brain, exulted madly in his blood. Stepping across the forgotten hammer, he embraced the Venus. . . . Her arms and bosom were cool as marble to his feverous touch, but they seemed to offer the firm softness and resilience of living flesh. . . .

IV

The absence of Brother Louis, together with that of three others, was noted by the monks at early dawn with much alarm and consternation. Sorrowfully, it was surmised that they had fallen under the spell of the statue, and would be apprehended in the same manner and for the same sinful deeds as their predecessors.

Later, two of the missing monks returned to the abbey of their own will; and a third was caught with the charcoal-burner's wife whom he had seduced into mad elopement. All made the same confession: laboring in the garden on the previous day, they had been prompted by a fatal curiosity to finger the forbidden image; and had been seized, as a result, by the pagan madness.

Brother Louis, however, was not found; and his fate remained a mystery for several hours. Then it happened that one of the older monks, on some errand or other, had occasion to cross the garden. Peering fearfully in the direction of the Venus, he was surprised and mystified to see that she had disappeared.

With much trepidation, deeming the vanishment an act of sorcery or Satanry, he went forward to the place where the statue had stood. There, with unspeakable horror, he found the solution of the riddle.

Somehow, the Venus had been overturned and had fallen back into the huge pit. The body of Brother Louis, with a shattered skull and lips bruised to a bloody pulp, was lying crushed beneath her marble breasts. His arms were clasped about her in a stiff embrace, to which death had now added its own rigidity; and later, when the horrified

Brothers had been summoned to consider the problem, it was deemed inadvisable to make any effort toward his removal. The iron hammer, lying beside the pit, was proof of the righteous intention with which he had gone forth—but certain other matters, putting him beyond all redemption, were equally evident.

So, by the order of Augustin, the pit was filled hastily to its rim with earth and stones; and the very spot where it had been, being left without mound or other mark, was quickly overgrown by grass and weeds along with the rest of the abandoned garden.

"O Golden-Tongued Romance"

We found, we knew it dimly
Within a dead life grimly
By guarding time inurned—
A glamour far and olden,
A fulgor night-enfolden,
A flame that in long-darkling Eden burned.

Though hardly then we claimed it,
We yet adored and named it
With a name forgotten now—
A faery word and dawn-like,
A word of gramarie, gone like
An opal bird from off a purple bough . . .

Ah! vain the lamp reluming
The unhaunted vault inhuming
The cold Canopic jar,
And vain the charm recovered
From out the daemon-hovered,
Worm-traveled page of pentacled grimoire.

And yet the thing we yearned for,
The thing that we returned for
From tomb and catacomb,
It may not wholly dwindle
While moon or meteor kindle
A phantom beacon on the ebon foam.

Through ghoul-watched wood unthridden,
By goblin mere and midden,
No ivory horn will blow,
No gold lamp lighten gloom-ward,
But we will carry doom-ward
The broken beauty caught from long ago:

An echo half evading
The ear, remotely fading
From a far-vibrant lyre,
A long-plucked flower blooming
In the dry urn, a fuming
Myrrh-fragrant ember in a darkened pyre.

THE END OF THE STORY

The following narrative was found among the papers of Christophe Morand, a young law-student of Tours, after his unaccountable disappearance during a visit at his father's home near Moulins, in November, 1789:

A sinister brownish-purple autumn twilight, made premature by the imminence of a sudden thunderstorm, had filled the forest of Averoigne. The trees along my road were already blurred to ebon masses, and the road itself, pale and spectral before me in the thickening gloom, seemed to waver and quiver slightly, as with the tremor of some mysterious earthquake. I spurred my horse, who was woefully tired with a journey begun at dawn, and had fallen hours ago to a protesting and reluctant trot, and we galloped adown the darkening road between enormous oaks that seemed to lean toward us with boughs like clutching fingers as we passed.

With dreadful rapidity, the night was upon us, the blackness became a tangible clinging veil; a nightmare confusion and desperation drove me to spur my mount again with a more cruel rigor; and now, as we went, the first far-off mutter of the storm mingled with the clatter of my horse's hoofs, and the first lightning flashes illumed our way, which, to my amazement (since I believed myself on the main highway through Averoigne), had inexplicably narrowed to a well-trodden footpath. Feeling sure that I had gone astray, but not caring to retrace my steps in the teeth of darkness and the towering clouds of the tempest, I hurried on, hoping, as seemed reasonable, that a path so plainly worn would lead eventually to some house or château where I could find refuge for the night. My hope was well-founded, for within a few minutes I

212

descried a glimmering light through the forest-boughs, and came suddenly to an open glade, where, on a gentle eminence, a large building loomed, with several litten windows in the lower story, and a top that was well-nigh indistinguishable against the bulks of driven cloud.

"Doubtless a monastery," I thought, as I drew rein, and descending from my exhausted mount, lifted the heavy brazen knocker in the form of a dog's head and let it fall on the oaken door. The sound was unexpectedly loud and sonorous, with a reverberation almost sepulchral, and I shivered involuntarily, with a sense of startlement, of unwonted dismay. This, a moment later, was wholly dissipated when the door was thrown open and a tall, ruddy-featured monk stood before me in the cheerful glow of the cressets that illumed a capacious hallway.

"I bid you welcome to the abbey of Périgon," he said, in a suave rumble, and even as he spoke, another robed and hooded figure appeared and took my horse in charge. As I murmured my thanks and acknowledgements, the storm broke and tremendous gusts of rain, accompanied by ever-nearing peals of thunder, drove with demoniac fury on the door that had closed behind me.

"It is fortunate that you found us when you did," observed my host. " 'Twere ill for man and beast to be abroad in such a hell-brew."

Divining without question that I was hungry as well as tired, he led me to the refectory and set before me a bountiful meal of mutton, brown bread, lentils, and a strong excellent red wine.

He sat opposite me at the refectory table while I ate, and, with my hunger a little mollified, I took occasion to scan him more attentively. He was both tall and stoutly built, and his features, where the brow was no less broad than the powerful jaw, betokened intellect as well as a love for good living. A certain delicacy and refinement, an air of scholarship, of good taste and good breeding, emanated from him, and I thought to myself: "This monk is probably a connoisseur of books as well as of wines." Doubtless my expression betrayed the quickening of my curiosity, for he said, as if in answer:

"I am Hilaire, the abbot of Périgon. We are a Benedictine order, who live in amity with God and with all men, and we do not hold that the spirit is to be enriched by the mortification or impoverishment of the body. We have in our butteries an abundance of wholesome fare, in our cellars the best and oldest vintages of the district of Averoigne. And, if such things interest you, as mayhap they do, we have a library that is stocked with rare tomes, with precious manuscripts, with the finest works of heathendom and Christendom, even to certain unique writings that survived the holocaust of Alexandria."

"I appreciate your hospitality," I said, bowing. "I am Christophe Morand, a law-student, on my way home from Tours to my father's estate near Moulins. I, too, am a lover of books, and nothing would delight me more than the privilege of inspecting a library so rich and curious as the one whereof you speak."

Forthwith, while I finished my meal, we fell to discussing the classics, and to quoting and capping passages from Latin, Greek, or Christian authors. My host, I soon discovered, was a scholar of uncommon attainments, with an erudition, a ready familiarity with both ancient and modern literature that made my own seem as that of the merest beginner by comparison. He, on his part, was so good as to commend my far from perfect Latin, and by the time I had emptied my bottle of red wine we were chatting familiarly like old friends.

All my fatigue had now flown, to be succeeded by a rare sense of well-being, of physical comfort combined with mental alertness and keenness. So, when the abbot suggested that we pay a visit to the library, I assented with alacrity.

He led me down a long corridor, on each side of which were cells belonging to the brothers of the order, and unlocked, with a large brazen key that depended from his girdle, the door of a great room with lofty ceiling and several deep-set windows. Truly, he had not exaggerated the resources of the library; for the long shelves were overcrowded with books, and many volumes were piled high on the tables or stacked in corners. There were rolls of papyrus, of parchment, of vellum; there were strange Byzantine or Coptic bibles; there were old Arabic and Persian manuscripts with floriated or jewel-studded covers; there were scores of incunabula from the first printing presses; there were innumerable monkish copies of antique authors, bound in wood or ivory, with rich illuminations and lettering that was often in itself a work of art.

With a care that was both loving and meticulous, the abbot Hilaire brought out volume after volume for my inspection. Many of them I had never seen before; some were unknown to me even by fame or rumor. My excited interest, my unfeigned enthusiasm, evidently pleased him, for at length he pressed a hidden spring in one of the library tables and drew out a long drawer, in which, he told me, were certain treasures that he did not care to bring forth for the edification or delectation of many, and whose very existence was undreamed of by the monks.

"Here," he continued, "are three odes by Catullus which you will not find in any published edition of his works. Here, also, is an original manuscript of Sappho—a complete copy of a poem otherwise extant only in brief fragments; here are two of the lost tales of Miletus, a letter of Pericles to Aspasia, an unknown dialogue of Plato, and an old Arabian work on astronomy, by some anonymous author, in which the theories of Copernicus are anticipated. And, lastly, here is the somewhat infamous *Histoire d'Amour,* by Bernard de Vaillantcoeur, which was destroyed immediately upon publication, and of which only one other copy is known to exist."

As I gazed with mingled awe and curiosity on the unique, unheard-of treasures he displayed, I saw in one corner of the drawer what appeared to be a thin volume with plain untitled binding of dark leather. I ventured to pick it up, and found that it contained a few sheets of closely written manuscript in old French.

"And this?" I queried, turning to look at Hilaire, whose face, to my amazement, had suddenly assumed a melancholy and troubled expression.

"It were better not to ask, my son." He crossed himself as he spoke, and his voice was no longer mellow, but harsh, agitated, full of a sorrowful perturbation. "There is a curse on the pages that you hold in your hand: an evil spell, a malign power is attached to them, and he who would venture to peruse them is henceforward in dire peril both of body and soul." He took the little volume from me as he spoke, and returned it to the drawer, again crossing himself carefully as he did so.

"But, Father," I dared to expostulate, "how can such things be? How can there be danger in a few written sheets of parchment?"

"Christophe, there are things beyond your understanding, things that it were not well for you to know. The might of Satan is manifestable in devious modes, in diverse manners; there are other temptations than those of the world and the flesh, there are evils no less subtle than irresistible, there are hidden heresies, and necromancies other than those which sorcerers practice."

"With what, then, are these pages concerned, that such occult peril, such unholy power lurks within them?"

"I forbid you to ask." His tone was one of great rigor, with a finality that dissuaded me from further questioning.

"For you, my son," he went on, "the danger would be doubly great, because you are young, ardent, full of desires and curiosities. Believe me, it is better to forget that you have even seen this manuscript." He closed the hidden drawer, and as he did so, the melancholy troubled look was replaced by his former benignity.

"Now," he said, as he turned to one of the bookshelves, "I will show you the copy of Ovid that was owned by the poet Petrarch." He was again the mellow scholar, the kindly, jovial host, and it was evident that the mysterious manuscript was not to be referred to again. But his odd perturbation, the dark and awful hints he had let fall, the vague terrific terms of his proscription, had all served to awaken my wildest curiosity, and, though I felt the obsession to be unreasonable, I was quite unable to think of anything else for the rest of the evening. All manner of speculations, fantastic, absurd, outrageous, ludicrous, terrible, defiled through my brain as I duly admired the incunabula which Hilaire took down so tenderly from the shelves for my delectation.

At last, toward midnight, he led me to my room—a room especially reserved for visitors, and with more of comfort, of actual luxury in its hangings, carpets and deeply quilted bed than was allowable in the cells of the monks or of the abbot himself. Even when Hilaire had withdrawn, and I had proved for my satisfaction the softness of the bed allotted me, my brain still whirled with questions concerning the forbidden manuscript. Though the storm had now ceased, it was long before I fell asleep; but slumber, when it finally came, was dreamless and profound.

When I awoke, a river of sunshine clear as molten gold was pouring through my window. The storm had wholly vanished, and no lightest tatter of cloud was visible anywhere in the pale-blue October heavens. I ran to the window and peered out on a world of autumnal forest and fields all a-sparkle with the diamonds of rain. All was beautiful, all was idyllic to a degree that could be fully appreciated only by one who had lived for a long time, as I had, within the walls of a city, with towered buildings in lieu of trees and cobbled pavements where grass should be. But, charming as it was, the foreground held my gaze only for a few moments; then, beyond the tops of the trees, I saw a hill, not more than a mile distant, on whose summit there stood the ruins of some old château, the crumbling, broken-down condition of whose walls and towers was plainly visible. It drew my gaze irresistibly, with an overpowering sense of romantic attraction, which somehow seemed so natural, so inevitable, that I did not pause to analyze or wonder; and once having seen it, I could not take my eyes away, but lingered at the window for how long I knew not, scrutinizing as closely as I could the details of each time-shaken turret and bastion. Some undefinable fascination was inherent in the very form, the extent, the disposition of the pile—some fascination not dissimilar to that exerted by a strain of music, by a magical combination of words in poetry, by the features of a beloved face. Gazing, I lost myself in reveries that I could not recall afterwards, but which left behind them the same tantalizing sense of innominable delight which forgotten nocturnal dreams may sometimes leave.

I was recalled to the actualities of life by a gentle knock at my door, and realized that I had forgotten to dress myself. It was the abbot, who came to inquire how I had passed the night, and to tell me that breakfast was ready whenever I should care to arise. For some reason, I felt a little embarrassed, even shamefaced, to have been caught day-dreaming; and, though this was doubtless unnecessary, I apologized for my dilatoriness. Hilaire, I thought, gave me a keen, inquiring look, which was quickly withdrawn, as, with the suave courtesy of a good host, he assured me that there was nothing whatever for which I need apologize.

When I had breakfasted, I told Hilaire, with many expressions of gratitude for his hospitality, that it was time for me to resume my journey. But his regret at the announcement of my departure was so unfeigned, his invitation to tarry for at least another night was so genuinely hearty, so sincerely urgent, that I consented to remain. In truth, I required no great amount of solicitation, for, apart from the real liking I had taken to Hilaire, the mystery of the forbidden manuscript had entirely enslaved my imagination, and I was loath to leave without having learned more concerning it. Also, for a youth with scholastic leanings, the freedom of the abbot's library was a rare privilege, a precious opportunity not to be passed over.

"I should like," I said, "to pursue certain studies while I am here, with the aid of your incomparable collection."

"My son, you are more than welcome to remain for any length of time, and you can have access to my books whenever it suits your need or inclination." So saying, Hilaire detached the key of the library from his girdle and gave it to me. "There are duties," he went on, "which will call me away from the monastery for a few hours today, and doubtless you will desire to study in my absence."

A little later, he excused himself and departed. With inward felicitations on the longed-for opportunity that had fallen so readily into my hands, I hastened to the library, with no thought save to read the proscribed manuscript. Giving scarcely a glance at the laden shelves, I sought the table with the secret drawer, and fumbled for the spring. After a little anxious delay, I pressed the proper spot and drew forth the drawer. An impulsion that had become a veritable obsession, a fever of curiosity that bordered upon actual madness, drove me, and if the safety of my soul had really depended upon it, I could not have denied the desire which forced me to take from the drawer the thin volume with plain unlettered binding.

Seating myself in a chair near one of the windows, I began to peruse the pages, which were only six in number. The writing was peculiar, with letter-forms of a fantasticality I had never met before, and the French was not only old but well-nigh barbarous in its quaint singularity. Notwithstanding the difficulty I found in deciphering them, a mad, unaccountable thrill ran through me at the first words, and I read on with all the sensations of a man who had been bewitched or who had drunken a philter of bewildering potency.

There was no title, no date, and the writing was a narrative which began almost as abruptly as it ended. It concerned one Gérard, Comte de Venteillon, who, on the eve of his marriage to the renowned and beautiful demoiselle, Eléanor des Lys, had met in the forest near his château a strange, half-human creature with hoofs and horns. Now Gérard, as the narrative explained, was a knightly youth of indisputably proven valor, as well as a true Christian; so in the name of our Savior, Jesus Christ, he bade the creature stand and give an account of itself.

Laughing wildly in the twilight, the bizarre being capered before him, and cried:

"I am a satyr, and your Christ is less to me than the weeds that grow on your kitchen-middens."

Appalled by such blasphemy, Gérard would have drawn his sword to slay the creature, but again it cried, saying:

"Stay, Gérard de Venteillon, and I will tell you a secret, knowing which, you will forget the worship of Christ, and forget your beautiful bride of tomorrow, and turn your back on the world and on the very sun itself with no reluctance and no regret."

Now, albeit half-unwillingly, Gérard lent the satyr an ear and it came closer and whispered to him. And that which it whispered is not known; but before it vanished amid the blackening shadows of the forest, the satyr spoke aloud once more, and said:

"The power of Christ has prevailed like a black frost on all the woods, the fields, the rivers, the mountains, where abode in their felicity the glad, immortal goddesses and nymphs of yore. But still, in the cryptic caverns of earth, in places far underground, like the hell your priests have fabled, there dwells the pagan loveliness, there cry the pagan ecstasies." And with the last words, the creature laughed again its wild unhuman laugh, and disappeared among the darkening boles of the twilight trees.

From that moment, a change was upon Gérard de Venteillon. He returned to his château with downcast mien, speaking no cheery or kindly word to his retainers, as was his wont, but sitting or pacing always in silence, and scarcely heeding the food that was set before him. Nor did he go that evening to visit his betrothed, as he had promised; but, toward midnight, when a waning moon had arisen red as from a bath of blood, he went forth clandestinely by the postern door of the château, and following an old, half-obliterated trail through the woods, found his way to the ruins of the Château des Faussesflammes, which stands on a hill opposite the Benedictine abbey of Périgon.

Now these ruins (said the manuscript) are very old, and have long been avoided by the people of the district; for a legendry of immemorial evil clings about them, and it is said that they are the dwelling-place of foul spirits, the rendezvous of sorcerers and succubi. But Gérard, as if oblivious or fearless of their ill renown, plunged like one who is devil-driven into the shadow of the crumbling walls, and went, with the careful groping of a man who follows some given direction, to the northern end of the courtyard. There, directly between and below the two centermost windows, which, it may be, looked forth from the chamber of forgotten châtelaines, he pressed with his right foot on a flagstone differing from those about it in being of a triangular form. And the flagstone moved and tilted beneath his foot, revealing a flight of granite steps that went down into the earth. Then, lighting a taper he had brought with him, Gérard descended the steps, and the flagstone swung into place behind him.

On the morrow, his betrothed, Eléanor des Lys, and all her bridal train, waited vainly for him at the cathedral of Vyônes, the principal town of Averoigne, where the wedding had been set. And from that time his face was beheld by no man, and no vaguest rumor of Gérard de Venteillon or of the fate that befell him has ever passed among the living. . . .

Such was the substance of the forbidden manuscript, and thus it ended. As I have said before, there was no date, nor was there anything to indicate by whom it had been written or how the knowledge of the happenings related had come into the writer's possession. But, oddly enough, it did not occur to me to doubt their veracity for a moment; and the curiosity I had felt concerning the contents of the manuscript was now replaced by a burning desire, a thousandfold more powerful, more obsessive, to know the ending of the story and to learn what Gérard de Venteillon had found when he descended the hidden steps.

In reading the tale, it had of course occurred to me that the ruins of the Château des Faussesflammes, described therein, were the very same ruins I had seen that morning from my chamber window; and pondering this, I became more and more possessed by an insane fever, by a frenetic, unholy excitement. Returning the manuscript to the secret drawer, I left the library and wandered for awhile in an aimless fashion about the corridors of the monastery. Chancing to meet there the same monk who had taken my horse in charge the previous evening, I ventured to question him, as discreetly and casually as I could, regarding the ruins which were visible from the abbey windows.

He crossed himself, and a frightened look came over his broad, placid face at my query.

"The ruins are those of the Château des Faussesflammes," he replied. "For untold years, men say, they have been the haunt of unholy spirits, of witches and demons; and festivals not to be described or even named are held within their walls. No weapon known to man, no exorcism or holy water, has ever prevailed against these demons; many brave cavaliers and monks have disappeared amid the shadows of Faussesflammes, never to return; and once, it is told, an abbot of Périgon went thither to make war on the powers of evil; but what befell him at the hands of the succubi is not known or conjectured. Some say that the demons are abominable hags whose bodies terminate in serpentine coils; others, that they are women of more than mortal beauty, whose kisses are a diabolic delight that consumes the flesh of men with the fierceness of hellfire. . . . As for me, I know not whether such tales are true; but I should not care to venture within the walls of Faussesflammes."

Before he had finished speaking, a resolve had sprung to life full-born in my mind: I felt that I must go to the Château des Faussesflammes and learn for myself, if possible, all that could be learned. The impulse was immediate, overwhelming, ineluctable; and even if I had so desired, I could no more have fought against it than if I had been the victim of some sorcerer's invultuation. The proscription of the abbot Hilaire, the strange unfinished tale in the old manuscript, the evil legendry at which the monk had now hinted—all these, it would seem, should have served to frighten and deter me from such a resolve; but, on the contrary, by some bizarre inversion of thought, they seemed to conceal some delectable mystery, to denote a hidden world of ineffable things, of vague undreamable pleasures that set my brain on fire and made my pulses throb deliriously. I did not know, I could not conceive, of what these pleasures would consist; but in some mystical manner I was as sure of their ultimate reality as the abbot Hilaire was sure of heaven.

I determined to go that very afternoon, in the absence of Hilaire, who, I felt instinctively, might be suspicious of any such intention on my part and would surely be inimical toward its fulfillment.

My preparations were very simple: I put in my pockets a small taper from my room and the heel of a loaf of bread from the refectory; and making sure that a little dagger which I always carried was in its sheath, I left the monastery forthwith. Meeting two of the brothers in the courtyard, I told them I was going for a short walk in the neighboring woods. They gave me a jovial "*pax vobiscum*" and went upon their way in the spirit of the words.

Heading as directly as I could for Faussesflammes, whose turrets were often lost behind the high and interlacing boughs, I entered the forest. There were no paths, and often I was compelled to brief detours and divagations by the thickness of the underbrush. In my feverous hurry to reach the ruins, it seemed hours before I came to the top of the hill which Faussesflammes surmounted, but probably it was little more than thirty minutes. Climbing the last declivity of the boulder-strewn slope, I came suddenly within view of the château, standing close at hand in the center of the level table which formed the summit. Trees had taken root in its broken-down walls, and the ruinous gateway that gave on the courtyard was half-choked by bushes, brambles and nettle-plants. Forcing my way through, not without difficulty, and with clothing that had suffered from the bramble-thorns, I went, like Gérard de Venteillon in the old manuscript, to the northern end of the court. Enormous evil-looking weeds were rooted between the flagstones, rearing their thick and fleshy leaves that had turned to dull sinister maroons and purples with the onset of autumn. But I soon found the triangular flagstone indicated in the tale, and without the slightest delay or hesitation I pressed upon it with my right foot.

A mad shiver, a thrill of adventurous triumph that was mingled with something of trepidation, leaped through me when the great flagstone tilted easily beneath my foot, disclosing dark steps of granite, even as in the story. Now, for a moment, the vaguely hinted horrors of the monkish legends became imminently real in my imagination, and I paused before the black opening that was to engulf me, wondering if some Satanic spell had not drawn me thither to perils of unknown terror and inconceivable gravity.

Only for a few instants, however, did I hesitate. Then the sense of peril faded, the monkish horrors became a fantastic dream, and the charm of things unformulable, but ever closer at hand, always more readily attainable, tightened about me like the embrace of amorous arms. I lit my taper, I descended the stair; and even as behind Gérard de Venteillon, the triangular block of stone silently resumed its place in the paving of the court above me. Doubtless it was moved by some mechanism operable by a man's weight on one of the steps; but I did not pause to consider its *modus operandi*, or to wonder if there were any way by which it could be worked from beneath to permit my return.

There were perhaps a dozen steps, terminating in a low, narrow, musty vault that was void of anything more substantial than ancient, dust-encumbered cobwebs. At the end, a small doorway admitted me to a second vault that differed from the first only in being larger and dustier. I passed through several such vaults, and then found myself in a long passage or tunnel, half-blocked in places by boulders or heaps of rubble that had fallen from the crumbling sides. It was very damp, and full of the noisome odor of stagnant waters and subterranean mould. My feet splashed more than once in little pools, and drops fell upon me from above, fetid and foul as if they had oozed from a charnel. Beyond the wavering circle of light that my taper maintained, it seemed to me that the coils of dim and shadowy serpents slithered away in the darkness at my approach; but I could not be sure whether they really were serpents, or only the troubled and retreating shadows, seen by an eye that was still unaccustomed to the gloom of the vaults.

Rounding a sudden turn in the passage, I saw the last thing I had dreamt of seeing—the gleam of sunlight at what was apparently the tunnel's end. I scarcely knew what I had expected to find, but such an eventuation was somehow altogether unanticipated. I hurried on, in some confusion of thought, and stumbled through the opening, to find myself blinking in the full rays of the sun.

Even before I had sufficiently recovered my wits and my eyesight to take note of the landscape before me, I was struck by a strange circumstance: Though it had been early afternoon when I entered the vaults, and though my passage through them could have been a matter of no more than a few minutes, the sun was now nearing the horizon. There was also a difference in its light, which was both brighter and mellower than the sun I had seen above Averoigne; and the sky itself was intensely blue, with no hint of autumnal pallor.

Now, with ever-increasing stupefaction, I stared about me, and could find nothing familiar or even credible in the scene upon which I had emerged. Contrary to all reasonable expectation, there was no semblance of the hill upon which Faussesflammes stood, or of the adjoining country; but around me was a placid land of rolling meadows, through which a golden-gleaming river meandered toward a sea of deepest azure that was visible beyond the tops of the laurel-trees. . . . But there are no laurel-trees in Averoigne, and the sea is hundreds of miles away: judge, then, my complete confusion and dumbfoundment.

It was a scene of such loveliness as I have never before beheld. The meadow-grass at my feet was softer and more lustrous than emerald velvet, and was full of violets and many-colored asphodels. The dark green of ilex-trees was mirrored in the golden river, and far away I saw the pale gleam of a marble acropolis on a low summit above the plain. All things bore the aspect of a mild and clement spring that was verging upon an opulent summer. I felt as if I had stepped into a land of classic myth, of Grecian legend; and moment by moment, all surprise, all wonder as to how I could have come there, was drowned in a sense of ever-growing ecstasy before the utter, ineffable beauty of the landscape.

Nearby, in a laurel-grove, a white roof shone in the late rays of the sun. I was drawn toward it by the same allurement, only far more potent and urgent, which I had felt on seeing the forbidden manuscript and the ruins of Faussesflammes. Here, I knew with an esoteric certainty, was the culmination of my quest, the reward of all my mad and perhaps impious curiosity.

As I entered the grove, I heard laughter among the trees, blending harmoniously with the low murmur of their leaves in a soft, balmy wind. I thought I saw vague forms that melted among the boles at my approach; and once a shaggy, goat-like creature with human head and body ran across my path, as if in pursuit of a flying nymph.

In the heart of the grove, I found a marble palace with a portico of Doric columns. As I neared it, I was greeted by two women in the costume of ancient slaves; and though my Greek is of the meagerest, I found no difficulty whatever, in comprehending their speech, which was of Attic purity.

"Our mistress, Nycea, awaits you," they told me. I could no longer marvel at anything, but accepted my situation without question or surmise, like one who resigns himself to the progress of some delightful dream. Probably, I thought, it was a dream, and I was still lying in my bed at the monastery; but never before had I been favored by nocturnal visions of such clarity and surpassing loveliness. The interior of the palace was full of a luxury that verged upon the barbaric, and which evidently belonged to the period of Greek decadence, with its intermingling of Oriental influences. I was led through a hallway gleaming with onyx and polished porphyry, into an opulently furnished room, where, on a couch of gorgeous fabrics, there reclined a woman of goddess-like beauty.

At sight of her, I trembled from head to foot with the violence of a strange emotion. I had heard of the sudden mad loves by which men are seized on beholding for the first time a certain face and form; but never before had I experienced a passion of such intensity, such all-consuming ardor, as the one I conceived immediately for this woman. Indeed, it seemed as if I had loved her for a long time, without knowing that it was she whom I loved, and without being able to identify the nature of my emotion or to orient the feeling in any manner.

She was not tall, but was formed with exquisite voluptuous purity of line and contour. Her eyes were of a dark sapphire blue, with molten depths into which the soul was fain to plunge as into the soft abysses of a summer ocean. The curve of her lips was enigmatic, a little mournful, and gravely tender as the lips of an antique Venus. Her hair, brownish rather than blonde, fell over her neck and ears and forehead in delicious ripples confined by a plain fillet of silver. In her expression, there was a mixture of pride and voluptuousness, of regal imperiousness and feminine yielding. Her movements were all as effortless and graceful as those of a serpent.

"I knew you would come," she murmured in the same soft-vowelled Greek I had heard from the lips of her servants. "I have waited for you long; but when you sought refuge from the storm in the abbey of Périgon, and saw the manuscript in the secret drawer, I knew that the hour of your arrival was at hand. Ah! you did not dream that the spell which drew you so irresistibly, with such unaccountable potency, was the spell of my beauty, the magical allurement of my love!"

"Who are you?" I queried. I spoke readily in Greek, which would have surprised me greatly an hour before. But now, I was prepared to accept anything whatever, no matter how fantastic or preposterous, as part of the miraculous fortune, the unbelievable adventure which had befallen me.

"I am Nycea," she replied to my question. "I love you, and the hospitality of my palace and of my arms is at your disposal. Need you know anything more?"

The slaves had disappeared. I flung myself beside the couch and kissed the hand she offered me, pouring out protestations that were no doubt incoherent, but were nevertheless full of an ardor that made her smile tenderly.

Her hand was cool to my lips, but the touch of it fired my passion. I ventured to seat myself beside her on the couch, and she did not deny my familiarity. While a soft purple twilight began to fill the corners of the chamber, we conversed happily, saying over and over again all the sweet absurd litanies, all the felicitous nothings that come instinctively to the lips of lovers. She was incredibly soft in my arms, and it seemed almost as if the completeness of her yielding was unhindered by the presence of bones in her lovely body.

The servants entered noiselessly, lighting rich lamps of intricately carven gold, and setting before us a meal of spicy meats, of unknown savorous fruits and potent wines. But I could eat little, and while I drank, I thirsted for the sweeter wine of Nycea's mouth.

I do not know when we fell asleep; but the evening had flown like an enchanted moment. Heavy with felicity, I drifted off on a silken tide of drowsiness, and the golden lamps and the face of Nycea blurred in a blissful mist and were seen no more.

Suddenly, from the depths of a slumber beyond all dreams, I found myself compelled into full wakefulness. For an instant, I did not even realize where I was, still less what had aroused me. Then I heard a footfall in the open doorway of the room, and peering across the sleeping head of Nycea, saw in the lamplight the abbot Hilaire, who had paused on the threshold. A look of absolute horror was imprinted upon his face, and as he caught sight of me, he began to gibber in Latin, in tones where something of fear was blended with fanatical abhorrence and hatred. I saw that he carried in his hands a large bottle and an aspergillum. I felt sure that the bottle was full of holy water, and of course divined the use for which it was intended.

Looking at Nycea, I saw that she too was awake, and knew that she was aware of the abbot's presence. She gave me a strange smile, in which I read an affectionate pity, mingled with the reassurance that a woman offers a frightened child.

"Do not fear for me," she whispered.

"Foul vampire! accursed lamia! she-serpent of hell!" thundered the abbot suddenly, as he crossed the threshold of the room, raising the aspergillum aloft. At the same moment, Nycea glided from the couch, with an unbelievable swiftness of motion, and vanished through an outer door that gave upon the forest of laurels. Her voice hovered in my ear, seeming to come from an immense distance:

"Farewell for awhile, Christophe. But have no fear. You shall find me again if you are brave and patient."

As the words ended, the holy water from the aspergillum fell on the floor of the chamber and on the couch where Nycea had lain beside me. There was a crash as of many thunders, and the golden lamps went out in a darkness that seemed full of falling dust, of raining fragments. I lost all consciousness, and when I recovered, I found myself lying on a heap of rubble in one of the vaults I had traversed earlier in the day. With a taper in his hand, and an expression of great solicitude, of infinite pity upon his face, Hilaire was stooping over me. Beside him lay the bottle and the dripping aspergillum.

"I thank God, my son, that I found you in good time," he said. "When I returned to the abbey this evening and learned that you were gone, I surmised all that had happened. I knew you had read the accursed manuscript in my absence, and had fallen under its baleful spell, as have so many others, even to a certain reverend abbot, one of my predecessors. All of them, alas! beginning hundreds of years ago with Gérard de Venteillon, have fallen victims to the lamia who dwells in these vaults."

"The lamia?" I questioned, hardly comprehending his words.

"Yes, my son, the beautiful Nycea who lay in your arms this night is a lamia, an ancient vampire, who maintains in these noisome vaults her palace of beatific illusions. How she came to take up her abode at Faussesflammes is not known, for her coming antedates the memory of men. She is old as paganism; the Greeks knew her; she was exorcised by Apollonius of Tyana; and if you could behold her as she really is, you would see, in lieu of her voluptuous body, the folds of a foul and monstrous serpent. All those whom she loves and admits to her hospitality, she devours in the end, after she has drained them of life and vigor with the diabolic delight of her kisses. The laurel-wooded plain you saw, the ilex-bordered river, the marble palace and all the luxury therein, were no more than a Satanic delusion, a lovely bubble that arose from the dust and mould of immemorial death, of ancient corruption. They crumbled at the kiss of the holy water I brought with me when I followed you. But Nycea, alas! has escaped, and I fear she will still survive, to build again her palace of demoniacal enchantments, to commit again and again the unspeakable abomination of her sins."

Still in a sort of stupor at the ruin of my new-found happiness, at the singular revelations made by the abbot, I followed him obediently as he led the way through the vaults of Faussesflammes. He mounted the stairway by which I had descended, and as he neared the top and was forced to stoop a little, the great flagstone swung upward, letting in a stream of chill moonlight. We emerged, and I permitted him to take me back to the monastery.

As my brain began to clear, and the confusion into which I had been thrown resolved itself, a feeling of resentment grew apace—a keen anger at the interference of Hilaire. Unheedful whether or not he had rescued me from dire physical and spiritual perils, I lamented the beautiful dream of which he had deprived me. The kisses of Nycea burned softly in my memory, and I knew that whatever she was, woman or demon or serpent, there was no one in all the world who could ever arouse in me the same love and the same delight. I took care, however, to conceal my feelings from Hilaire, realizing that a betrayal of such emotions would merely lead him to look upon me as a soul that was lost beyond redemption.

On the morrow, pleading the urgency of my return home, I departed from Périgon. Now, in the library of my father's house near Moulins, I write this account of my adventures. The memory of Nycea is magically clear, ineffably dear as if she were still beside me, and still I see the rich draperies of a midnight chamber illumined by lamps of curiously carven gold, and still I hear the words of her farewell:

"Have no fear. You shall find me again if you are brave and patient."

Soon I shall return, to visit again the ruins of the Château des Faussesflammes, and redescend into the vaults below the triangular flagstone. But, in spite of the nearness of Périgon to Faussesflammes, in spite of my esteem for the abbot, my gratitude for his hospitality, and my admiration for his incomparable library, I shall not care to revisit my friend Hilaire.

To Klarkash-Ton, Lord of Averoigne

A time-black tower against dim banks of cloud;
Around its base the pathless, pressing wood.
Shadow and silence, moss and mould, enshroud
Grey, age-fell'd slabs that once as cromlechs stood.
No fall of foot, no song of bird awakes
The lethal aisles of sempiternal night,
Tho' oft with stir of wings the dense air shakes,
As in the tower there glows a pallid light.

For here, apart, dwells one whose hands have wrought
Strange eidola that chill the world with fear;
Whose graven runes in tones of dread have taught
What things beyond the star-gulfs lurk and leer.
Dark Lord of Averoigne—whose windows stare
On pits of dream no other gaze could bear!

—H. P. LOVECRAFT

Averoigne: An Afterword

By putting *The Averoigne Chronicles* together, Ronald Hilger in the immediate editorial tradition of Lin Carter has rendered a genuine and singularly creative service not only to the Klarkash-Tonophiles, the solid core of Clark Ashton Smith aficionados here and abroad, as well as to the specialist audience consisting of the devotees of fantasy and science fiction, but just as much to the general reading public, especially those individuals who value modern imaginative fiction in some of its more intense manifestations. Quite unintentionally, by gathering these more or less related materials into the over-all form exhibited here, Ronald Hilger has come up with something that is very much like a novel or a romance, a development that neither he nor his editorial precursor could have anticipated. Such an historic achievement as this collection represents deserves not only to be generally noticed but also to be signalized and even celebrated.

The late Lin Carter certainly takes an eminent rank among the other notable Klarkash-Tonophile connoisseurs of the latter half of the twentieth century, as witness the series of four Ballantine paperbacks made up of the writings of Clark Ashton Smith that he compiled and edited. During his extensive and fruitful career as a poet, a writer, a general man of letters, and above all else as an editor, Carter often expressed a certain enthusiastic desire in person, and at least a number of times in print while he was editor in chief of the Adult Fantasy Series published by Ballantine Books. Although he expressed it in a slightly different way, the essence of this desire was that he very much wanted to read an authentic novel by Ashton Smith as a master of perfervid imagination and polyphonic prose, that is, as a master of certain unique gifts in prose fiction, especially as exemplified in the genre(s) of the short story and the novelette. Moreover, Lin Carter astutely reckoned that, had Ashton Smith written (and finished, we should probably add) such a novel worthy of his best abilities in prose, something rare and choice might very well have resulted—something quaint and curious that at least would have united grand melodramatics and magnificent outré pageantry with pungent grotesquery—and thus, in rarity and choiceness, something comparable to the definitely unorthodox *History of the Caliph Vathek* by William Beckford, or the historical romance *Salammbô* by Gustave Flaubert.

Sometime between his early and late adolescence, Smith did in fact write and apparently complete a number of long novels laid in that particular Orient (at once real and mythical) revealed by, and extrapolated from, *The Thousand and One Nights*, one of the pivotal texts that had enchanted his childhood and early adolescence. Smith once described these extensive narratives of his as "long adventure novels dealing with Oriental life." In such experimental fiction as these very long and evidently rambling stories, as well as in his imitations of European fairy tales, Smith was directly learning for the first time his craft as a concoctor of make-believe, that is, as a fictioneer. Apparently only two of these early novels have survived, *The Black Diamonds*, (almost 250 pp in all) and *The Sword of Zagan*, (much shorter at just over 100 pp). Technically, however, such early work ranks, of course, as juvenilia, and apart from such overt as well as latent tendencies as they may disclose in anticipation of those of the adult fictioneer, this early work has no particular importance or interest except for specialist scholars. Certainly, upon attaining his maturity as an active fictioneer during the early and middle 1930s, their author never wanted or anticipated their serious publication!

In a different class from his acknowledged juvenilia are such novelettes as he produced in the 1930s as "The City of the Singing Flame," "The Ice-Demon," "The Dark Eidolon," "The Letter from Mohaun

Los," "The Monster of the Prophecy," and many others, including as well "The Colossus of Ylourgne," collected herein as the single longest of *The Averoigne Chronicles*. These are not only some of his longest and most characteristic adult fiction, but they are also some of his best and most original work. Still, these and other similarly long tales are only novelettes, and still are not full-length novels. However, Smith did leave behind him at his death one unpublished and unfinished novel which emerged, like the stories just cited, as a product of the 1930s, his busiest and most creative period as a fictioneer. This fragment was *The Infernal Star*, comprising c. 12,000 words (Smith's own estimate), begun and completed in February 1933. Its author had originally conceived it as a book-length fantasy novel, and he once reckoned that he had at least achieved one third or one half of the over-all work. He had first planned the novel as a serial for *Weird Tales*, but when the magazine's editor Farnsworth Wright discouraged him in this plan, he then put it aside indefinitely. Much later, Smith considered finishing it; this was during the late 1950s. Apparently by means of the regular postal service, he showed it as it was to August Derleth in February 1958 in the hope of its eventual publication by Arkham House, which had become Smith's book publisher starting in 1942. It would have thus appeared either as a separate book or as part of one of the ongoing series of Smith's hard-cover collections. However, these tentative plans also came to nothing, and by the time of Smith's death in August 1961 the fragment remained unpublished, and apparently more or less as the author had left it almost thirty years before.

When the unfinished novel was finally gathered into *Strange Shadows* (Greenwood Press, 1989), a final but final collection of hitherto unpublished fiction and miscellanea by Smith, Steve Behrends as editor well summed it up as "an unfinished novelette [sic] that expertly mingles elements of fantasy, horror, and science fiction." Even though the work is in fact a novel, albeit in fragmentary form, and even though it does have a certain originality about it, *The Infernal Star* would still not answer, anymore than would his juvenile novels, to Lin Carter's desire or expectation of an exotic and idiosyncratic novel by Smith of the type either of *Vathek* or of *Salammbô*. However, on the other hand, the present volume might possibly have satisfied Carter's wish. As gathered and arranged by Ronald Hilger more or less chronologically (that is, according to the inner chronology of the individual tales), *The Averoigne Chronicles* in their present embodiment does indeed shape up into what is possibly the closest thing that we shall ever have to an authentic novel by Ashton Smith. Explicitly, by including, and even having the stories open with, the virtual prose-poem "A Night in Malnéant"—a tale closely related in theme, atmosphere, and mood (and apparently even geography) to the narratives concerning Averoigne—Ronald Hilger has greatly enriched and extended the tone, concept, and feeling of this collection, and has heightened even further its resemblance to a novel or a romance, especially as interspersed with poems in verse or in prose, most of them by Smith—poems chiefly of a mediaeval flavor or imagery—carefully selected to echo, reflect, or comment upon, sometimes ironically, the stories in whose proximity they appear.

Even if it does nothing else, the present compilation—with its more or less alternating sections of verse and prose, its narratives long, short, or middling, as well as major or minor—does at least rather strongly resemble one of those multifarious bodies of lore favored for narrative use during the Middle Ages. Mediaeval storytellers were accustomed to utilize subjects or themes from three principal bodies of narrative material. *The Matière de Rome*, or *Matter of Rome*, included subjects from Roman and Greek history, as well as mythology, embracing (among other things) Thebes in Greece, the Trojan War, and Alexander the Great, especially his presumed fantastic adventures in India. *The Matière de France*, or *Matter of France*, concerned itself mainly with Charlemagne and those of his knights, such as Roland, revolving around the court of that monarch, first as King of the Franks and later as the first Holy Roman Emperor. *The Matière de Bretagne*, or *Matter of Britain*, involved itself, of course, with King Arthur and his Knights of the Round Table, Arthur having been transformed by this time into another Charlemagne thanks to Geoffrey of Monmouth's monumental Historia Regum Britanniae. However, as this last body of lore developed into its most characteristic form, it concerned itself above all with the machinations and amours of Lancelot and Guinevere, Tristan and Yseult, and other lovers. Indeed, it was primarily from such stories as these last ones, as well as from the poetic activity of the troubadours and trouvères, that our modern concept of romance first emerged and crystallized. The present Chroniques d'Averoigne seems to hint at an apparently otherwise unknown, forgotten, or overlooked *Matière d'Averonne*, or *Matter of Averoigne*.

But can this compilation indeed technically qualify as a novel? That would obviously depend on how we define the form. First, we must peremptorily dismiss from our minds the concept of the evolved modern literary novel of the twentieth century; such has absolutely no relevance or application here. We must return instead either to the ancient Mediterranean world or, more appositely, to the Middle Ages for the more appropriate models that might have influenced Ashton Smith, however vaguely, and even if he himself might not have been consciously thinking of them in quite the same terms as indicated by our present discussion. If we define the novel in terms of its original and historically most fundamental form—which in brief is simply that of a genuinely long piece of fiction, whether in verse or in prose—then, yes, this collection can qualify in some sense as a kind of novel, not so much a novel of one person or of several persons, but rather a novel of a specific place or an over-all region. We must not forget that, whether cast in verse or in prose, the mediaeval epics and romances, as well as the epics and romances of the Renaissance which succeeded them, were in fact the direct precursors of the modern novel, overtly literary or not.

Unexpectedly, and almost paradoxically, *The Averoigne Chronicles* as a concept emerges with a greater degree of cohesion than what the original author himself may have consciously thought possible, or than what the material itself may have promised, or may have seemed inherently to possess before being put into this more coherent form, even if that very, and more ample, cohesion may seem, at least at first consideration, to be the result of mere happenstance. After all, one form or shape or arrangement of the material is as good as another, and surely it is the substance that is important, at least more so than the form—or are they?! Considered as a novel—in the present case as an explicit or implicit over-all narrative frame or structure as embodied and developed in a series of highly diverting and original tales or episodes taking place over a long historical period—*The Averoigne Chronicles* thus becomes the story or history of a French province apparently otherwise unknown to orthodox culture and chronology.

Undeniably, even if perceived as the result of seeming happenstance, the present arrangement of *The Averoigne Chronicles* still possesses a greater cohesion and, equally important, a greater variety than those possessed by Lin Carter's own editions of Smith's prose tales of a similar nature, that is, *Zothique* (1970), *Hyperborea* (1971), *Xiccarph* (1972), and *Poseidonis* (1973). We may well ask why this should be so, and why *The Averoigne Chronicles* should succeed in this way to a greater degree than what those previous volumes have done.

We know from his letters to his fellow scriveners of the 1930's, as well as from *The Black Book*, the notebook that he used from the late 1920's until his death in 1961, that Ashton Smith obviously intended at one time to gather in an appropriate manner his various series of tales laid in certain general ambiances. In *The Black Book* we find these titles with attendant lists of stories for such seriously proposed collections as *The Book of Hyperborea, Tales of Zothique, Tales of Atlantis*, and *Averoigne Chronicles*. This original intention he never did accomplish, but had he done so, we may be sure that there would have been yet a further and final stage of shaping and filling in. It is quite evident that the various series of tales as now collected in various forms lack here and there obviously needed echoes as well as entire sequels to previous and often monstrous events, something that probably would only have become apparent once Ashton Smith had gotten the various series up to this final stage. Also, at the same time, he might then have perceived the equally obvious need of an even greater variety of theme and content than what the divers materials already possessed, and might then have supplied such an evident deficiency. We may regret that for whatever reason he never did thus gather the relevant stories and shape them into the appropriate overall forms that he might have done. We can only speculate as to what he might have made of them in an over-all sense, and furthermore, in the case of *The Averoigne Chronicles*, exactly into what kind of potentially glamourous composite he might well have transformed them.

Why then does an Averoigne volume possess at once a greater cohesion and a greater variety than those put together by Lin Carter? Why is it that, in the specific case of *The Averoigne Chronicles*, the concept seems to function more effectively than in the case of Zothique, Hyperborea, Xiccarph, and Poseidonis? In asking such questions, we are not belittling in any way Carter's achievement with the original four paperbacks. First, there is the primary and determining nature of the geography involved. Zothique and Hyperborea are large and far-ranging continents with considerable geographical variation within the margins formed by their coastlines. Xiccarph is an entire planet (and about which Smith wrote only two stories), and Poseidonis is the last and considerable remnant of Atlantis (and about which he completed only a handful of extant stories)—a continent that, it is obvious, had originally no less geographical variation than Zothique and Hyperborea. Similarly to the present collection, the volumes Zothique and Hyperborea are presented as interconnected series according to the inner chronology of the stories involved. However, in the case of these two volumes, the tales themselves deal almost unrelentingly with doom, death, and necromancy, and when assimilated *en masse*, one right after the other, the over-all impression is one of considerably less variety of theme, content, and mood than what at first we might expect from the variegated backgrounds against which they are set. Apart from this one caveat, many of the stories are nevertheless individually outstanding, often outrageous, and startlingly original. Conversely, although not without their own structural logic, the volumes Xiccarph and Poseidonis offer for the most part an obvious variety of stories and poems to fill the collections out, and clearly have no pretention of being other than overt miscellanies of prose and verse.

As developed and presented by Ashton Smith (in manifest imitation of Auvergne), Averoigne by contrast, while still exhibiting some variety of form and feature, is nevertheless geographically, as the former Roman province of Averonia, a patently cohesive area, and represents the Massif Central, the mountainous and forested heartland not only of southern France but also of France over-all. Culturally the people living there are predominantly auvergnat, or (more properly) averoïgnat, speaking more or less the same dialect of French. But beyond the common geography, and in addition to Smith's omnipresent themes of death, loss, and necromancy, the Averoigne stories are super-romantic, patently more so than any other connected group of tales by this author, and feature love and romance in a variety of forms and appearances. Furthermore, in the instance of these especial tales, the women characters, many of whom literally are enchantresses, have obvious charm, fascination, savoir-faire, and that undeniable glamour which, in the perspective of the chief male character, the paramour, transforms the chief woman character, the enchantress, into a manifestation of the supernal and the ideal. Moreover, with all the attendant picturesqueness and grotesquery of those times, most of the extant stories take place during the long cavalcade of the Middle Ages, which is, of course, exactly when our modern, now rather generic, and curiously enduring concepts of romance and romanticism first came historically into being in all their outrageous efflorescence.

The note of supreme and uncompromising romance is struck at once by "A Night in Malnéant" as the opening story, which apparently occurs in a realm immediately contiguous to Averoigne. But beyond love and romance, and contained within the shared topography, inhering as a constant and ineluctable presence, there looms the vast and all-embracing Forest of Averoigne, concealing, revealing, interconnecting almost everything, or so it would seem, and extending from the mountains and woodlands on the north, south, east, and west all the way down to the marshes on the southeast where the now meandering Isoile, the chief river of the province, after leaving the great forest and passing through the extensive marshland, changes to the yet Lower Isoile, and ultimately flows into the yet greater Rhône.

It is perhaps incumbent on us to continue this Festschrift in that spirit of exploration, discovery, and invention so characteristic of those various "matters," or bodies of material, favored for narrative use by mediaeval storytellers. In the essence of that very spirit we should consider some of the ramifications of known French history vis-à-vis this little known French province. Due to a variety of reasons, by a miracle of historical accident, Averoigne like Auvergne was evidently spared the worst excesses of the Albigensian Crusade, which—conducted in Toulouse and Provence, among other areas, with such ferocity during the first half of the thirteenth century under the direction of Simon de Montfort—virtually destroyed not only the Albigensian heresy which had previously flourished during the eleventh, twelfth, and thirteenth centuries primarily in southern France, but also ruined the brilliant Provençal culture and lifestyle of the Middle Ages. The principal reason why Averoigne like Auvergne evaded the terrible fate meted out to Toulouse and Provence was elementary: richer and more easily accessible prizes existed elsewhere. What had started out as a religious war soon degenerated into an excuse for the princes of northern France to massacre and plunder at will, and thus to aggrandize and enrich themselves with goods and lands at the expense of the princes of southern France.

Some five hundred years or so later, again by a miracle of historical accident, Averoigne was also patently spared the worst excesses of the French Revolution during the 1790s. Likewise, it would seem, the province's great forest escaped, almost unscathed, the direst effects of the Industrial Revolution which followed. The ancient forest survived thus more or less intact into the nineteenth century, just as it does into our own time in the twentieth. Now, thanks to some enlightened legislation emanating from Paris, the major portion of the extensive forest enjoys virtual immunity as an enormous nature preserve as well as a national treasure, unique in France.

The fact and effect of this fortunate preservation vis-à-vis certain selected temperaments during the 1800's were sensitively recorded in the latter part of that century by the poet and general man of letters Gabriel d'Ysère, among other writings, in his picturesque itinerary *A Walking-Tour of Averoigne* (*Un Tour à pied d'Averoigne*, first published in Lyon, 1881; translated into English by Sir Frank T. Marzials, and published in London, 1912). A native of the town of Tournon on the west bank of the Rhône but north of the Lower Isoile, d'Ysère became fascinated with the idiosyncratic area of Averoigne to the west and northwest early on in his childhood and adolescence. As a young adult, he began recording the curious traditions and legends from Graeco-Roman antiquity and from the Middle Ages that had survived among the peasantry of Averoigne.

A Walking-Tour of Averoigne details the route followed by two youths in 1851 during the middle part of summer. They both came from the same extended family of Néanvair but, oddly enough, each from one of its two principal branches, the older and major one being centered in Lyon east of the northernmost section of Averoigne, the younger and minor one in Moulins north of the same geographic area.

The story of the itinerary taken by the two youths and its aftermath passed down to d'Ysère, among other reasons, by virtue of his own family's distant but longstanding relationship with the Néanvair branch in Lyon. The account by d'Ysère not only includes some unusually lyrical descriptions of the ancient forest, but can still serve to this day as a practical guide to the chief legendary as well as historical sites of the old province.

To what extent—if indeed any—Ashton Smith was influenced in his depiction of Averoigne by the preceding account and other writings of d'Ysère, as well as by those of other writers, has not yet been completely or even partially determined. Certainly, in regard to the over-all geography as well as the flora and fauna peculiar to the area, Smith developed and presented his conception of Averoigne in manifest imitation of Auvergne. In "The Maker of Gargoyles," the earliest extant completed story that we have in terms of the (revealed) inner chronology of the over-all cycle of tales, the poet-author adumbrates the entire locale of Averoigne in a concise but sufficient style while overtly describing just the general situation of Vyônes.

> At that time, in the year of our Lord, 1138, Vyônes was the principal town of the province of Averoigne. On two sides the great, shadow-haunted forest, a place of equivocal legends, of loups-garous and phantoms, approached to the very walls and flung its umbrage upon them at early forenoon and evening. On the other sides there lay cultivated fields, and gentle streams that meandered among willows or poplars, and roads that ran through an open plain to the high châteaux of noble lords and to regions beyond Averoigne.

This description correlates well enough with Auvergne in a general way. As borne out by other chronicles in the same series, Averoigne is quite well forested and semi-mountainous in the same fashion more or less as Auvergne is both well forested and genuinely mountainous, rather than just semi-mountainous. Both Averoigne and Auvergne obviously have oak and beech forests, usually at the lower levels, together with stands of evergreen trees, including larches and pines, usually at the higher ones. Pursuing our imaginative equation of the two areas, we should note that, apparently in the same way as Averoigne, Auvergne is rich in lakes, ponds, pools, streams, and mineral springs. Rugged mountains alternate with rolling farmlands, stark summits contrast with sprawling forests of great oaks and beeches.

We know for a fact that Ashton Smith also definitely identified, in certain respects both actual and imaginative, his own native area with Averoigne. This native area included both Long Valley and Auburn, California, together with their general surroundings, located in the lower foothills of the Sierras. The Klarkash-Tonian identification of the general Auburn area with Averoigne is not only confirmed by external evidence such as that stemming from the visits to Smith by Rah Hoffman in the early 1940's, and as recorded by the same and other visitors in various memoirs.—But the identification is also corroborated by the direct textual evidence preserved in Smith's own writings (including his personal letters), and especially (for one salient example) in such a poem as "To Howard Phillips Lovecraft," dated March 31st, 1937, and created almost immediately after H.P.L.'s death on March 15th of the same year.

> And yet thou art not gone
> Nor given wholly unto dream and dust:
> For, even upon
> This lonely western hill of Averoigne
> Thy flesh has never visited,
> I meet some wise and sentient wraith of thee,
> Some undeparting presence, gracious and august.

The imaginative equation of the Auburn area with Averoigne is also clearly borne out to some extent geographically. As regards the Auburn area's general topographical situation, rolling parklike expanses alternate with yet higher hills, fruit ranches or farms of fruit orchards alternate with stands of oaks and forests of pines. While Northern California gradually dries up during the summer and autumn until the rains arrive in the latter autumn, the weather is cool or cold and wet throughout the winter. During the rainy season and after, the land actually becomes green and lush, and while it still remains in this condition, the area could sustain a generic resemblance to Averoigne. However, unlike the mountains of Auvergne and the semi-mountains of Averoigne, the high Sierras of Northern California are still some considerable distance away, even though distinctly visible on a clear day. In a similar manner, Smith's native Auburn area has pines, larches, oaks, willows, and poplars, among other species of trees, but relatively few beeches.

In the corpus of Smith's works whether in verse or in prose—to pursue our imaginative equation of Auburn with Averoigne as a kind of generic principle of locale—Cocaigne also becomes, as does Amithaine, the imaginative equivalent of Averoigne. The landscape presented in the prose-poem "In Cocaigne" is an imaginative projection of Smith's native Auburn area. Two lovers, the poet and his sweetheart, go forth into the vertumnal forest. They pass first through a parklike area of oaks alternating with zones of vernal flowers, and then they enter the lonely woods of pine trees. There they find Cocaigne at last in each other's kiss and embrace.

In our imaginative equation of Auburn with Averoigne and other similar places, we have put considerable emphasis on woods and forest because such locations loom large in both Smith's literary and artistic output whether as physical realities or as imaginative projections or as both, whether they are Smith's own native Californian forests, the dangerous and often lethal jungles featured in Smith's own concept of Hyperborea, or the gorgeous but patently lethal woodland that overcomes the child Natha in Smith's prose-poem "The Forbidden Forest," among many other examples that we could cite. Many, if not indeed most of, Smith's extant Averoigne stories take place completely or partially in the forest or ineluctably close to it. Two of the three unwritten chronicles that now survive only in the form of plot-sketches—these two being "The Oracle of Sadoqua" and "The Sorceress of Averoigne"—also take place almost completely in the forest.

Like the mountains, the desert, or the ocean, the forest from time immemorial has almost always functioned as a prime and primordial place of adventure, whether it is perceived or presented as mercilessly forbidding or miraculously beautiful. Like Longfellow's forest primeval in Evangeline, or like Dante's dark forest, or *selva oscura* (as described in the first canto of The Divine Comedy), the ancient Forest of Averoigne is a place not only of "equivocal legends" but of an ambiguous reality as well, whether sometimes grimly threatening, or at other times gorgeously inviting, or merely curiously affording consolation. The great forest allures us with its beauty and mystery as much as it can repel or deter us with its darkness and peril, as well as with its adumbration of the unknown and the otherworldly.

As for the writer of this afterword, he is himself actively planning, as a future tourist, an imminent vacation in Averoigne, aided not only by Ronald Hilger's useful map as well as by d'Ysère's Walking-Tour of the same area, but also, and especially, by the immediate advice of a close local friend whose profession is that of travel agent. The present writer must allow at least a month for his trip, or possibly even much more than that, since there is so much to see and to do in that ancient province. He has long desired to linger among the hallowed stones making up the imposing pile, half Romanesque, half Gothic, that is the Cathedral of Vyônes. He wishes to loiter among the no less hallowed stones of the venerable Abbaye de Périgon rising not very far from Vyônes. Perhaps he will visit the village of Ste. Zénobie, or further afield, the unhallowed ruins of the Château des Faussesflammes where it dominates the level area at the top of its own hill.

Or travelling much further afield, going eastward, he might spend the day (but certainly not the night!) at the grim and ruinous mass of the Château d'Ylourgne where it still lifts up from its semi-mountainous eminence. Or crossing the valley which gives birth to the river Isoile in the form of a small stream, he might pass to the other side, and visit the Cistercian Monastery, about a mile distant from the castle. The monastery sits more or less midmost on the western slope of the valley. Here he might pause awhile and possibly say a silent prayer or two in the austere quiet of the monastery chapel, where the depredations wrought by the Colossus of Ylourgne have long since been repaired. The new stained-glass windows installed around the middle of the nineteenth century have been recently restored, and indeed look magnificent, especially at sunset and sunrise, when the light passing through them creates a kaleidoscope of shifting colors.

Then, rambling further south, along the banks of the Isoile, he will come eventually to the estate surrounding the still inhabited and superbly maintained Château de La Frênaie, and from there pass on by the Tomb of Malinbois. Perhaps he will wander on further until he reaches that inn once called the Auberge de la Bonne Jouissance, and then later the Auberge de la Haute Espérance, where he might spend the night after consuming a gourmet dinner in the excellent restaurant kept up there, accompanied by the still exceptional wines of Averoigne, especially those produced in the winecellars of La Frênaie. Or later, the next morning, crossing the main road that leads from Vyônes to Ximes, he will visit the lonely but still somehow extant Tower of Moriamis where it rises amid the dense woods of the ancient forest. Or strolling back across the road, perhaps he will ford the Isoile where it flows not far away, and then climbing some high hill, he might catch a rare glimpse of the other-dimensional Tower of Séphora sitting somewhere near the top of her demesne of Sylaire.

At last he will arrive in Ximes, where he will visit that town's very own cathedral, perhaps not as large as that of Vyônes, but surely a magnificent example of Gothic Flamboyant. Built between 1450 and 1530, it replaced the earlier Romanesque structure destroyed by fire in 1445. From there it is only a few steps to the grandiose Bishop's Palace, brought to its height of architectural splendor in the latter part of the twelfth century through the efforts of the thrice-blessèd Bishop Azédarac. Linking the palace and the cathedral is the huge mausoleum reared for the selfsame St. Azédarac, duly canonized after his death in or around 1198. Evidently it never contained his body; the local legends hint that, like the Virgin Mary, he was transported to heaven alive.

Perchance next the traveller will move on from there to spend a few days in the charming and unpretentious village of Les Hiboux, located some real distance away to the south and west of Xîmes. The village presently sits in the midst of dairy farms, and north of the extensive marshland formed by the now meandering Isoile. Then wandering north along the banks of the river, the traveller will come again to the main road that leads from Xîmes to Vyônes, and following this westward, he will arrive at the ancient *Auberge de l'Oracle*, where he will put up for the night. Then he might very well spend the better part of the next day visiting the subterranean *Caverne de St. Sodagui*, once the dread *Oraculum Sadoquae*, and a favorite spot for tourists since the days of the Romans. The entrance to the cavern lies amid the deeper woods that extend towards the mountains of southwest Averoigne, an area still relatively uninhabited.

However, most of all the present writer wishes to pass as much time as possible taking long, long walks through whatever part of the great Forest of Averoigne that he happens to find himself near.

In the vertumnal season the forest becomes a riot of burgeoning verdure and vernal color as the trees and flowers unfold or unfurl into blossom. In the autumnal season the infinitely variegated green of the forest becomes a blaze of kaleidoscopic red, orange, yellow, brown, purple, and rust. But whatever the season, the forest is ever supernally beautiful, and forms a welcome retreat away from the bustling towns.

Nevertheless, for those readers who cannot at this time actually travel to Averoigne, the present volume—whether chronicle, romance, or novel—can suffice as a source of equivalent experience. To such readers the present writer can only say: Bon voyage! He can but envy those who have picked up this volume for the first time. In the venerable tradition of the best mediaeval storytellers, Ashton Smith serves indeed as an exemplary guide to the old province of Averoigne.

—DONALD SIDNEY-FRYER

ACKNOWLEDGMENTS

"Amithaine." *Different* 7, No. 3 (Autumn 1951): 9. In *The Dark Chateau* (Arkham House, 1951).

"Averoigne." *Challenge* 1, No. 4 (Spring 1951): 6. In *The Dark Chateau* (Arkham House, 1951).

"The Beast of Averoigne." *Weird Tales* 21, No. 5 (May 1933): 628–35. In *Lost Worlds* (Arkham House, 1944). Text taken from *The Maze of the Enchanter* (Night Shade Books, 2009).

"The Broken Lute." In *Ebony and Crystal* (Auburn Journal Press, 1922).

"Cambion." In *The Dark Chateau* (Arkham House, 1951).

"Canticle." *Troubadour* 3, No. 8 (July 1931): 26. In *Selected Poems* (Arkham House, 1971).

"The Colossus of Ylourgne." *Weird Tales* 23, No. 6 (June 1934): 696–720. In *Genius Loci* (Arkham House, 1948). Text taken from *A Vintage from Atlantis* (Night Shade Books, 2007).

"The Dark Chateau." In *The Dark Chateau* (Arkham House, 1951).

"The Disinterment of Venus." *Weird Tales* 24, No. 1 (July 1934): 112–17. In *Genius Loci* (Arkham Hosue, 1948). Text taken from *The Maze of the Enchanter* (Night Shade Books, 2009).

"The Enchantress of Sylaire." *Weird Tales* 35, No. 10 (July 1941): 25–34. In *The Abominations of Yondo* (Arkham House, 1960). Text taken from *The Last Hieroglyph* (Night Shade Books, 2010).

"The End of the Story." *Weird Tales* 15, No. 5 (May 1930): 637–48. In *Out of Space and Time*. Text taken from *The End of the Story* (Night Shade Books 2006).

"The Holiness of Azédarac." *Weird Tales* 22, No. 5 (November 1933): 594–607. In *Lost Worlds* (Arkham House, 1944). Text taken from *A Vintage from Atlantis* (Night Shade Books, 2007).

"In Cocaigne." In *Ebony and Crystal* (Auburn Journal Press, 1922).

"The Maker of Gargoyles." *Weird Tales* 20, No. 2 (August 1932): 198–207. In *Tales of Science and Sorcery* (Arkham House, 1964). Text taken from *A Vintage from Atlantis* (Night Shade Books, 2007).

"The Mandrakes." *Weird Tales* 21, No. 2 (February 1933): 254–59. In *Other Dimensions* (Arkham House, 1970). Text taken from *The Maze of the Enchanter* (Night Shade Books, 2009).

"Mother of Toads." *Weird Tales* 32, No. 1 (July 1938): 86–90. In *Tales of Science and Sorcery* (Arkham House, 1964). Text taken from *The Last Hieroglyph* (Night Shade Books, 2010).

"Necromancy." *Fantasy Fan* 1, No. 12 (August 1934): 188. *Weird Tales* 36, No. 10 (March 1943): 105. In *Selected Poems* (Arkham House, 1971).

"The Nevermore-to-Be." In *Selected Poems* (Arkham House, 1971).

"A Night in Malnéant." In *The Double Shadow and Other Fantasies* (Auburn Journal Press, 1933). *Weird Tales* 34, No. 3 (September 1939): 102–5. In *Out of Space and Time* (Arkham House, 1942). In *The End of the Story* (Night Shade Books 2006).

"O Golden-Tongued Romance." In *The Dark Chateau* (Arkham House, 1951).

"A Rendezvous in Averoigne." *Weird Tales* 17, No. 3 (April–May 1931): 364–74. In *Out of Space and Time* (Arkham House, 1942). Text taken from *The Door to Saturn* (Night Shade Books 2007).

"The Satyr." *La Paree Stories* 2, No. 5 (July 1931): 9–11, 48. In *Genius Loci* (Arkham House, 1948). In *The End of the Story* (Night Shade Books 2006).

"Song of the Necromancer." *Weird Tales* 29, No. 2 (February 1937): 220. In *Selected Poems* (Arkham House, 1971).

"The Witch with Eyes of Amber." *Auburn Journal* 23, No. 32 (24 May 1923): 6. *Agenbite of Inwit* 2, No. 5 (November 1945): [16]. *Epos* 1, No. 4 (Summer 1950): 14. In *Selected Poems* (Arkham House, 1971).

"To Klarkash-Ton, Lord of Averoigne" by H. P. Lovecraft was first printed in *Weird Tales* 31, No. 4 (April 1938): 392 (as "To Clark Ashton Smith").